PLEX PRESENTS

YOUNG -N- THUGGIN

By Troy 'Disco' Jones & PLEX

I0671557

Ain't Nobody Pen'in Like Us Man!!!

YOUNG -N- THUGGIN

A PLEX PRESENTS BOOK
Published With Permission By BGM, Inc.
PO Box 11623, Riviera Beach, FL 33149-1623
ISBN: 978-0-9839123-8-5

www.badlandpub.com

Acknowledgements

I would like to dedicate this book to Troniyah and Tronaye Jones. You two truly make this world a better place...

First, I would like to give thanks to The Man upstairs because without Him I wouldn't have a mom like Mrs. Diane [my heart and soul] and a big brother like PLEX [I hope you didn't think I forgot about you. We gon' ride this bitch 'til the wheels fall off – like we used to ride in Uncle Ronnie's Monte Carlo beating that Poison Clan! Bruh, all I got is my word and I'm gon' own up to that. I GOT YOU! I know you need a support team out here and I'm putting that together. You feel me?! I GOT YOU!].

I would like to give a special thanks to a very special young lady in my life - Tekiae Parrish [God put us through this for a reason]... To my sister Cybriane Jones, Rosa Marshall, and Shira Yearby [Y'all keep your heads up!].

To John-John [You never had a friend like me].

To WaWa and Cuz [If I could do it all over again I wouldn't change nothing!].

To Charles Smalls, Anthony Lewis, Maron Jones [I ain't even mad atcha].

To Tymekia Marshall [It's just the little things you do that means so much to me!]...

I had to save the best for last – BADLAND! Ain't Nobody Pen'in Like Us, MMaann!!!

Troy 'Disco' Jones

OFF DA' RULER'S DESK

Been down a few minutes.   Lost a few things. Can't say I don't miss 'em, though I realize I never quite had 'em...

Had a few ideas over the years. Tried a few things. Can't say they were all absolute, though I thoroughly believed in 'em all...

At my lowest point I've tried to stay my highest. Maintain my creativeness. Yet, they didn't see what I saw. Couldn't quite feel what I felt...

Still, I kept on looking. At last, I saw somebody. Believed in a nigga. Saw what I saw, kind of felt what I felt...

We fell a few times. Got up more times! Now there are others – with opinions and suggestions. We blow by 'em! 'Cause we no longer need 'em...

Still-in-all, I'm elated. To be here is a blessing because I got 'em all seeing what I saw. And together, they feeling what we felt...

You feel me?!

Some of the truest shit I ever wrote. And I wrote it for you all, the people that saw what I saw and loved a nigga through it all – even when it was hard and felt like it wasn't going to work – on my Grandma, I love y'all: Kimberly Adams, Mike Harper, Cedric Killings, Dorothy Killins, Cindy Killings, Etta D. Jones-Gates, Troy Jones, Troy Cannon, Bo Brown, Jonathan Carter, Palmer Bradshaw, Bernard Moore, Christopher Freeman, Seth & Diane Ferranti, Robert Thomas, Dwayne Gladden, Damon Causey, Lisa Banks, Antonice 'Treasure' Hills, Pam 'Sweet' Quigley, Summer Rose, Steven Polk, Pam Little, Skip & LaLa Coleman, Dewey Hound, and my homegirl Coach Latonya.

How 'bout the ones that fell to the wayside, didn't see what I saw? I wrote it for y'all – nameless, not really worth my ink

– more than others. Say you love a nigga?! But right now I'm not seeing you and I can't quite feel what it is you feel. Feel me?!

To all my niggas – behind these walls and fences – don't never [ever-ever!] get dependent on anyone! It'll be your downfall. Believe that! The key is to always stay in motion and stay emotionless. Motion – stay networking and building positive contacts. Emotionless – whether it's business or pleasure, know what it's worth and never hesitate to cut your losses and move on because as long as you've been networking and building positive contacts you'll always have something/someone to move on to. Believe that! Male or female, no monkey stops your show!

Enough with the smart shit! Where my dumb-niggas at? If you're a dumb-nigga stand up! Time for that dumb-nigga roll call: K-1 [four papers?!] you a dumb-nigga!!! Playboy Wayne [ATL Shawdy] I'm fucking with you, boy! You a super dumb-nigga. Believe that!... Benny Red, it's calibrate, not ciliate! I told you to ask the people, "when is the last time the breathalyzer's been calibrated [turned or adjusted]," not ciliated! You would've beat your write up just like Flaco. Slim, you a dumb-nigga!... I got to holla at that dumb-ass-nigga General. I thought you put them guns up?! Mmaann, she lied on you, dog... Soulja Boy [guns and drugs in the whip?!] you a dumb-ass nigga!... Whatever label signed and released that last DMX shit, y'all some dumb-niggas!... V-Nasty from White Girl Mob, you a dumb little white-nigga, but I'm feeling you on some dumb shit... And everybody that say my little dog Wizzy [Wiz Khalifa] is dumb for fucking with Amber Rose [y'all must ain't seen them naked flicks of Amber!] y'all some ultra-dumb-niggas! Believe that... Leroy Bethal [oh you a Muslim now, no more Blood Gang?!] You a dumb-nigga!

Let me stop playing so much... what up Blind [Napoleon Lee]... what up Bio [Shakim]... what up Tray [out of Titusville]... what up Roe [I'ma boss like my nigga Rozay! That hoe asked me for a check. I told that bitch like NO WAY! You feel me?!]... what up Ken [my dog out of Tampa]... what up Shelton Terry [my dog Black]... what up Fresh [my little dog out of Miami-Lil River-over by the Diamonds. I got your letter, boy. It's all love]... what up

Red [Reginald Walton – you a real nigga!]... Keenan Lawson, Theodore Merchant, Jiri Simon, William Wheat, Brian Marshall, Kashevia Brown, Joseph Wells, Pat Derrell, Luther Williams, Horace Allen – what up, what up? Thank y'all so much for the love!... Melissa "Mess" King [I know you miss me!]... what up Vert [my closest road-dog Corey Chambers]... what up though K-Girl [your ass better be swallowing by the time I get there or it's $25]... Monica Hardy [bullshit aside. You-are-that-baby! Holla at me therealestyouevermet.com]... what up E4 [I'm working on that book homeboy!]...what up Travis [my dog out of VA]... what up Vee [my dog out of Brownsville, NY]... what up Lue [DC]... what up Falon [you a bad lil' girl! One day we might have to vibe...y'all niggas check her, Skittles, Lisa Banks, and Treasure out! They are hurting them with that 2011-2013 TREASURE ISLAND EYE CANDY CALENDAR. Get it right now from BADLAND!!!]... what up Slim & Beam [Y'all are my real niggas! Jim Beam/CapoCat/PLEX Presents until the world blow up!] ... what up authors and publishers [y'all still going to act like y'all don't see me?! I did GET IT HOW YOU LIVE, ONE LOVE, NO TURNING..., LOVE & THUGGIN, CRUMBS TO BRICKS, LIL ONE: Blood Investment, and sOmEtHiNg 2 dIe 4 in 2011. With my deuces in the air I shitted on the game and y'all still going to act like y'all don't see me?! For real, y'all some dumb-niggas!]... Guillermo Zara Bozo [You're a real dude! Thanks for the Spanish and the love!]

Tracey-Tracey, let's just get married and retire to a small house in a small town. How does that sound? No more books, no more bitches, no more big duffle bags, no more big cars. We could walk to the store and push the groceries back in a basket, eat ice cream and fish while the sun sets. In my dreams, right? ☺ You know I had to try...

You know it's Book Gang or nothing muthafuckas! So know it's real and always honest – from the heart even if it's fiction. I give it to you with the best intents – no matter how it may turn out. I was sincere – even when I lied. Why? Because even though we may have wanted other things, the moment had its own demand. Think about it! If it makes sense, feel it. If it don't, be mad, but let's move on... Book Gang forever: President Big Gemo [Thanks for writing Chapters 3, 4 and 5 of this book. You did that!], Big Breed [M. Moore], Big Fridge [LaMont Needum], Jimbo [Jimmie Williams], Big Joe Hollywood, The Boss Lady [Ms. Pam Q], Seven Supreme, Ivette [The Super Typist!], Jahhead [Arab Money], My Heart [Susan Gibson], Emmanuel Cadillon [Thanks for the love homeboy!], James Frye, Von Hamilton, Bee Brown, Tracey Brown, Leslie Taylor, Fred Palmer, Avonda Dowling, Diane Hughes, Marvin Brown, Top Cat, Adrain Hadley, Erica Thomspon, Kahelia Adams, Demetrice Hill [Bling, I love you, boy!], Big Bino [Melvin Jones], Samuel Cadillon, Latoya Clinton, Derrick Howard, Trenise C. Blaylock, [My dog Blue] Davaus McCown, Anthony Davis, Danielle McDonald, [Fast Black] S. Culbert, William Roker [Bet that up, bruh!], Darnell Wilson, John Watford, Shanika Brown [My little sister and one of the prettiest and realest females in the world!], Sabrina Walden, Abman Glaster [One love, bruh!], Montreal Brown [What up, boy?! Keep your head up and your pen-in-the-wind!], Ashley Hamm [Keep up the good work. It all pays off!], Penelope Willaims [Anniston Stand Up!], K. Rozier [I love you Big Homie!], Keon Flint, Sam [CrackaBlack], Jimmy Cox, Mark Bell, Gerald Adams [Blue], Jimmy Barkley, Herbert Battle, Devon Tyler, David Harris, David Trotter, Rahmin Jefferson [Bet that up, homie!], Jernard Jackson, [Nasty] Nate Pitts, Green Eyes [P-Cola], Mykael Thompson, Jason Dixon, Dip Skywalker [Tampa], Thomas Coates, Ronald Smith, Roberty Hernandez, Darryll Capers, Debra Harrell, Ricky Curry, Julius Holmes, Derry 'Bougie' Evans, Danielle Sears [Thanks!], Jessie Cage [What up!], and Roy Johnson... all of y'all have truly helped to facilitate more dreams than you could possibly imagine. Because this is truly bigger than urban-fiction. THANK YOU ALL WITH ALL I'LL EVER BE!!!

My dog Pito [V-P/Pito/R-A], Sombra, [R-I-P] Jabai Dixon [Dap], Troy Davis [R-I-P], Amy Winehouse [R-I-P], [R-I-P] Col. Muammar Gadhafi... Love Pam Oliver and Wahida Clark's lips, love Nicki Minaj's body, love Kelly Rowland's face and voice, would love to get naked, get drunk and curse with Zoe Saldana [and we ain't got to do nothing, I promise!]... Mrs. Vera Berman [Thanks for the letters and colorful words. They meant the world! And I can't wait to read your book], Donnie Mac [You're the real one! Your father was/is my main man! So you're now my main man. Be smart and do better than me with what he gave you. Holla if you ever need me]...

ONE LOVE,
PLEX

Prologue

Beep....Beep....Beep...Beep...Beeeeeeep! The monitor screamed.

"We're losing him!" the nurse said, excitedly.

"Everybody, calm down," the doctor said, rubbing the two fibrillator pads together. "Clear!"

Boop! The electrically charged pads sounded, causing the patient's body to jump.

The doctor rubbed the pads together again. "Clear!"

Boop! The body jumped again.

Beep... Beep... Beep... Beep.

"We've got a pulse!" the nurse yelled. "It's not very strong... if he goes under again, we'll lose him."

"Prep him for surgery...he's lost a lot of blood."

The team of nurses and doctors quickly scrambled to save the young man's life. He'd taken five shots to the back, neck and leg. Shots that were meant to end the life of Troy 'Disco' Jones. Yet, through God and the steady hand of the surgeon, his chances of surviving were increasing by the minute. Either the Grim Reaper had missed his mark or the young certified gangsta was too stubborn to call it quits...

90 DAYS LATER

A month had passed since Disco had been air lifted to Ryder Trauma Center, full of holes and bleeding like a muthafucka. During the course of his stay, he'd caught the attention of Nurse Parish. Ever since she'd laid eyes on him, barely holding on to life, she could not get the handsome young man off of her mind. Everyday after she finished her rounds she would go into his room to check on him, and for the entire time of his stay she never ran into any ladyfriends of his. She found that quite odd, as handsome as he was.

Nurse Parish was open and aimed to see exactly what it was about Mr. Troy 'Disco' Jones that attracted her so strongly and seemed to repel all others...

BOOK 1NE

THE INTRODUCTION

...I'm 'bout an ounce from a millionaire... and a boat load from a billionaire... wherever my coke sold... hell, I'm livin' there... I'm sucka free nigga... for every gun you got... I got three nigga... you don't wanna see me nigga... I'm just a thug nigga from the M-I-A... down to do any fuck nigga in my way...

—Trick Daddy [Off Book of Thugs]

Chapter 1

17 MONTHS EARLIER

Disco, Lil Will and Maine were sliding down 27th Avenue on their way to Lil Will's babymomma's crib. Normally Disco didn't hang with dudes his age, but with his older brother Pretty Pulla away in Federal prison, he'd hooked up with Lil Will, Maine and their man Jay, and made a few things happen.

"Aye, Sco!" Lil Will called, choking from the lace-blunt he was smoking. "You finna chill wit' us over Trisha crib or what? You know Londa keep askin' about you."

Disco sucked his teeth and cut his eyes at Lil Will, pushing the Chevy Vert like a true big-boy. "Lil Will, you need to keep that mutt-ass-hoe from 'round there, wit' that big, sloppy-ass, nasty pussy...and her head-game ain't on nothin' anyway."

"Man, at least say something to the hoe, 'cause I'm tired of her ass always askin' me 'bout you," Lil Will lightweight begged.

"Will, my nigga, you might as well let Maine hit the hoe, I'm straight. I gotta go pick up Jay and go handle some

10

shit, for real...besides, my nigga, I ain't tryna be 'round no hoe like that. She know my lil' wife and all."

When the '71 Impala convertible pulled up to Will's baby-momma's house, a black Chrysler 300 was leaving. Lil Will and Maine jumped out and Disco rolled off 'olo. TRILLA by Rick Ross was beating from the black-on-black convertible as the top slowly came down and the 24" Ashantis rolled towards Choppa-Locka.

$$$

"Trisha, who that was just pulled off in that black 300?"

"I'on know dude. He was here to see Londa," Trisha answered Lil Will with a slight attitude.

"When that pussy-ass-cracka got out the feds?"

Trisha popped her lips. "See, boy, you need to touch yo' nose, because White-boy Dave is still in the feds. That was some new dude Londa just met."

"Well why the stupid-ass hoe got the nigga comin' round here?" Lil Will stated. "She need to meet buddy somewhere else. You know a nigga got sack in here... you should know better."

No sooner than Lil Will had completed his statement, Londa came out of the front door onto the porch where Trisha, Lil Will and Maine stood talking. She was a bad little chick as far as appearence was concerned. Yet too many dicks in her mouth and pussy had fucked up her reputation.

"Wuz up, Lil Will, Maine?" Londa popped like a true hoodrat. "Ain't that was Disco who just dropped y'all off?"

"Yeah, that was fool," Lil Will said. "But, Londa, check this out, I need to holla at you right quick."

"'Bout what?"

"'Bout buddy who just left the house. Who was that?"

"Oh, that was my new friend, Varray. He from Overtown."

"Why you met the nigga over here? You know this crib off limits," Lil Will barked.

"Nah, Will, he seen all us together on Maine's birthday at the Rollexxx, anyway. It ain't like I just met him. We don' been out a couple times and he asked me to introduce him to Disco. He wanna cop some work or whatever. And I knew that Disco was bringin' y'all back."

"Bitch, you don' bumped yo' muthafuckin' head!" Lil Will snapped.

Londa rolled her eyes and sucked her teeth. "First off, Will, I ain't no bitch. I was just tryna plug y'all and make me a few dollars. Shit been crazy for me since the feds snatched Dave up."

Stupid ass bitch, Lil Will thought. "Well, yo' ass lucky that nigga pulled off, 'cause Disco woulda fucked you and that nigga up for steppin' to him sideways wit' that bullshit. I gotta lil' love for you on the strength of you bein' Trisha's best friend, but you better get yo' fuckin' mind right."

"Well, will you holla at Disco for me, please, Will?" Londa begged.

"I'll see what's up," Lil Will said and pulled Trisha in the house.

$$$

Disco pulled up in front of Jay's ole-girl crib in Choppa-Locka. He was beating so hard that he didn't need to blow the horn. Everybody in the eight block vicinity heard his sound system.

Jay came walking out of the house like an old man. "Say, bruh, turn that music down. You know that old lady 'cross the street be trippin," he whined, hopping in the vert.

Disco said, "Fuck that lady! You need to move yo' ole-girl from 'round here anyway."

Smashing the gas, the vert snatched off, smoking up the block as Disco cut rubber. He'd just had Alex put a super-charger in his shit and he loved the way it snatched. They balled off of Jay's street and got into the flow of traffic.

12

"Say, bruh," Jay began, talking slow. "You really need to park this shit and jump behind some tints, for real-for real."

Disco ignored him, steady punching the vert. "And you need to stop trippin', we good."

The two *always* went through it. Jay was older than Disco and had been good friends with Disco's older brother, Pretty Pulla. The two met over ten years ago in Largemont Projects, some of the toughest projects in Miami Dade County. Those projects groomed them into the gangstas that they were.

Jay turned down the radio so that Disco could hear him clearly. But Disco didn't even give him a chance to speak. He simply reached over and turned the radio back up, laughing. He loved to fuck with Jay, because even though they were good friends and business partners, Jay somewhat feared Disco. Not that Jay was pussy, he had one or two bodies under his belt, but he simply knew that he could not stand in the paint with Disco. Mainly because Jay or nobody else ever knew Disco's next move.

They were headed to Broward to holla at Disco's little partner, Boe. Disco needed to introduce him to Jay, because he had plans on making Boe part of the family.

"You sho' we can trust buddy? 'Cause I really don't be feelin' these outsider-ass niggas, for real-for real," Jay stated.

"I feel you, bruh-bruh, but when I did that lil' bid up at Coleman, all them niggas that was from the crib, always 'round a nigga smokin' a nigga goods and eatin' up a nigga shit, all them hoe-ass niggas left a nigga out there when that shit jumped off wit' me and fool at the poker table... my nigga, them chico's upped swords on me and all. And the only nigga that stood in the paint wit' a nigga was Boe. So yeah, I trust buddy... He gotta mind on him too. While we was locked down behind that fuck-shit, me and him came up wit' a lil' plan. Now it's time to put it down. Feel me?"

$$$

Maine and Lil Will were still at Trisha's house cooking up hard and handling the table work. Maine was an animal over the stove. He could easily turn 36 ounces into 54 with his golden wrist and still have tension. For every two ounces that he dropped in the three ounce beaker, he brought back another. And after every 18 ounces he had to change the beaker because they would break under the pressure of his whip game.

After laying down the last three cookies Maine went and sat at the table with Will, the top-table-man in the world. Lil Will could bag up 95 DP's [*$10 bags of cocaine*] off of an ounce, without using cut and still have enough to roll a lace-blunt. That was $34,200 and 36 lace-blunts a brick!

With Maine's wrist, Will's table game, Disco's hustle and Jay's cocaine connect, they were eating real good.

After they were done, Lil Will and Maine jumped in Trisha's white-on-white SRT Hemi Charger and hit all of their traps, making sure that the workers had plenty of work for their shift.

Pulling out of Silver Blue Lakes, Will made a left on 103rd and then hit I-95 headed North. When he reached the fish-bowl he caught 826 West, headed to Miami Lakes to drop Maine off.

Even though Disco paid Maine and Lil Will top dollar to lieutenant his spots, they had established their own thing on the side, which was robbing banks. Being from Robin Hood, robbing shit was second nature to them. They'd been snatching pocketbooks, jacking niggas coming out of the Flea Market, and breaking in dope-boys' cars and cribs since they were ten and eleven years old. That's how they met Disco in the first place.

Trisha was fucking around with a *green-ass-nigga* from Coconut Grove named Lil Buddy. After Lil Will found out and beat *her* ass, he made Trisha copy the dude's house keys and give them to him and Maine. The two of them then ran off in Lil Buddy's spot and came out of that bitch with 20 pounds of 'Zona, *good green weed,* and 5,000 grams of Olean, *raw cocaine.* Young and ultra-dumb, they sold everything to Disco for $67,000, which they quickly blew on chunk, clothes and two Chevys. Yet they were cool because the deal had made them family.

$$$

Maine and Lil Will had been handling banks for a little over a year now. Besides Trisha, nobody knew about their extracurricular activities, and the only reason that she knew was because she was their driver. They'd been together since Westview Junior High and Lil Will trusted her with his life.

"Yo, bruh, I been checkin' out this Bank of America in Hialeah and that bitch sweet."

"Yeah? When we gon' slide out there so I can see just how *sweet* it is?"

"Shiid, we can slide through in the morning if you get yo' ass up, yo," Maine said, cutting his eyes at Lil Will. "'Cause you been sleepin' like a bitch lately...Let me find out you got Trisha pregnant again, fool."

Lil Will shook his head. "I don't know, dog. I might've fucked up."

Maine bussed up laughing at his dog. "Ain't no pressure, fool... that's just another reason to tear these crackas off and throw another *big-boy* party. You feel me?"

"Yeah, whatever."

The two rode in silence until they reached Maine's crib. He'd had the house for a little over a year. He bought it with his first bank robbery money and he'd spent a very attractive piece of change remodeling it.

"Damn, Maine," Lil Will said, pulling up to the house. "I like what you're doin' to the crib. That bitch tight."

"Bet that up, boy... I'm just tryna keep up wit' that nigga Jay. I done dropped 'bout $85,000 remakin' that bitch."

"Yeah, well you gon' have to drop 'bout another $85,000 to keep up wit' fool. His shit plushed out!"

"For real," Maine said, getting out of the car. "But yo, fool gettin' all that bread and livin' in a *big-boy* crib like that...my nigga, why he got his ole-girl still squattin' in the hood like that?"

"I don't know, but that's something that Jay gotta worry 'bout. I'm worryin' 'bout Bank of America in Hialeah."

"I heard that," Maine shot back.

The two exchanged dap and Maine walked off towards his front door.

His crib really was nice. He smiled to himself, admiring his work and feeling good about how far he'd came. Maine never noticed the dude dressed in all black squatting beside the hedges. Without warning the man spung from the bushes, pointing an AK-47.

"Yeah, buddy! You know what time it is!"

No sooner than those words left his mouth two more dudes with guns ran from the side of the house. They made Maine open the door and disarm the alarm system. *Damn!* Maine cursed himself. The three men were wearing ski masks, so Maine figured that they hadn't came to kill.

"We came for the money and the work, playa. Simple robbery, buddy. Don't make it a homicide, nigga!"

The dude with the rusty looking Choppa was doing all of the rapping.

Maine was a seasoned jack-boy before he ever knew anything about drugs, so he knew two things: one was that they didn't want to splash him or they wouldn't have wore masks; and two, he could see that they weren't real robbers, because they were too jumpy and they were talking too damn much. That alone made him want to buck bad-as-hell! But like Boo Baby said, "when you know better, you do better." So Maine laid it down and followed their instructions.

They led him to the car garage and handcuffed him to the crash bar of his Range Rover. There was thirty-something thousand in the headboard of his King size bed, his Cuban-link chain and bracelet, plus his 14kt gold Jaeger LeCouitre watch was all in his dresser draw, and he did not waste anytime telling them where it was all at. He even told them about the case of Armand De Cognac [Ace of Spade] that he had in his storage closet. Maine wanted to let them know about the 14 grams of clean and the five dime bags of weed that he'd just got out of Silver Blue Lake Apartments, but he knew that when they left he was going to need something to smoke, to calm his nerves.

Now what he didn't tell them was about the big hidden wall safe in the guest room closet with the $240,000 re-up money and Disco's Audemars Piquet watch in it. He also didn't tell them that they were all dead niggas once he figured out exactly what the lick read and who put them on it. However, they found the former and would eventually find out about the latter.

"You thank a nigga playin' wit' you? Bitch nigga, open that muthafuckin' safe!" the dude yelled and slapped the shit out of Maine with his gun.

Blood leaked from Maine's head as he was led to the safe and forced to open it up. He knew that Disco was really going to be fucked up about the money and watch being taken; however, there was nothing that he could do about it at the time.

The three masked robbers took everything and slid off, but not before Maine peeped the tattoo on the wrist of the dude with the AK-47. It read T4L [*Towner For Life*].

$$$

As Lil Will whipped off from Maine's crib, he came to a four-way stop sign and noticed that the police were camped out up ahead of him with their lights off. *Fuck!* Lil Will said to himself and yoked it hard to avoid a problem with the crackas. That's when he noticed Maine's cell phone slide off of the seat and onto the floor. He didn't even pick it up, he just bussed a U-turn and flushed it back to Maine's crib to give him his phone....

Chapter 2

Disco and Jay were doing about a ball-twenty, northbound on I-95. They were racing two white girls in a silver 2010 Camaro SS, Raw-Nitty's SPEED BALLIN thundered through the Vert's 15" speakers as they whipped through traffic. The two cars were neck-at-neck until the Camaro suddenly slowed up and eased over into the exit lane on Broward BLVD. As the Camaro coasted the pink-toes lowered the window smiling and both blew kisses towards the Vert. Disco, being the damn fool that he was, shot the two white broads the bird and kept smashing the gas.

Approaching the Sunrise East exit, Disco slowed the Vert and let the automatic top up. He then grabbed his phone and called his partner Boe. There were two missed calls from Lil Will. He made a mental note to hit Will up later as he scrolled through his call log for Boe's name. The phone rung three times before Boe's voice came across.

"Where you at, nigga?" asked Boe.

"Comin' off Sunrise East right now. Which way I go?"

"Buss a right on 16th and come down 'til you see a gray Dodge in the yard."

Doing as he was told, Disco hung up and made a right on 16th. He slow-rolled the Vert as he searched for the gray Dodge. At the end of the block they came to a stop sign. A corner store sat before them. There were about eight young niggas posted up, looking crazy. Jay eased his .40 from his waist and jacked one into the chamber.

"Chill," Disco told his man and redialed Boe's number.

"Yeah?"

"Yo, I don't see no Dodge, fool."

"Where you at?"

"In front this store, 'bout to kill one of these young wild-ass niggas."

Boe laughed, knowing that his man was always on one. "Yo, you on the wrong street."

"You said 16th!"

"Yeah, street, not terrace... you straight, though. Just come one block over."

"Aiight, I'm on it."

Disco hung up and slow-rolled past the store, eyeing the young niggas as the Vert crawled. Seeing that there was no pressure he turned the music back up and bent the block.

"There go the gray Dodge," Jay pointed.

The Vert came to a stop behind the Dodge. Disco spotted Boe and another dude coming around the side of the house. The dude with Boe carried an AK-47. Disco jumped out and greeted his man before introducing him to Jay. They all dapped each other up and circled back around the side of the house. Once inside, Boe sparked up the lace-blunts, laid out the brown liquor, and the men got right down to business. The focus of their conversation was the corner store that sat on 16th Terrace.

"So lil' fool 'em on yo' line?" Disco asked Boe.

"Nah, but they gon' get on my line or get the fuck."

"What if they buck?" Jay asked, pulling hard on the blunt.

The young dude with the AK-47 spoke up for the first time. "If they do, this muthafuckin' stick gon' get they muthafuckin' mind right, believe that!"

Disco glanced at the young dude and turned his attention back to Boe. "Man, what you think the spot gon' do?"

"Shiid, befo' I left we had 17th doin' 'bout a nine piece a day, straight double-ups. So if we get 16th Terrace too, my nigga, we gon' do at least about $18,000 a day, easy."

Disco looked at Jay. Jay nodded his head yes. But before either man could speak Jay's cell phone started ringing. It was Lil Will.

"Yeah?" Jay answered and listened for a few seconds. "What? Where the fuck y'all at?... stay right there! We on our way."

Chapter 3

When Lil Will finally pulled up in front of Maine's crib he noticed that the front door was slightly cracked. The sight of the open door did not raise alarm with Lil Will because Maine's house sat in such a good neighborhood. That was one of the main reasons why Disco had chosen to keep the re-up money there. Maine's neighborhood was a close-knit group of wealthy white folk and upper-middle class blacks – struggling to keep in step with their rich counterparts. Both groups thought highly of young Maine because he'd conned them all into believing that Bishop Victor T. Curry of the New Birth mega church was his parental uncle.

Lil Will continued to blow his horn and flash his lights, however, Maine never came out of the house. *What the fuck this nigga doin' in there?* Lil Will asked himself. Frustrated, he grabbed Maine's cell phone and his heat from the floor board and hopped out. *I got shit to do while this nigga playin'*, Lil Will continued mumbling to himself as he pushed the cracked door wide open.

"What the fuck?" Lil Will said out loud after seeing Maine's living room furniture all flipped and tossed about. It looked as if Hurricane Andrew had spun through it. "Maine! Aye, Maine! My nigga, where you at?"

"Back here, boy!" he heard Maine yell.

His voice was coming from the garage. With his nerves on fire, Lil Will made his way through the messy kitchen and into the garage where he found Maine handcuffed to the crash-bar of his

Range Rover. *Damn!* Lil Will cursed himself, knowing that this shit was his fault. *Disco's gonna be fucked up 'bout this!* he thought as he searched for something to cut the handcuffs and free his dog. *If my stupid ass woulda stuck to the code* [which was to wait until the person you dropped off made it inside of the house and flicked the porch light three times before you pulled off] *my dog wouldn't be cuffed up and leakin'*, he mused. Yet he also knew that Maine's ass could've been dead, because rarely did niggas leave niggas living to seek revenge. Especially when they knew that the niggas were seriously thugging.

"Man, hurry the fuck up, my nigga!" Maine complained as Lil Will worked the small bolt cutters on the cuffs.

"What happened, my nigga?" Lil Will asked after freeing his partner.

"Nigga, whatchu thank happened?"

"I mean, what they got?"

Maine rubbed his face and sighed. "Dog, them fuck niggas got everythang except this lil' weed and coc', and I'm 'bout to put that in the wind."

Lil Will rubbed his head and looked at Maine building the lace-blunt. The magnitude of the situation weighed heavy on him. "My nigga, Disco gon' nut up."

"I know," Maine said, hitting the lace-blunt extra hard before passing it to Lil Will. "He gon' really be fucked up 'bout that fuckin' watch."

"They got the watch?!"

Maine nodded his head and gave Lil Will the complete run-down of events that took place. "So we gotta do somethin', bruh."

"Like what?"

"Get that fuckin' money back and kill them fuck-niggas!" Maine answered.

Lil Will thought for a minute. "You ain't see the niggas' face or recognize none of them?"

"Nah," Maine replied then searched his memory. "But they was Towners."

23

"How you know?"

"The nigga wit' the choppa had T4L tattooed on his arm."

Lil Will hopped up all of a sudden. "Hold up, my nigga! Ain't that hoe Londa said them niggas in the 300C was from Town?"

"Yeah, why?"

"'Cause, my nigga, *bumb!*" Lil Will said and began explaining his point.

After bussing the U-turn to bring Maine his cell phone, he'd almost ran into a black Chrysler 300C, and whoever was driving it was in a big rush to get somewhere.

"So you think it was the same one?"

"My nigga, I know it was the same 300. Plus they from Town and the nigga that laid you down had T4L on his arm. Shit ain't hard! Them niggas jumped out there, now we on one," Lil Will finished with murder in his eyes and tone.

"Get Disco on the phone," Maine ordered like he was the official boss.

Chapter 4

The three slimy Overtown robbers sat in Varray's small Overtown apartment counting their take. They'd been counting for the last hour. Varray, the leader of the jack-boy crew, was a little disappointed with the almost $300,000 that sat before him. However, Jack and Mac-90 were both cheesing their asses off. They'd never seen so much money before in their young lives.

The three of them, with Varray controlling the whole lick, had been squatting on Maine for a long minute. After watching the way that Maine and his men *balled-out-of-control* in the Rolexxx that night, Varray knew that he had to have him.

The key to the whole lick had been Varray's ability to get next to the dumb, *shoning-ass-bitch* Londa; which wasn't much of a problem for him because she wasn't nothing but a gold-digging bitch, looking for her next mine to mine. So Varray played the sucker role just long enough for the big mouth bitch to unknowingly give him all of the missing information that he needed to pull off the easy lick.

"Aye, Varray, my nigga," Mac-90 whined with his squeaky voice. "You ain't gon' count all that money you got in yo' pocket?"

"What money?" Varray asked, feigning offense, even though he knew he'd been caught cuffing.

Mac-90 pointed at the huge bulge in Varray's pockets. "That money, my nigga!"

Varray sucked his teeth and grilled Mac-90. "Nigga! This my muthafuckin' money! I keep money, nigga!" Varray bassed, because even though he *kept money*, the money in question was from the robbery.

"Mmmaaannn, my nigga, you trippin'." Mac-90 threw his hands up in surrender. "I just asked, my nigga... you still gon' let a nigga get the chain?"

"Hell nah! I'm gettin' that chain!" Jack, the third member of the crew, spoke for the first time.

"Nah," Varray said, sliding $50,000 across the table to Jack. "Let the lil' nigga get that punk ass chain, Jack. All this bread we got, I know you ain't 'bout to spazz 'bout no chain."

Jack grilled Mac-90. "Yeah, aiight... y'all niggas gon' stop tryin' me... always takin' up for this nigga 'cause you fuckin' his *animal-ass* sista."

"My nigga, you gon' watch yo' mouth 'bout my sista!" Mac-90 stood up.

"Nigga, fuck that *mutt-ass-hoe*, and fuck you!" Jack stood up. "I'll fuck yo' lil' light-ass up."

"Y'all niggas chill!" Varray yelled and upped his .40. "Both of y'all sit the fuck down and leave that lil' shit 'lone. We homeboys and we gettin' money. What y'all trippin' 'bout?"

Jack mugged Mac-90 for a few seconds longer and sat down. Mac-90 looked at Varray, who was still holding the gun, and followed Jack's suit. There was a serious East-Unit on his face, but deep inside, Mac-90 was glad that Varray had intervened.

With the situation deaded, Varray sat down also and tossed some weed, coc' and cigars on the table. Jack took the cue and started building a lace-blunt. After perfecting it he fired it up and passed it to Varray, who hit it twice and tried to pass it to Mac-90.

"I'm straight, my nigga," Mac-90 whined and removed a pack of Newports. "I ain't finna be smokin' wit' this nigga and he done tried me."

Varray laughed at his little dog, because even though he played that Frankie-Blaze/Johnny-Go-Hard shit to the 'T', him and

Jack both knew that Mac-90 was a cold coward that didn't really want no problem. They'd all grown up together in Overtown, however, they rarely hung out together and this was only their sixth lick together.

Mac-90 dumped some of the tobacco out of his cigarette and removed the filter. Once that was done he laced both ends of the Newport with cocaine. After admiring his work, Mac-90 wet the *choppa* with his saliva and fired it up. The smell was loud as hell and the smoke was black. Mac-90 hit it twice more before he began mumbling.

"...niggas 'round here fakin'... got the Mac-man fucked up... like they want that pressure for real... niggas better fall back..." he damn near whispered. After smoking the *choppa* to the butt, he smashed it out in the ashtray and turned to Varray. "Yo, Varray, you... you thank maybe, my nigga, that uummm... that maybe that other nigga coulda peeped yo' whip when we almost wrecked out wit' him?"

Varray looked at his little dog and saw that he was a bit fearful. *Look at him, scared to death, but always poppin' that rah-rah*, Varray thought to himself. But before he could speak his mind Jack spoke up.

"Yeah, that lil' *scary-ass-nigga* might gotta point," Jack said.

"Scary?! Nigga, who scary?! I'm Mac-90! And I ain't 'bout *ann* game... shiid, I hope *ann* nigga would fuck wit' Tamika son. Nigga, bet that! I'm from Overtown, not outta town," Mac-90 snapped.

Varray shook his head. *Boy, if it wasn't for that fi' ass and head yo' animal-ass sista got, Lord knows I wouldn't be fuckin' wit' yo' bitch-ass*, Varray thought, but simply stated, "Calm down, killa, we on the same team, and y'all might be right. I'ma holla at the *loose-deep-ass-bitch,* Londa and see what the play read. Meanwhile, here." He slid Mac-90 $25,000 and the chain. "Don't spend it all in one spot."

"What's up wit' the watches?" Mac-90 asked, putting on the chain.

"Nigga, I'm keepin' both watches!" Varray said, picking up the expensive Audemars Piquet that belonged to Disco. It had been a gift from his big brother, who was now in the Feds. "Here, Jack, you can get the bracelet."

"Bet that up, boy!" Jack smiled, putting the four-link bracelet on.

They smoked another lace-blunt and talked some more shit before Jack bounced, leaving Varray there with his brother-in-law.

Mac-90 recounted his money again for the sixth time. *I'm 'bout to be on one!* he told himself, pocketing the cash. He was ready to hit the club, buy some bitches, pop some pills, and fuck a few animals.

"I'm up, bruh."

"Hold up," Varray said. "Befo' you dip, ride wit' me to the Pitt right quick."

"Aiight, shiid, we can ride in my shit."

Varray looked at Mac-90 like he'd lost his *rabbit-ass-mind*. Without even bothering to respond to Mac-90's comment, Varray snatched his own keys off of the counter. *I hope the fuck I would go somewhere in that boy truck*, he thought to himself as he headed for the door.

True enough, Mac-90 did have an all black Benz truck with peanut butter guts and 23" rims. He even had screens and wall in it. The problem was, It was now 2011 and fool-ass Mac-90 had a muthafuckin' '98 model, pushing that bitch like he was really coming through.

"Man, come on," Varray ordered.

Mac-90 sucked his teeth and whined, "Mmaannn, why y'all don't never wanna ride in my shit? Like I ain't snatchin'."

Chapter 5

Disco and Jay were back in the 3-0-5 after having to cut their business meeting with Boe short, because of the emergency call that Lil Will made to Jay's phone. At Maine's crib, the two sat and listened as Lil Will and Maine ran the story down to them. Jay kept shaking his head and Disco looked like he wanted to cry, especially when Maine got to the part about the $240,000 and the watch being gone.

"Well, my nigga, at least they ain't buss you," Disco said sadly.

But inside, he was truly pissed! Niggas had tried him and he took the whole situation as a punch in the face. And being as his mother and big brother had always taught him *when somebody hits you in the face you hit their ass back*, Disco was preparing himself for what he knew needed to be done.

"So you sho' it was the same 300?" Jay asked Lil Will for the hundredth time.

"Yeah, my nigga, I'm positive."

"So what we gon' do?" Maine asked.

"Fuck you mean?" Disco stood up. "Boy, my momma ain't no hoe and my brutha ain't no hoe, so ain't no niggas finna play me like no hoe! Fuck you mean? We gon' kill them fuck-niggas!"

Jay nodded his head. Disco was starting to sound and act more like Pretty Pulla everyday.

"Yo, I'ma hit my man Pimp from Town and see what the lick read on that black 300," Jay said and whipped out his cell phone.

"Yeah, do that. And Lil Will, get that bitch Londa on the phone, right now!" Disco ordered and passed Maine the weed and cocaine so he could build another lace-blunt.

As soon as Londa answered Lil Will gave Disco the phone.

"Hello? Londa."

"Who is this?"

"Bitch! You know who the fuck this is!" Disco checked her.

"Oh, hey, Sco. What's good witchu?" she shot back, sounding all sexy.

"Who is the nigga in the black 300?"

"Black 300?"

"Londa, if you play wit' me I'll beat yo' funky ass! Now who drive the fuckin' car?"

"Varray, okay, damn. You ain't gotta be actin' like that Disco and treatin' me like I'm just some hoe or somethin'. 'Cause me and fool ain't done nothin'. He just be givin' me money. I swear—"

"Whatever, Londa. Where the nigga stay?" Disco asked, cutting off her lies.

"He from Town."

"Where at in Town?"

Londa sucked her teeth. "Shit, I don't know! He always come over here to give me money or we meet up at the Grand Familiar. I ain't never been to his spot. 'Cause like I said, Sco, baby, me and that boy ain't never did nothin'."

Hearing that, Disco hung up on the bitch.

"What she say?" Lil Will asked.

"That stupid bitch don't know no more than us."

Just then Jay hung up his cell phone and said, "Got they ass!"

"Who?" Maine asked.

"The nigga in the 300. He at the Pitt right now."

"Shiid, let's get it!" Maine yelled and led the way to his Range Rover.

30

They all climbed in, strapped up like the Taliban, and sped off toward Overtown, all hoping that their targets were still there when they arrived.

Chapter 6

Disco didn't sleep much that night. He tossed and turned all night long. All that he could think about was running down on Varray and his crew. When they'd arrived at the Pitt earlier that day they'd just missed him, and the feeling of being disrespected had Disco sick to his stomach. He needed blood, because blood was the only thing that could ease the queasiness that troubled his insides. No matter what happened though, money still had to be made. Their spots, especially Silver Blue Lakes apartments and the Diamonds apartment complex, were jumping like the Carters from the movie New Jack City. But with his $240,000 gone he only had half a brick and about $12,000 to his name.

When the sun peeked through his blinds Disco was up and at it. After cleaning his person and space, he got fresh and called up Jay before smoking a lace-blunt for breakfast. With his head now right he jumped in the Vert and smashed off towards Silver Blue. Everybody was sitting around smoking and kicking it when he walked into the apartment. Disco made his greetings and got right down to business.

"My nigga, I'm fucked up. Niggas hit me for everything. I got enough bread to pay everybody and I gotta half left. We gon' have to just concentrate on the Blue and pump that shit back up.... Jay, my nigga, we gon' have to put that shit wit' Boe off for a lil' minute. Once –"

"Nah, man, nah." Jay cut him off. "I got you, fool. Long as I'm here and the plug's in place we gon' always be straight, bruh.

I s'posed to pick up six tomorrow, so that shit wit' Boe is all green lights."

"Yeah, my nigga, you don't owe us shit!" Lil Will said. "Pay the bomb-men and the look-outs, but me and Maine straight. When you lose, we lose. We take that shit together, just like we gon' kill them niggas together."

Maine nodded his head yeah to confirm what his partner had just said.

"My nigga, that's why I fucks wit' y'all boys," Disco said, smiling.

"Ain't shit, that's what real niggas do," Jay replied and headed for the door.

Everybody got up and headed out as well.

Disco called Lil Will over to the Vert. "Get in, fool. Ride wit' me right quick."

Lil Will sighed and jumped in. He just knew that Disco was about to snap on him for his fuck up, so he beat him to it. "Look, Sco, my nigga, I know I fucked up, but I'ma make it right, dog."

"Man, fuck all that! I ain't trippin' off that shit. We all make mistakes. Just don't let that shit happen again, my nigga. I know you young and we thuggin' out here, but slippers count. Shit like that could cost a nigga his life, feel me?!" Disco preached as the Vert skated up 103rd Street.

Lil Will nodded his head and Disco continued. "That's why we got rules in place. 'Cause doin' the shit we do come wit' a lotta *fuck-shit.* Stick to the script and we untouchable, dog. Feel me?!"

"Yeah, I feel you, my nigga."

"Aiight, but check this out... My nigga, between me and you, that *pussy-ass-hoe,* Londa, keep an eye on that hoe, my nigga. Real nigga shit, I don't trust that hoe and somethin' tellin' me that that bitch know more than she say she do."

Lil Will sat listening, occasionally nodding his head. He heard everything that Disco was saying loud and clear. However, he wasn't feeling the same way towards Londa. His girl Trisha and Londa had been best friends for years, so he couldn't possibly imagine her doing anything to hurt anyone close to Trisha. True enough, she had her little faults – chasing sack, being nosey, talking too damn much and always fiending for dick – but everybody had faults and hers didn't make her a bad person in Lil Will's eyes. Maybe a little stupid, but nonetheless harmless. But Lil Will didn't bother sharing his feelings with Disco, he just continued to shake his head and say, "I hear you."

Chapter 7

"Ooooh, shit, lil' boy, yeeesss! Lick momma right there... yeah, lick it... just... like... that!" Londa whined as she lay with her legs bussed wide open, getting *boss-bitch-face*.

Whenever she wasn't chasing money, gossiping or sucking grown man dick, Londa enjoyed picking up young high school boys and teaching them how to suck pussy and eat ass. Rarely, if ever, did she actually fuck any of them or show them pleasure. Today was no different. The young high school junior that she now had eating her fat, wet pussy was a little more experienced than her normal pick ups. She'd found him in Westland Mall while shopping. He was cutting school.

"Ooooh! Oooh! Godddaaaammmmmnnn!" she yelled as her second oral orgasm poured out of her. Her entire body shivered as her mind whirled. Thoughts of maybe giving the little nameless figure, with his working tongue between her thighs, some pussy or head crept into her lustful mind, but then her phone rung. She thought about ignoring it, but not too many people had her new home number, only six to be exact – her mother, Trisha, White-boy Dave, Disco, Lil Will and Varray. Everybody else had her cell number.

Hesitantly, with closed eyes and shaky hands, Londa answered the phone in a deep moan, "heelllloooo?"

"Hoe, ut'un, who chile you got over there? And I do mean chile, as in under age," Trisha asked somewhat knowingly. Her and Londa always talked and kept no secrets with each other.

"Girl, who you askin'? I picked his ass up in the mall...but, mmmm, hmmmm... baby, right there..." she left her conversation with Trisha to instruct her boy-toy, whom was still busy pleasing her while she talked. "Damn, girl, this lil' boy is the bomb. Somebody done taught his ass good. You should come get you some of this fi' head."

Trisha laughed at her crazy ass. "Hoe, whatever. I'm good at home. I ain't got time for nobody's children but my own."

"Damn, baby, hold up ... oooh," Londa moaned as the young boy stroked her asshole with his tongue. "Tr-Tri-Trisha, girl, this young nigga eatin' my ass. I gotta ca-call you ba-back, girl."

"Bye, hoe," Trisha laughed.

Londa didn't say shit, she just hung up and turned over on her stomach. With her ass up in the air and her face in a pillow, Londa gave her young friend full access to her naked ass, and using his skilled young tongue, he took full advantage of it.

With her whole body tingling, Londa groaned and rotated her ass on his tongue as he ate her anus and played with her throbbing clitoris. Another thundering orgasm rocked her as her home phone began ringing again. But Londa ignored it, too weak to answer it. She laid there, her pussy now being tickled again with loverboy's mouth, hoping she hadn't missed any money by missing that call. *I wonder who that was?* she asked herself. *Couldn't have been my ole girl, she at work. Trisha just called...probably was Lil Will or Dave's worrisome ass... or maybe it was Disco callin' for some make-up pussy.* Her questions were answered when she picked up the phone.

"Hello?"

"Damn, you busy?"

"Who is this?"

"Girl, don't play. This Varray."

"Oh, boy, I'm 'bout to cuss yo' ass out! Hold on..." she said and looked over her shoulder at the fully clothed little boy that was still sucking and lapping her fat, wet pussy. "Excuse me, you! Lil' boy, whatever yo' name is, will you please stop... thank you."

36

She then turned back to the phone. "Okay, you! What the fuck you done done? Got my peoples questionin' me 'bout you! I know you ain't 'round here talkin' on yo' dick like you ain't never had no pussy befo'!"

"Bit-" Varray started but caught himself. "Baby, whatchu talkin' 'bout? I ain't said nothin' to nobody 'bout us doin' nothin'."

"Well, Disco called me trippin', askin' 'bout you, and I'm 'bout to cut yo' ass off 'cause I don't need the bullshit."

Bitch, if yo' stupid ass only knew. Varray laughed to himself and continued to play the game. "Damn, ma! Why you wanna cut me off? I ain't said shit."

"Boy, you fulla games—"

"Nah, hold up." Varray cut her off. "I don't play no games, ma. But yo, let me make it up. Letta nigga come scoop you up and spend some money on you."

Money? Okay, nigga, now you talkin', Londa thought to herself and smiled. "How much? How much cash you gon' splurge on a chick?"

"Bands, lil' momma."

"When?"

"When you ready?"

"Well, I was baby-sittin', but I'ma drop this lil' boy off and I'll call you to come through."

"Cool."

"Okay, baby, bye," Londa sang and hung up.

Chapter 8

Varray smiled to himself after hanging up the phone with Londa – the thick, sexy red-bone with the ghetto Toni Braxton looks. At 5'6" and a real sexy 130 pounds, Londa was stopping all traffic. Varray just couldn't believe that someone so pretty and fine could be so stupid.

Varray looked around himself at all of the traffic that came through Town Park Apartments. It seemed to never cease. Removing a fat lace-blunt from his pocket, Varray put the flames to it and leaned back against his ride. Life was looking good, he thought. That's until Mac-90 whipped up in his old-ass Benz truck.

"Yo! Varray! Check this out, my nigga! Lemme holla atcha right quick!" he yelled out after lowing the truck's dark tinted window.

Mmaann, this nigga ain't on shit! Varray told himself as he walked over and climbed into the truck. "What's up, lil' nigga?"

"You know the punk Bertto?" Mac-90 whined excitedly.

"Bertto?" Varray thought, trying to remember where he'd heard that name at. After a few seconds of recollection it hit him. Bertto was the Spanish punk with all of the major work. Varray had once considered robbing the faggot, but after doing his homework on him he saw that Bertto was too well connected. If a nigga touched Bertto he was as good as dead.

Mac-90 jumped in before Varray could speak again. "My nigga, the faggot-ass-Spanish nigga that got that work! Wit' the soft-purple G-Wagon."

"Yeah, I know him. What about him?" Varray asked, a little puzzled that Mac-90 would be asking him about Bertto. *I sho' hope this boy ain't fucked that man,* he thought. Because Mac-90 was crazy as a muthafucka, and rumor had it that Bertto was always breaking young handsome niggas off with dope and big money to fuck him.

"I stunted on that punk!" Mac-90 said excitedly and began explaining how he'd broke into one of Bertto's cribs an hour ago. "My nigga, I got some packs of dope, money, and all these DVD's..." he said and pulled two big gym bags off the backseat. "You the only nigga I told, so we straight."

We my ass! You the one broke in that punk's shit! Varray thought. "Man, you trippin', dog!"

"Trippin'?" Mac-90 whined. "That punk was slippin', dog!" He opened the bag and showed Varray his work. There was about $15,000 in cash and four ziplock bags with nine ounces of raw cocaine in each bag.

"*Hundones!*" Varray yelled, clapping his hands. "Break a nigga off!"

"Here, sell this shit. One bag yours and three of 'em mine. When you gon' hit a nigga off?"

"Just call me later tonight. I'ma shake this wit' no pressure, yo." Varray grabbed the bag of work and hopped out of the truck. Mac-90 sped off beating Juvenile's song... *I'd rather see it on TV/ Than to see it in person/ Have my fuckin' head hurtin' when them 30's be burstin'...*

Varray laughed at the irony of the song's lyrics, because he felt that same way! He wanted to be far away from Mac-90 when Bertto's hitmen's *30's started bursting.* Which was sure to happen, because nothing happened in Overtown without somebody seeing something. And just as sure as somebody saw, somebody was sure to tell it. Especially after Bertto's faggot-ass put out a big reward.

With the gym bag full of work firmly in his grip, Varray jumped into his ride and shot over to Jack's crib, which was only a few blocks away from Town Park. When he pulled up Jack was standing outside on the third floor with his baby-momma. *Good! Just the person I need to see!* Varray thought as he parked. Jack's baby-momma's people pushed all of the street-level nickels and dimes [$5 and $10 bags] of cocaine in the building, so Varray's plan was to sell them the 36 ounces.

$$$

"Look, bay, there go yo' schemin' ass partner," Jack's baby-momma said, seeing Varray's 300C pull up.

"I hope his schemin' ass gotta nother lick, 'cause my baby need shoes and my partner need bail money," Jack replied and kissed his baby-momma on her lips before jogging off.

He quickly slid into the passenger side of Varray's whip and watched as Varray unzipped the gym bag of cocaine.

"Damn, boy! You in the dope game now?" Jack asked, eyeballing the work.

"Somethin' like that..." he said, smiling his crooked smile. "Yo' girl people still doin' they thang out here?"

"Hell yeah."

"Good, I'm tryna off this."

Jack thought for a minute. "What I get for playin' middle-man?"

The two discussed the situation for a few minutes and agreed to sling each nine-piece for $4,250. Jack would get the $250 off of each one and everybody would be happy, except the punk Bertto...

Chapter 9

At the gambling house off 95th Street and 17th Avenue [Robin Rood/Little River area], Mac-90 was drunk, high off two good pills, and trying his hand at C-low. He had the bank, the bet was $250 or better and he had a little over $6,000 in there. So gamblers and dope-boys, both big and little banks, were trying to get a piece of Mac-90's money.

"You *poe* niggas know what it is. Money on the wood and it's all good... suckas, money outta sight gon' start a fight," Mac-90 capped, shaking the three small dice. "And I fight real good. They call me Mac-90 Roc, not Rocky Balboa. Now play wit' it!"

Mac-90 released the dice and they tumbled, stopping on trip-sixes.

"Nobody move, nobody get hurt!" Mac-90 yelled. "Sweep house! Collect my muthafuckin' money! And when these broke-ass-niggas run outta money, I take chains, bracelets, car titles, Visa and Rush cards!"

Mac-90 was on a roll. He shook the dice and slowly tossed them again... six... four... five showed up.

"Gotdamn-it! Somebody stop me!" he yelled and watched the houseman collect the bets.

Everything was clicking. However, a strange feeling crept over him. His *creep-sense* were ringing like crazy in his mind. Smooth and slowly, Mac-90 turned and scanned his surroundings. He peeped a dude in the corner of the room peeping him. The nigga looked real familiar. *Where I know this soft-ass red nigga from?* he asked himself.

"You gon' shoot or what?!" one of the losing bettors popped slick.

Mac-90 stared at the smart-mouth and capped back. "Or what, my nigga! I just four-five-thang'd, so bank pass, I'm out this bitch," he finished and scooped up all his money. It had to be at least $13,000.

"Hold up, my nigga! That ain't how shit work in here!" one of the pissed off gamblers yelled.

"House, you better check this nigga befo' I do," Mac-90 said, placing his hand under his shirt and backing out of the crowded little house.

Faking like shit, Mac-90 made a beeline for his truck, where his real gun was. As he walked he continued glancing back over his shoulder. *Fuck!* he said to himself upon seeing someone walking behind him. It was the same dude that had been eyeing him from the corner of the room.

"Aye, fool, check this out!" the man called out to Mac-90.

Fuck all this! Mac-90 thought and quickened his step at the sound of a gun being cocked.

$$$

From the far corner of the room, Jay sat drinking shots of Remy. He'd been in the gambling house for three hours and had loss about three-bands before the lucky nigga with the big mouth had arrived. Jay lived in the gambling house and had never seen dude before, so he just sat and continued to watch. It was clear that the nigga had plenty money and he wasn't scared to shoot it or his mouth. Seeing one of his old partners that visited the gambling house just as much as himself over whispering to the new man in question, Jay waved him over to holla at him. He really needed to know who this new big money nigga was.

"What they do, Henry Black?" Jay asked his partner while offering him a shot of Remy.

Henry Black readily accepted the drink and sat down. "Same ole shit, Jay, just a different day."

"I heard that, my man," Jay said with a chuckle. "How the dice treatin' you?"

"Like a black fag wit' AIDS! They ain't showin' me no love," Henry Black replied.

Jay laughed and slipped a C-note onto the table. "Here, you might wanna try yo' hand on the lil' black-jack table."

Henry Black quickly lifted the bill and slid it into his empty pocket. He then poured himself another shot of Remy and leaned in closer to Jay before downing the drink. "Thanks for the *hundone,* man, but what's up? 'Cause you done loss way more than me and I knows for sho' that you don't just go 'round handin' out bread."

Jay smiled and nodded his head towards the big C-low game. "The new nigga you was just rappin' wit', wit' the big mouth and all the money, who is that nigga?"

Henry Black downed another shot. "Mac-90 Roc. He from Town. Why, what's up?"

Jay lied with no pressure. "Nah, nothin' serious. He just approached me 'bout some business and I wanted to get a quick read on him befo' I committed myself. Feel me?!"

"Well, the nigga's a *arch-fuck-up!* And he ain't no muthafuckin' good. He be wit' the pretty brown-skin nigga, Varray."

"The nigga wit' the black 300C?"

"Exactly!" Henry Black said and downed one more shot before standing. "Well, be careful. I gotta go."

Jay flipped open his cell phone and called Disco. After making the connection he told Disco what was what and hung up, still keeping an eye on Mac-90. He hoped that Disco would hurry up and get to the gambling house before the fool left. *We gon' see what yo' luck really like when the real shootin' start,* Jay said to himself, steadily eyeing Mac-90. And as if the dude had somehow heard his malicious thoughts, Mac-90 suddenly turned his way and the two made eye contact. *Shit!* Jay cursed himself

43

and quickly turned away. Waiting a few long seconds before sneaking another peek, Jay cursed himself again, because Mac-90 was exiting the room. He quickly got up and followed the fleeing man out, for he could not stand to let him get away. As soon as he was outside of the gambling house Jay pulled out his gun and quickened his pace. His heart-rate also increased because he knew for certain that it was about to go down. He only hoped that this move didn't land him in prison for life. *Can't thank 'bout that fuck-shit now*, Jay told himself, because it was all in thuggin'. With his .45 pressed behind his thigh, Jay noticed Mac-90 looking back over his shoulder at him.

I gotta do somethin' now, Jay thought.

"Aye, fool, check this out!" Jay yelled to the fleeing man and cocked his .45.

$$$

Mac-90 was almost at a fast jog when he hit the alarm on his truck, which automatically unlocked the door. *Check this out my ass!* Mac-90 said to himself as he snatched the door open and lifted the Mac-90 assault rifle that sat on his passenger seat. But before he could spend around shots went off.

Boom! Boom! Boom! One shot shattered the truck's window and two struck the rear passenger door. The loud booming of the big .45 scared Mac-90 so bad that he involuntarily pulled the trigger of the Mac-90. *Tat! Tat! Tat!* The big assault rifle jumped in his hands, while also shattering his driver side window and peppering his dash board.

Mac-90 quickly dove to the pavement, thinking that someone else was shooting at him, and closed his watery eyes. *Tat! Tat! Tat! Tat! Tat! Tat! Tat!* He squeezed off.

Boom! Boom! Boom! Come back in return.

Mac-90 could hear the huge slugs tearing into the truck's metal. He kept his eyes closed and continued to fire wildly, waving the gun as he sprayed. *Tat! Tat! Tat! Tat! Tat! Tat! Tat! Tat! Tat!*

Tat! Tat! Click! The clip emptied. Tears ran down Mac-90's face, because he just knew that he was now as good as dead. Slowly opening his eyes, he looked and saw the dude that had followed him out of the gambling house and took shots at him. He was now stretched out dead beside a Toyota Camry.

"Fuck nigga!" Mac-90 yelled and jumped up.

People were now rushing out of the gambling house.

Mac-90, with his empty assault rifle still in hand, knew he had to get missing. He began to walk around to the driver side of his truck, when out of nowhere a blue rental sped up. *Boom! Boom! Boom! Boom!* Shots came from the car, missing Mac-90 but ripping through his already shot up Benz truck.

"Fuck!" Mac-90 screamed and ran out into the busy traffic before the shooter could jump out of the car.

$$$

"Bitch-ass-nigga!" Disco yelled as he jumped out of the rental. He was about to run out into the traffic behind Mac-90 when he heard somebody screaming his name.

"Sco! Yo, Disco!"

He looked and saw Henry Black kneeling beside a Toyota Camry. Henry Black was waving him over. The closer he got to the Camry, the madder he got. Blood was all over Henry Black and the ground beneath him and Jay.

"Damn, dog... Damn! Why you ain't wait?" Disco asked, but knowing that Jay couldn't answer him.

There were sirens in the distance, so Disco picked up Jay's .45 and ran back to the rental. But before getting in, he carefully slid into the old-ass Benz truck. The first thing he did was take the registration and insurance papers. He then looked and saw a gym bag on the rear seat. Disco quickly snatched it up and jumped into his rental. He was up 17th and flying past the new park before the first squad car arrived.

Chapter 10

Varray laid across his couch watching re-runs of *Cheaters*. He'd just came home from *fucking-the-air* out of Londa's hoodrat-ass. During the course of their trip to the mall and their three hour *fuckathon*, he'd spent $2,600 and gained some valuable information. Based on the line of questioning that the nigga Disco had used with Londa, Varray was positive that he'd been made out as the home invader. He also knew that they were looking for the 300C, so he had to park that bitch quick and hop behind some fresh tints. *I gotta cut that bitch Londa off too. The hoe talk too much. Plus the pussy bussed up and the head ain't really on shit,* Varray thought and decided to cop a new phone asap.

His mind continued to flip through different scenarios as he attempted to outline a sure course of action, when the TV screen flashed and *Cheaters* was interrupted with a special news flash. Varray sat up and watched.

"Just hours ago, in Northwest Miami Dade, a terrible shooting took place, leaving one man dead and others seriously wounded. It happened right outside of this house," the reporter stated and the news cameras zoomed in on the gambling house.

"Police believe," the news anchor continued. "That robbery was the motive. Over here we have this vehicle, an early model Mercedes truck—"

"Mercedes truck?" Varray yelled and jumped up off of the couch.

He no longer heard anything that the reporter was saying. All he could do was stare at the image of Mac-90's old-ass Benz truck with bullet holes running all through it. Then the scene flashed to the dead body with the white sheet covering it.

"Damn, lil' fool," Varray said out loud.

A tear escaped his eye. Because even though Mac-90 was a pain in the ass at times, and an arch-coward, he was loyal and an all around good little partner to Varray.

What coulda happened? Varray asked himself. He knew for a fact that it wasn't a car jacking, because nobody wanted that ancient-ass truck. It could've been Bertto's people; but how could they have found out that fast? *Nah, it wasn't them,* he mused while pacing the floor. Varray knew how scary Mac-90 was, but he also knew how crazy he was. *A nigga probably tried to jack lil' fool and his crazy ass done bucked on 'em,* Varray thought. It made sense, however, Varray felt deep down inside that the incident stemmed from the robbery they pulled off together. Which made him partly responsible. Which also meant that he had to do something, because nine times out of ten he was next.

Boom! Boom! Boom! Came the knocks from his front door.

Varray sighed heavily. He just knew that it was Mac-90's sister coming to tell him the bad news, cry on his shoulder, then blame him for everything that happened. *Shit, I wasn't even there,* he thought before picking up his pistol and opening the door.

"Boy!" a familiar voice whined and shot past him. "Lock that muthafuckin' door!"

Varray turned and looked at Mac-90. "Nigga, I thought you was dead!"

"Shiid, ain't *ann* nigga finna do shit to Tamika son!" Mac-90 screamed in his high-pitched voice. "Nigga, lock that door!"

Closing and locking the door, Varray looked at his little partner. He was sweating bad and looked scared as hell. His Mac-90 was held tightly in his left hand.

"Man, what happened? I seen yo' truck on the news."

"Bruh, my nigga, some fuck-niggas tried to ambush me! It was 'bout eight of them niggas! And they all had K's, my nigga! I had to shoot my way up outta that shit like Method Man did on Belly," Mac-90 told more lies than truth.

"Who was it, jackas or killas?"

"Killas!"

"You seen they faces?"

"Two of 'em. That soft-ass red nigga from the Rolexx who be wit' the nigga Maine that we touched. Him and the nigga Disco."

"Which one you painted?"

"The red nigga," Mac-90 said and sat down on the couch.

"Why you left yo' truck on the scene?"

"I had to! I told you it was twelve niggas wit' AK's! Everytime I flipped one nigga two more jump out on a nigga. Lucky I had like ten extra clips. I had to carjack a bitch and all to get away. But one thang 'bout it, I bet them fuck-niggas won't jump out on the Mac-man no mo'. Bet that!"

Varray shook his head and picked up the phone. He called Mac-90's sister so she could report the Benz truck stolen. Next he called Jack to see if his baby-momma's people had came up with the cash for the cocaine he'd left him with, because shit was getting crazy and he knew that him and Mac-90 was going to have to lay low for a while. So they needed all of their money.

$$$

The next day Varray and Mac-90 picked up the money from Jack. They then copped new cell phones and bought a new *slider* – a used 2006 Mercury Grand Marquis with dark tinted windows. The black Chrysler 300C, he parked in Mac-90's sister's backyard and placed a car cover over it.

For the next few days the two never left the apartment. Jack would come every morning with liquor, weed, blunts, cigarettes, cocaine, beer, and food. He'd stay as late as he could, however, his baby-momma wasn't having it, so he left every night only to return bright and early the very next day. And everyday they had to listen to Mac-90 *buck da dice* about the situation at the gambling house.

"Like Tupac say, my nigga, 'in times of danger, ain't no time to freeze, it's time to be a G'. You feel me?! That's why I let them fuck niggas have it, my nigga! All head shots," Mac-90 lied. "Whatever y'all niggas thank, if somebody gotta die, it won't be Tamika son, bet that!"

Chapter 11

...up early in the morning/ dressed in black/ don't ask why/ a nigga dressed in a suit and tie... They killed a nigga that I went to school wit'/ Damn! I tell ya life ain't shit to fool wit'... I still hear the screams from his mother/ as my nigga lay dead in the gutta...

Ice Cube's DEAD HOMIES beat from Disco's Vert as he followed the hearse. Jay's funeral had been a grand event. Everybody was there from corner-boys to professional athletes, prostitutes to female doctors. Jay had been loved in his lifetime. However, it was all over now. And as much as it pained those close to him, the feelings of loss would subside in time and life would go on. He'd be forgotten like so many before him.

The black Phantom hearse slowly pulled in the cemetery and came to a stop beside the large white tent. The long line of cars that followed stopped also and everybody got out, their expressions solemn. Disco's wifey, Shoniece, accompanied him and she was looking damn good. She'd flew in from Anniston, Alabama to attend the funeral. And even though she wasn't from Miami everybody at the funeral knew her, because not only was she the baddest bitch at the funeral, she was *top-5* wherever she went, but Disco flew her in at least once a month to hang out. They'd met five years earlier while Disco was up in Anniston scrabbling with his big brother.

Londa and Trisha, also looking good as hell, walked over and stood with Shoniece while Disco, Maine, Lil Will, Boe and Cuz, and Jay's cousin did their duties as pallbearers.

Jay's young son and daughter stood next to their mother. It fucked Disco up to see them and Jay's mother crying, because that could've easily been him laying in the casket with his family sad and heart-broken. A tear escaped his eye. It was the first time he'd cried in five years – the last time being when Pulla had gotten sentenced.

His mind flashed back through time as Jay's casket was lowered into the Earth. He thought of all the times they'd shared over the years. *Damn, dog...you shoulda waited, dog... damn,* he said to himself. *I'ma miss you, dog. And don't you trip. I'ma kill everybody that I think was wit' it! And I got yo' people, don't even trip. You wasn't thuggin' for nothin'.* He was so caught up in his thoughts that he didn't realize the service was over until Shoniece grabbed his arm.

"Baby, you aiight?" she asked him.

Without answering her, he wiped his tears away and looked around him. Londa, Maine, Lil Will, and Trisha were all standing off to the side staring in his direction. Anger and confusion washed over his tired mind, because he knew that everybody was waiting for answers. They all depended on him for their livelihood. Yet he'd always had his brother or Jay to help lead the way. Now they were both gone and he wasn't so sure he could do it. For the first time in his life he was alone.

With Shoniece on his arm, Disco made his way over to the others. Almost everyone had left already, so the cemetery was somewhat empty. Maine pulled out two fat-ass lace-blunts and fired them both up. And even though Trisha nor Londa smoked lace, they did blow big lace smoke on that day in Jay's memory. As they stood smoking and reminiscing, Lil Will tapped Disco on the arm and pointed over towards Disco's Vert. There was a group of about six Spanish dudes standing next to the Vert and they were all focusing their gazes on Disco.

"Who them crackas is, dog?" Lil Will asked.

Disco strained his eyes for a minute before realizing who they were. "Just who I need to see," he said and walked off alone.

The tall fair-skinned man with the long black ponytail extended his hand for Disco's shake. There was a queer grin on his handsome face. His hands were large and very soft. This wasn't Disco's first time in the powerful man's presence, however, it was the first time without Jay.

"How are you today?"

"I'm cool. How 'bout you, Bertto?"

"Could be better," Bertto answered and led Disco off.

The two of them walked alone, leaving everyone else at the cars. Bertto had seen Disco on many occasions with Jay and had also heard a lot of good things concerning his character. As they walked along the peaceful cemetery Bertto explained a few things to the young ambitious hustler, after of course, expressing his condolences for his partner Jay and the family. After all, Disco had been introduced to Bertto as Jay's first-cousin. Once that was out of the way the high-level Cuban drug dealer got down to business. A lot of what Bertto explained Disco already knew. Nevertheless, he was totally dumbfounded to learn that Jay owed Bertto for fifteen kilos.

"So, umm, whatchu want me to do?" he asked, staring at the soft spoken man with the girlish features.

"I want you to pay. Jay was your partner, true."

"Yeah, but not like that. I mean, we done some shit together, but fifteen units?! Man, Jay ain't never showed me no muthafuckin' fifteen units," Disco shot back in all sincerity and hoped that Bertto believed him, because he already had enough bullshit going on.

Bertto stared at him as if he were trying to read him. A crooked smile replaced his chary look. "I like you, Disco."

Disco liked what he'd heard, however he didn't like the manner in which it was said. He knew Bertto was a *boss-sausage-stuffer,* everybody knew that.

"Say, Bertto, I don't really know where you goin', but I see you as a man and we gon' always carry our relationship *just like that,* as two men doin' what we can to help each other. You feel me, man?" Disco capped, checking Bertto's tone more so than what he'd actually said.

Again Bertto smiled. "I do feel you, my young friend. You are young and... umm, how do you say?" Bertto thought for a second and snapped his fingers when he remembered the word in question. "Thugging! That's it. And I like that about you. I sense that you will always keep your mouth closed about our business and I am confident that whatever I give you will be in safe hands because you are not soft – so to speak."

Disco smiled inside but continued to wear his game face. Bertto had just spoken on *giving him some work*. Things were looking super-hopeful until Bertto finished his little speech.

"But! Before I can give you anything, you must first pay your partner's debt."

Damn! Disco thought before saying, "I feel you Bertto... but, man, I ain't got no $400,000 layin' 'round like that."

Bertto looked at him. A frown covered his face. "Your math is wrong. No $400,000. Only $255,000."

"$255,000?" Disco repeated. "That's only $17,000 a bird."

"Correct."

Damn! Disco thought. Jay had been hitting him in the head for $20,000 a piece and swearing by God that that was his price.

"Look, gimme 'bout two weeks. I'ma get yo' money, Bertto."

"Good!" Bertto clasped his hands together and smiled like the faggot he was. "I will give you seven days. And please, do not disappoint me, because I am bisexual... not a bitch."

With that being settled the two parted ways...

Chapter 12

The day following the big funeral, Londa and Trisha sat around Trisha's house drinking miniature bottles of Moet and being roxy as hell. Lil Will had hopped up extra-early and disappeared with Maine. The two of them had been gone all day.

"Bitch, did you see that badass dress that Shoniece was rockin'?" Trisha stated. "That bitch was killin' 'em!"

Londa drank from her bottle and sucked her teeth. "She was aiight," Londa replied with a nasty frown on her pretty red face.

"What?!" Trisha said, eyeing her friend hard. "Girl, you know wasn't *nann* bitch doin' it like Shoniece at that funeral. That bitch had 'em all on pause. Disco makes sure she be straight for whatever event."

"*That bitch had 'em all on pause... Disco makes sure she be straight for whatever event...*" Londa mimicked her friend sarcastically. "Bitch, puleez, get off the hoe clit!"

"Do like this," Trisha said, brushing the corner of her own mouth with her hand. "You got somethin' right there."

Londa put her bottle down and brushed her mouth. "What? I got it?"

"Yeah, I think it's gone. You had a lil' bit of hate on yo' mouth," she said laughing.

"Bitch! Fuck you!" Londa laughed with her friend. "She was tight, I can't lie. But! She only be *actin' up* like that 'cause of

Sco's money. That bitch wouldn't be shit wit'out Disco! And the fucked up part is the bitch don't love him. She just usin' his ass."

Trisha almost choked on her Moet when Londa said that shit. "Hoe! No-the-fuck-you didn't. Much as niggas you use?! All you do is fuck niggas for money!"

"But that's different, Trisha. They be *fuck-niggas*, so I s'posed to play they ass. Sco a *real nigga* and he deserve better."

"Lord, God, I done heard it all... bitch, what about White-boy Dave?"

Londa drunk some more of her drink and thought for a minute. "Girl, I'm 'bout to leave his ass. All his lil' money 'bout gone, and the bitch keep callin' me talkin' 'bout help him get a time cut. I told his ass, b*oy I don't know nothin' 'bout settin' nobody up. So no!* His ass wanted to be a balla, now he gotta pay his dues. But me, I can't wait no longer. I'm finna change my numbers."

"Girl, you a mess... you and Shoniece is the damn same."

"No the fuck we ain't! 'Cause I'ma real chick. I'll do whatever for my nigga if he's real wit' me. If Sco fell off, that bitch gon' be in the wind."

Trisha laughed. "Well, we 'bout to see."

"Whatchu mean?!" Londa asked, always eager to get the 'T' from her friend.

"Disco fucked up," Trisha said simply.

"Fucked up? Or fucked up-fucked up?"

"From what I heard, fucked up-fucked up!"

"Bitch, stop!" Londa said with her eyes wide and her manicured hand over her luscious mouth. "Noooo! That bitch broke?!"

Trisha nodded her head yeah.

"What happened? How you know?" Londa asked, not truly believing her ears.

"Well, look, girl, you ain't heard this from me. So if it come back to me I'ma beat yo' red ass."

Londa feigned offense. "Trisha, don't play. You know I don't discuss other peoples' business wit' other peoples... now tell me!"

"Whatever, bitch... anyway, you know some niggas stuck them for 'bout half-a-ticket."

"Bitch, noooo! When this happened?"

"A lil' while ago, maybe 'bout a week ago. But anyway, they ran up in Maine's house and took everythang," Trisha said and downed her bottle.

"Whatchu mean, *everythang*. I thought them niggas was playin' wit' mills."

"Ppsstt! Jay mighta been, but you know how Disco, Lil Will and Maine like to show off. So since the lil' robbery and Jay got killed, they fucked up."

"Dddaaammmnnn!" Londa said, shaking her head sadly. She really liked Disco. Plus the fact, even though Trisha hadn't said it, if Disco was broke, so was Lil Will. Which meant that Trisha was fucked up too.

"And that ain't the worst, girl."

"What else done happened?"

"Remember them Spanish dudes that was at the burial?"

"Yeah, Bertto. Some niggas just broke into one of his lil' stash houses and he got money on them bitches' head. They took some money, drugs, and DVD's. And Bertto want his shit back, bitch."

"How you know him?"

"Bitch, everybody knows Bertto gay-ass. He eatin' major," Londa replied, excitedly. "What about him?"

"Well, he was Jay's plug. And-"

"They was fuckin'?" Londa asked, cutting Trisha off.

"No! Dumb-ass-girl... when Jay got killed he owed dude for fifty of them thangs, and Disco gotta pay it. I heard Lil Will tellin' Maine that Disco gon' sell the Vert."

"Fifty?! That bitch lucky Bertto ain't kill him! Girl, Bertto got hitmen and everythang on his line... yeah, you right, them boys fucked up-fucked up!"

The two sat quiet for a minute. Each thinking about the shit that had just been shared. Londa felt sorry for Disco. Trisha felt sorry for herself. Shit was about to get ugly for every party involved.

Before either of them could utter another word, Lil Will walked in all happy-go-lucky. "What y'all two roxy-asses in here gossipin' 'bout?" he asked in good humor.

"Ut'un! Nigga, no you didn't just call us roxy when yo' ass always wanna be in on the 'T'," Londa said, standing up in her tight white sweat pants. They were all up in her big pussy.

Damn! Lil Will said to himself as he stared at her camel toe.

Londa peeped his glance and smiled. *You wish, nigga!* she thought, *because not only is you the help, but yo' boss-man is broke.* "I'm outta here, Trisha. I gotta few runs to make."

"Aiight, girl." Trisha stood to walk Londa outside.

"Hold up, Londa," Lil Will said and turned to Trisha. "Lemme holla at Londa for a minute, bay."

Trisha sucked her teeth. "Gon' head. She gon' tell me anyway."

"Whatever," Lil Will said and turned back to Londa. "Aye, what's up wit' Varray?"

"Whatchu mean?" Londa got on the defense. "I already done told Sco that me and that boy ain't did shit. He just be breakin' me off. And-"

"Hold up, Londa. This ain't 'bout that."

"Then what it's 'bout?" she asked, shifting her weight to one bowleg and putting her hands on her hips.

Lil Will sighed. "Look, I don't even s'posed to be talkin' to you 'bout this, but the nigga Varray's the one that ran up in Maine's crib. And his man killed Jay."

"What?!" Londa replied. *That's why that bitch kept askin' me all them questions 'bout Disco and shit. And that's why his ass was nervous last time we hooked up,* she thought.

"Yeah, he did that... but yo, you haven't been rappin' wit' fool 'bout us, have you?"

"Hell nawl!" Londa lied.

"Do you know where fool stay?"

"Nah, Will. I don't know, but I'ma damn sho' try to find out."

"Aiight. But yo, keep that between us."

"You got that, Will."

$$$

Londa felt like shit as she navigated the clean gray-on-gray Volvo C70 convertible. She'd just tried Varray's cell phone and found his number disconnected or changed. Either way, she was pissed, because she realized that she'd been played like a punk-bitch. She also felt bad because her loose lips and hunger for money had cost the people that she truly cared about.

Turning right off of 103rd, Londa cruised past the security booth into her apartment complex – Silver Blue Lakes. Making a right, she drove past the children playing football. They all waved at her. Londa smiled and blew her horn. Her apartment was on the second floor, above the rental office.

After checking her messages, Londa ate some Hot & Spicy Noodles and jumped in the shower. She'd hoped to have gotten a message from Varray explaining that he'd changed his number for one reason or another and left her the new one. It would've surely helped to ease the uneasy feeling that floated in her mind and her unsettled gut. However, that was not the case. There was no message from Varray and no easy answer to her plight.

Stepping from the shower, Londa stood naked in the bathroom's full-length mirror. Her image, its perfection, stared back at her, so ripe and sexy that looking at herself was like listening to Ms. Keri and R. Kelly trade verses of seduction. Loving what she saw, Londa lotioned up and slipped into her T-shirt and panties. Her next endeavor was to find sleep. Yet after twenty minutes of staring at the glow-in-the-dark stars on her bedroom's ceiling, she realized that her troubled mind was not going to let her rest. The clock on her nightstand read 12:38 a.m. *I know what I need*, she thought to herself and got out of bed.

Within minutes Londa was dressed and walking down the hallway towards the end of the building, whistles and cat-calls insued. She loved the attention, only wishing it was coming from a wealthier class of drug dealers. All of these were corner-boys, and far below her standard, because Londa had standards that she lived and died by: never fuck with the help [her man's underlings], never fuck with a corner-boy [whether he worked for himself or someone else] and always step-it-up [never fuck with a nigga that didn't have more money or status than her last].

When she got to the stairwell of the second to the last building, Londa stood, staring over the cement railing. It was dark because the dealers had shot out most of the lights. Just below her on the first floor, Londa saw a fine young brown-skin dude running to cars and catching smokers in the hallway, but he wasn't who she was looking for. Walking down a little further she spotted two dudes huddled by the trash shoot.

"Blue, lemme get two bags," Londa said.

Seeing her, Blue smiled his sixteen gold-teeth smile. "Damn, Londa, you coulda just called a nigga and I woulda brung this to you when I came home to you," Blue capped.

"Boy, my house ain't yo' home and you'll never be comin' off nobody's block to me."

"Not even for 'bout an hour? I just want you to sit on my face," Blue said, still smiling.

"Boy, take this lil' $10 and gimme my damn weed."

Blue dug in his briefs and came out with a small brown paper bag. He then went inside that bag and pulled out two small envelopes of good-green. The envelopes were stamped FIREBALL with the Miami Heat logo on them.

"Don't worry 'bout the $10," Blue said, handing her the weed. "You need to let a nigga smoke one of them fire-bags witcha and show ya how it have a real goon beatin'."

"Ppsstt! Is you sho' you don't want these $10, boy?"

"You good."

"Thank you, then." Londa put the $10 and the two bags of weed in her bra and walked off.

When she rounded the stairwell that sat at the edge of her building, a figure sat mid-way the stairs counting money. The bills were crumbled up $5's, $10's, 20's, and a gang of $1's. A black .40 caliber sat beside his thigh. It was the very same brown-skin young dude that she'd just seen a little while ago running to cars. Hearing Londa's footsteps, the dude reached for his gun and looked up. Londa froze in her tracks.

"Damn, Sco, what's up?" she said, displaying a curt little smile.

"Ain't shit," Disco replied and sat the gun back down.

Londa stood there as he folded and rubber-banded the two stacks of money that he'd been counting. He placed one stack at the bottom of his Jordan's and pulled a brown paper bag out of his briefs. In the brown paper bag was more crumbled bills. Disco began counting it, but suddenly stopped and looked up at Londa.

"What? What's up?" he asked her.

"Oh, umm, ain't nothin'," she stumbled on her words. Londa couldn't believe that Disco was out on the block going hand-to-hand. "Umm, you ain't gotta be out here on no steps countin' yo' money. You can come in my-"

"I'm straight!" Disco cut her off and went back to counting.

Londa stood there for a few more minutes, wrecking her brain for something to say, or hoping maybe he'd say something. Yet nothing came to her mind and no word left his mouth. He didn't so much as look back up to acknowledge her presence. Londa sighed and walked on home.

BOOK 2WO
LET'S GET IT

...Remember me from back in the days... we used to slang a lil' crack in the days... now he broke and he lackin' these days... now he feel like I owe him somethin'... sendin' messages like a hoe or somethin'... talkin' 'bout throw him somethin'... Oh, if I ain't got it I ain't yo' dog no more... This lil' flow worth warrin' for... Well, in that case I ain't got it then... I'm in the hands of yo' fake ass 'bout it men... 'Cause only real niggas roll wit' me... get dough wit' me... fuck hoes and get on blow wit' me... pussy nigga!

- Trick Daddy [SITTING ON D's]

Chapter 13

"So what time you gon' be back to get me," Shoniece asked with her juicy lips poked out. She'd been nagging and complaining ever since the funeral, but the shit had really hit the fan when Disco came in at 3:30 that morning, so to shut her the fuck up he agreed to treat her to a day at BUFFY'S HAIR & BODY WORKS.

"I'ma be on the block, so just call Trisha, she'll pick you up and drop you home," Disco responded, busy strolling through his call log for a particular phone number.

"Who said I wanted Trisha comin' to get me?" Shoniece was full of attitude.

Not even bothering to look up from his cell phone, Disco continued strolling. "Catch a cab, then."

"Boy, I am not gettin' in nobody's cab!"

Disco looked up at her with *kicking ass* in his eyes. "Get out of the car, Shoniece. Get home however you want to."

She knew not to push it. "When you comin' home?"

"When I get this money... now, I gotta go."

Shoniece sucked her teeth and got out of the car.

With his phone to his ear and a big black .40 on his lap, he eased the rental car out into the flow of traffic. His mind calculated as he drove along, waiting for the other party to answer. At least he hoped that they answered, because he'd stayed out all night and *bammed* the whole twelve ounces that he'd bought the day before [actually he'd bought a nine-piece and whipped it to twelve], and now had $9,000 to spend – after just giving Shoniece $1,500.

"Hello?"

"Damn, boy, what's up?"

"Ain't shit, 'bout to shoot down South for a minute."

"Look, I need to see you right quick befo' you dip," Disco stressed.

"Well you better hurry up, 'cause I'm out the door."

"Chico, my nigga, hold up! I'm 'bout ten minutes from you."

"Whatchu want?"

"I wanna ride that Benz, nigga."

"The 500?"

"Yeah."

"Eleven thousand."

"Got-damn, my nigga!" Disco exclaimed. "This me, nigga!"

"My nigga, it is what it is," Chico stated.

"Dog, I got nine, lemme-"

"Nah," Chico cut him off. "I told you I'm 'bout to go down South. So come get this dirt bike and let me get up outta here."

"Aiight, my nigga." Disco hung up the phone.

At this rate he'd never get the $255,000 that Bertto was lightweight pressing him for, because even with his whip-game he was only seeing $800 off of each ounce, which only meant $9,600 off each quarter-key. Of course, the profit was only $4,100 – give or take a few hundred for shorts. That's why he'd let his other traps fold for a minute and chose to concentrate on Silver Blue Lakes – where he could easily boom a half-kilo a day in double ups. He even had to let his three workers go because shit wasn't adding up.

Only for a minute thought, he told himself. By hook or crook he was going to get Bertto's money up and secure the plug. Once that $17,000 a brick was in place, it was going to be *THUG LIFE AGAIN!*

$$$

63

...you can go to sleep broke/ wake up in a Benz/ talk 'bout you when you down/ muthafuck friends/ Gggeeetttt Mmmooonnneeey Bbaaabbbyyy/ I just get money, baby... my block is scorchin'/ Feds tryna peep my swag/ jack boys on my ass/got the camera in my tag... choppa on my front seat/ I'ma give 'em what they want/ turn the Kenwood down/ dump the ashes off the blunt... my chain cost a fortune/ watch'll make the time freeze/ purp in my system/ call me black and Chinese...

The flow of Soul's GET MONEY boomed through the living room as Disco poured the water off of the third and last four-ounce cookie. He wrapped it in a dry towel to dry it and then placed it on his digital scale. A smile covered his handsome brown face as 103 appeared on the scale's display.

It took him four hours and two lace-blunts to chop and bag all 960 juggler-rocks. Then, after breaking the pile of rocks into about seven bombs, he took off his Bally's for Jordan's and headed off to work.

$$$

Disco parked the rental car on the *sucka-side* of Silver Blue Lakes [The 17th Avenue Side] near the fence by Popeye's. With his .40 in his front-right Dickie pocket and two $1,200 bombs on his nuts, he made his way through the hole in the fence and strolled over to Popeye's.

"Gemme a three-piece wit' dirty rice and a large cherry," he told the cute, young black girl.

She smiled and took his order along with the $10 bill that he handed her. The smell of the fried chicken caused his empty stomach to rumble. He hadn't eaten anything since 10:00 the night before and he was hungry as fuck.

"Thank you, lil' momma," Disco told her. "Keep the lil' change."

Cutting through the hole in the gate on the *Slump-You-Side* of Silver Blue [The 1-0-3 Side], he hit the first stairs and walked the second floor. It was best to always stay off of the first floor, because the robbers and police were down there, and you could always see them down there and make your move before they could see you and make their way up the stairs.

Niggas spoke and hoes sweated as Disco walked along eating his food. He'd always been a hustler, and to him this was just part of the hustle. It was where he'd started. His big brother Pretty Pulla had given him his first bomb at fourteen and his first half-brick at sixteen. And though moving weight and giving work to workers was preferred, lacing up his Jordan's and beating the block for fives and ones wasn't contrary to his hustler's nature. The bottom was where he'd started, so starting over was just like being at home.

Rounding the corner by the rental office, Disco froze and damn near dropped his food.

"Gotdamn!" he slipped up and said out loud.

Londa was bent over in front of her apartment, pussy and ass cheeks hanging everywhere.

Hearing Disco's voice, Londa, still bent over, looked back over her shoulder and smiled at him. "What's up, Sco?" she asked, standing now, facing him. "What got you 'round here?"

Disco looked past the colorful flyer that she'd just picked up and zoomed in on that fat, fist print between her thighs. The little nasty booty-shorts that she had on were wedged deep in that big pussy of hers.

"I'm chasin' my dreams," he said sarcastically.

"Why you walkin'? You usually be comin' through, stuntin' on 'em." Londa pulled her shorts out of her pussy and bounced on her bowlegs.

"I'm walkin' 'cause I ain't learned how to fly yet," Disco capped at her and frowned. "Don't play wit' me, girl. You know exactly what it is wit' me... I'm gettin' it how I live."

Londa sucked her teeth. She wished she could rub his losses in his face, but she couldn't because she wanted to see him win. Only she wanted to be at his side when he did. Problem was, she knew that Disco was not feeling her. Why, she just could not understand. After all, she was one of the top-five baddest hoes in Dade County.

"Yeah, I know what it is wit' you. So if you need me for *whatever*, just holla, Sco."

He looked at her nipples pressing through her wife beater and glanced once more between her legs and felt his dick jump. But money came before bitches and Londa wasn't worth his time.

"Aiight, I'ma holla," he said and walked on.

Chapter 14

Jack gave the old Spanish woman the money for his, Mac-90 and Varray's order. They'd been ordering from the Pitt damn near everyday and he was sick of it, so he'd decided to hit Laguna's on 17th Avenue and 29th Street. It was a popular Spanish eatery that every *big-boy* in Miami frequented on their way to the top.

Taking the three big bags of food into his arms, Jack spun around and took two steps before freezing up like a statue. His mouth fell open and his right leg trembled. Had his hands not been full he would've surely yanked at the .357 that rested beneath his shirt. Like a deer caught in the headlights of a speeding eighteen wheeler, Jack stood staring as the two men approached him.

"Fool, you good?" Lil Will stopped and asked the dude that was openly staring at him and Maine as they walked in.

"Umm, yeah, I'm, I'm good," Jack stuttered, thanking God that they didn't know who he was. "But, umm, was, was you in the Panhandle?"

"What?" Lil Will asked, frowning his face.

"Prison, up in the Panhandle?" Jack asked, covering his ass.

"Hell nawl, yo. You got the wrong nigga."

"My bad, dog," Jack fake chuckled. "You looked like a nigga I did time wit' up there."

Lil Will didn't make any further comments, he just mean mugged Jack and walked off to the ordering counter with Maine.

"You see that fuck-nigga, Maine?" Lil Will asked, looking back at Jack as he exited the restaurant. "Starin' all in a nigga shit."

"Yeah, I seen lil' buddy. But he ain't want no pressure." Maine laughed and added, "You reminded him of his boyfriend in prison."

"Nigga! You got me fucked up!" Lil Will said, laughing with his homeboy.

The two young killers for the cause ordered their food and found an empty spot in the back. They'd been in and around the Overtown area for the past three days – day and night. Every morning the two got together, stole a new *splack* and headed out – AK-47, .40 caliber and Spec-90 ready to rock. Their first stop would always be the address that Disco had given them off of the registration and insurance he'd gotten out of the old Benz truck that Jay's killer had been driving the day of the murder. After sitting and watching that house for about three to four hours they'd hit the streets of Overtown. The nigga Varray or his Chrysler 300C had yet to be spotted. They'd even taken the time to follow the fine-ass dark-brown skin chick that lived at the address Disco had given them, but she'd led them nowhere but the grocery store, the weed hole, the beauty supply store and the strip club [P-POOPA'S] where she apparently worked as a stripper.

"So how we gon' do this shit today?" Maine asked, raking the big chunks of baked fish from the bone.

"Shiid, how we been doin' it," Lil Will replied.

Maine sighed. "Mmaannn, this shit gettin' played, dog. I'm sayin', I wanna kill them bitch-ass niggas bad as fuck, but they ducked off, dog. And for real, you know what we s'posed to be doin', dog."

Lil Will chewed and swallowed his steak and eggs. "I feel you, my nigga. But Disco want 'em dead, so they dyin'... my nigga, Jay was family! And I know if a fuck-nigga woulda killed me, Jay woulda been ridin' day and night for me... so, fool, that other shit gotta wait."

Maine sucked his teeth and began mixing his fish with his grits. "When the last time you holla'd at Sco?"

"Shiid, the night of the funeral when we was all at my crib."

"You thank he gon' really sell the Vert?"

"I'on know. But that's what he said."

"Mmaann, we can't let that nigga sell his Vert. He love that car," Maine stated, eyeing Lil Will.

"Shiid, we can't stop him either," Lil Will responded and continued eating his food.

$$\$\$\$$$

Boom! Boom! Boom! Boom! The loud banging sounded on the small apartment's front door.

Mac-90 jumped up, leaving his gun on the cheap coffee table, and jogged wide-eyed towards the third floor window. "Boy! That's them crackas!"

Varray put the lace-blunt that he'd been smoking down and picked up his gun. "Scary-ass-nigga, if you can't fly you might as well get from by that window." He frowned on Mac-90 and nodded his head towards Mac-90's gun. "Come on, nigga."

Boom! Boom! Boom! Boom! The knocking kicked off again.

With guns in hand, the two slowly approached the door. Big beads of sweat popped up all over Mac-90's face and bald head.

"Who is it?" Varray asked from beside the door.

"Jack, nigga! Open the door!"

Varray sighed a big sigh of relief and unlocked the three dead bolt locks. Then he reached for the door knob, but the door came flying open and nearly knocked him on his ass. Jack shot by in a blurr.

"Close the door!" Jack yelled.

The already scared Mac-90 stuttered, "B-b-boy, wh-what happened?"

Jack caught his breath and began explaining who he'd just seen and what had transpired between them. Varray stood stoic as he listened, though a sliver of fear did consume him. When Jack was finished telling his tale Mac-90 was the first to speak up.

"It was just two of 'em, my nigga, and you ain't get off?" Mac-90 asked Jack, shaking his head as he spoke. "My nigga, ain't no way that coulda been me! Fuck that food, fuck witnesses, and all that shit! I'da fi'd them fuck-niggas up, just like at the gamblin' house. It was twelve of them fuck-niggas gunnin' at a nigga and I still *set-it-off* like them hoes in the banks... my nigga, you flaw! Let two niggas run you."

"Nigga, fuck you!" Jack yelled, walking towards Mac-90.

"Nah," Mac-90 responded, waving the gun in his hand. "Fuck wit' me! Tamika a bitch if *ann* nigga fuck wit' Mac-90. Now bet that!"

Varray stepped between them. "Y'all niggas trippin'! We together!" he yelled. "Y'all chill and let me figure this shit out."

"Yeah, you better holla at fool. 'Cause he got the Mac-man fucked up!" Mac-90 stated and sat down on the couch.

Varray cursed himself for not killing Maine the day of the robbery when he had the chance, because had he killed the nigga then he wouldn't have been worried about killing him now.

Chapter 15

"Hey, who got them green bags?" the dirty forty-something-year-old man asked as he hopped out of the silver Dodge Wagon.

Disco, standing in the cut with Ziggy, Blue, Jit and Shelton, peeped the smoker and then the car. Behind the wheel sat a medium built white woman with glasses and dirty-blonde hair. She'd came through the night before with the same dude, but in a different car. They'd spent $450.

"Right here, yo-boy!" Disco yelled.

Seeing Disco, the forty-something-year-old, a black man, briskly strolled over.

"Damn, Disco, let somebody else get some money, my nigga." Ziggy was one of the workers that Disco had laid off. He had a little bomb of his own but couldn't move shit while his former boss was out. Nobody could.

"You heard the man, my nigga, he want green bags," Disco responded, serving the man for a $600 lick. He only had sixty-five slabs left, so he went ahead and gave the man the extra five for free.

When Disco walked back over to the group of dudes, Ziggy was still bitching like a hoe on her rag and Shelton had joined him.

"Look, my nigga, y'all can stop cryin' 'cause I'm out. But y'all better get it-get it, 'cause I'll be out wit' a fresh bomb in the morning and they gon' be bigger, so y'all lil' shop gon' be closed again," Disco said, counting out his money. That was the very last of the 960 rocks he's chopped and bagged this morning.

Blue just laughed at Ziggy and Shelton because he sold weed, so Disco's big-ass-rocks didn't affect his money. Jit didn't care either because he sold clean [raw cocaine in powder form].

When Disco had counted the $2,000 and rubber-banded it, he pocketed the cash and looked over at Blue and Jit. "Y'all can laugh, but next week I'm closin' y'all shop too. So get it-get it, my niggas."

"Whatever, my nigga, build one!" Jit said.

"I got ten on it," Disco said.

"Give it here," Jit shot back and took a $20 bag of cocaine out of his bomb.

Blue put up four nickel-bags of weed and Shelton got two El Po's out of his Delta. Since Ziggy's crab-ass didn't put anything up they made him mix and roll the blunts. The four smoked the two lace-blunts and were sitting in the cut talking about bitches – who had the best pussy in Silver Blue – when Disco heard somebody calling his name. He stood and walked out of the hallway's shadows and saw Londa standing at the corner of the second floor's concrete railing. She looked good in her loose fitting cream colored silk short-set and four-inch gold heels. Her short wrap was perfect as always – not a hair out of place, and Mac lip gloss had her juicy lips looking as sexy as ever. Disco just stared at her, wondering what the hell she wanted.

"What's up?" he finally asked, a puzzled expression on his face.

"Oh, ain't nothin'. I figured you was out here so I brought you this plate from Ester's when I went to get me somethin' to eat... and no, I ain't get you no pork," she said, smiling as she handed him the food.

"Damn, Londa." Disco took the food. "Bet that up."

"Ain't nothin', Sco. Be safe out here," she said and walked off. Her round ass jiggled and swayed in the thin material.

The food smelt good and he was hungry, yet at the moment her ass looked better than the satisfaction the food promised.

Londa looked back as she *slung-nasty* up the hallway and caught him staring at her ass. She giggled like a little girl and held her pinky and thumb to her ear and mouth like a phone and mouthed the words, *call me if you need me.*

$$$

The next morning Disco woke up to Shoniece's pretty head bobbing up and down the length of his early morning erection. He'd came in around 3:45 and fell out sleep without taking a shower or even taking his clothes off. But that didn't stop Shoniece from giving her boss boss-fellatio. With only her fat, wet lips and tongue, she gormondized his dick. Disco looked beyond her arched back and big naked ass at the mirror on the dresser. Seeing her pretty shaved pussy hanging beneath her perfect ass cheeks like ripe fruit in a bush, he started working his hips, grinding his dick into the back of her deep throat.

"Mmmmm! Mmmm, hmmm!" Shoniece moaned, pleased that her head-game was still top-notch.

Disco grunted and continued to maul her throat.

Shoniece spat his long slippery dick out and jacked the length of it while whining, "Come on, baby, gimme that nut." She then sucked his dick back into her mouth.

Within seconds his children were running over her tongue and down into her belly. Shoniece continued to suck and pull until he was drained of his next generation.

Pleased with her work, she climbed out of bed and walked naked to the bathroom. He lay their catching his breath. When she returned, wearing a bright smile, she climbed back into bed and cuddled up next to her man. Times such as these had been rare since she'd came down for the funeral. In fact, this was only their second sexual encounter in five days. Yet she remembered a time back in Anniston, when they'd first met, when he couldn't go five minutes without digging in her *good-good* or cracking for some of her *firecracker* head. Now it seemed that he was always too busy or too tired. She damn near had to beg for the dick, which really was not her style. For that matter Shoniece had already concluded that Disco was fucking around on her. But thinking further, on life and her own actions, *doesn't everybody fuck around*, she mused. Especially since she'd once been labeled the Anniston-animal and was in fact a first-class gold-digging slut. Only Disco hadn't seen that side of her. When he and his brother had travelled to Alabama some five years ago, Shoniece had given him a safe place to lay his head and had also plugged him with a few local dudes to move his work. He had to love that.

"Bay," Shoniece whispered as she slowly massaged Disco's semi-erection.

"What's up?"

"What's wrong witchu?"

"Nothin'," he lied, because he'd learned early in life to keep bitches [as well as bitch-niggas] out of his business.

"Then why you be gone all the time? And why you always sooo tired?" She had no idea that he'd loss over a quarter-mill' and owed Bertto a little over a quarter-mill'.

"'Cause I work sooo hard, that's why. A lotta shit changed since Jay got killed and it's up to me to make shit right."

"Make what shit right?"

By now her soft hands had his dick rock-ass-hard. "Shit that you don't need to be worryin' 'bout 'cause it's thug-business, not wifey-business..." Crowning the top of her pretty head, he pushed her face down to his swollen dick. "I'ma handle the streets, you handle everythang between the sheets."

And with no pressure Shoniece handled her business like a big-girl was supposed to.

$$$

Either Disco was extremely tired or Shoniece had sucked and fucked the life out of him, because when he finally woke up from their forty-five minutes of thug-passion, the clock on his dresser read 1:45 p.m.

"Fuck!" he yelled and jumped up. Shoniece was gone and only her sweet smell remained. The very last thing that he remembered was her babbling something about Trisha, shopping, and some money. He immediately checked his pants pocket. $1,200 was missing. "Slick bitch!" he said and hit the shower, reminding himself to curse her ass out for playing money-games.

Dressing in Familiar Line cargo-shorts, all black soldier Rees and a fresh Arab, he snatched up his .40, cell phone and the $11,000 that he'd neatly stuffed in a brown paper bag. He hoped that he hadn't missed Chico, because he was out of drugs.

"Damn, I'ma miss that money!" he said as he whipped off in the rental, dialing Chico's number with his free hand.

"Yeah," Chico answered on the third ring.

"What they do, boy?"

"Shiid, whatever you need 'em to," Chico shot back.

"I'm ready for that Benz you denied a nigga the other day."

"Aiight, I'm here."

"Bet that, one!" Disco ended the call and fired up half a lace-blunt that was sitting in the rental's ashtray.

Jay-Z's REASONABLE DOUBT beat at a whisper as he rode. It had been Jay's favorite CD.

The ringing of his cell phone interrupted the groove.

"Yeah-yeah?" he answered.

"What it do, my nigga?"

"Ain't shit, Boe. What's good witchu?" Disco said, recognizing his little partner's voice. They hadn't seen each other or talked since Jay's funeral.

"Nothin' for real. I'm tryna see 'bout that thang we talked about."

Disco wanted to help his main man but he couldn't stand it at the time.

"It's fucked up, you feel me? I'm seein' somethin' but it ain't a lotta room, you feel me?"

Boe thought for a minute and then sighed heavily. He knew that Disco was a fair nigga, so he put it out there.

"Look, my nigga, I ain't like these other fuck-niggas, my nigga. I fucks witchu. So if you need a nigga to hit the block for you, it's all good. You ain't gotta give me shit. Just look out for Cuz, 'cause he gon' be out there wit' a nigga, and I'm straight, my nigga. 'Cause I know shit gon' get greater later."

Disco smiled to himself. It felt good to be trusted and respected by a real nigga.

"Boe, my nigga, bet that up, boy. I'ma hit you tomorrow night," he stated as he pulled up in Chico's front yard.

"It's all good, my nigga. One!"

"One," Disco replied and jumped out with the $11,000 brown paper bag.

He rung the doorbell three times before the door finally swung open. Standing before him was Black Girl, Chico's extra-sexy, but ultra-mean sister. He'd always had a lightweight crush on her, but because she was always short with her words and constantly frowning her pretty face, he never said anything to her except, "hello" or "where that boy at?" Today was no different.

"What's up, Black Girl. Where that boy at?"

She frowned and pointed towards the back room.

After stealing a few peeks at her nice ass and pretty dark legs, Disco walked off towards Chico's room, which was situated at the rear of the house. As he neared the room door he heard loud moaning, the type of moaning that resonated from a bitch getting her back beat out. The closer he got to the door, the louder the sounds of hardcore fucking got.

"Oh shit, Chico, baby, you killin' this pussy!" he heard a female voice yell so loud that it sounded like it was coming from a stereo system. The cry was followed by a gang of laughter.

"Fuck this nigga doin'?" Disco said and knocked on the door with three quick raps before walking into the semi-dark room.

"Disco, check this out, dog! Watch me hit her wit' the Flex!" Chico said, pointing at the huge plasma screen and doing the Flex dance.

76

Disco looked over at the screen and saw Chico punishing a hoe from the back. Everytime he plunged into her pussy the force of his stroke made her big D-size breasts bounce and jiggle. Disco laughed along with everybody else as Chico's crazy ass actually did the Flex as he fucked her from the back.

"You a wild nigga, my nigga!" Disco said, laughing his ass off.

The broad was a real tight piece of work – brown skin with big titties, a big ass, nice sexy lips and a short sexy hair style. He'd seen the chick somewhere before but couldn't place a name with the face.

"What's up, lil' nigga?"

Disco turned and saw the twins [Boe and Nard], E-4, Rat and Doc were also in the room watching Chico's triple X sex tape.

After greeting everybody and watching a little more of the footage, Disco and Chico walked into the kitchen to conduct business. While he placed the 500 grams of fish-scale on the old triple-bean, Chico gave the $11,000 to Black to count. When that process was complete, Disco dapped Chico up and hit it, because he had money that needed to be made, and the only way to get it was to *get* it.

"I ain't even gon' whip this shit," Disco talked to himself as he drove home with the half a kilo. "I'ma straight drop this shit and *bam-bam* every dime. I ain't comin' back home or leavin' the block until all 1,600 jugglers is gone!"

Motivated by his predicament, Disco fired up a lace-blunt and turned up the radio.

...I hustle 'til the sun come up/crack a forty when the sun go down/it's a cold winter y'all niggas better bundle up... bet it be a hotter summer/it's hot now listen up/don't you know the cops whole purpose is to lock us down/and throw away the key...[Even though what we do is wrong] 'Cause wit'out this drug shit/my kids got no way to eat... still tryna keep mine, smilin'/when the stomach start growlin' and the teeth stop showin'/I'ma rob me a person/caught a nigga slippin' while he out in the open... ['Cause even though what we do is wrong]...

Freeway rapped on WHAT WE DO.

Chapter 16

The money-green 2011 Infiniti QX56 floated South on 27th Avenue. Londa sat on the passenger side daydreaming as she stared throught the SUV's dark tinted windows. Tamia's ALMOST played softly through the truck's Bose sound system. Trisha's voice brought her back to the present.

"Damn, hoe, you aiight over there?" she asked her friend as she stopped at the red light on 119th Street, just past Club Lexx. They'd just dropped Shoniece off at Disco's house after hitting the mall.

"Yeah, I'm good," Londa replied, still staring out the window.

"Well, I just wanna thank you for the two outfits."

Londa sucked her teeth and frowned at her best friend. "Chick, thank them hoes that don't really fuck wit'chu, don't thank me, 'cause you like my sista, so that lil' $800 wasn't no pressure."

Trisha smiled and pulled off when the light changed. "You just gotta play tough, huh?"

"Girl, I am tough!" Londa said and they both laughed. "But, Trisha, for real, next time you wanna hang out wit' me don't bring that wannabe, fake bougie-ass-bitch, Shoniece."

"Shoniece aiight, Londa. You just gotta-"

"I ain't gotta do shit but be me, okay. I don't like that bitch. Plus, how would you like it if I brought Lil Will's other hoe 'round you?"

Trisha bussed out laughing again, but Londa just looked at her like she was crazy.

"Londa, first off, Lil Will ain't got no *other hoe*. Second, you say *other hoe* wit' Shoniece like Sco yo' man or somethin'. Girl, give me the 'T' 'cause I honestly didn't know."

Londa rolled her eyes at Trisha. "Hoe, don't play. You know me and Sco done fucked."

"And?" Trisha shot back.

"And, that mean I don't do his *other hoes*, so don't bring that bitch 'round me."

Trisha cut her eyes at Londa. *This bitch is really trippin'*, she thought to herself.

Londa had gotten up that morning to the ringing of her phone. Trisha had called to see if she wanted to hang out, however, she'd said nothing about bringing Disco's *other bitch*, Shoniece.

Before arriving at Trisha's house, Londa had gone to her bank and withdrew all of her savings except for $100, which was $5,850. She'd then drove to the pawn shop on 79th Street and 19th Avenue and pawned the last of White-boy Dave's jewelry. The man gave her $3,600 for it. So after spending $1,800 in the mall on Trisha and herself, she had $7,650 to her name.

As Trisha pulled up into her driveway, Londa took $650 of the money and dropped it back into her purse. The $7,000 she sealed in the white bank envelope and slipped it in her panties for safe keeping.

"So whatchu 'bout to do, chick?" Trisha asked as she walked Londa to her car, which was parked outside of her gate.

Londa opened the car door on her convertible Volvo and dropped her big designer handbag on the car's floorboard. "I'on know. Probably just go home and stare outta my project window."

"Well, that's better than goin' 'round pickin' up them lil' boys," Trisha said and cracked up laughing.

"What-ever-hoe!" Londa shot back and got in her car. "Trisha, you think I'ma dog? Like, maybe somebody like Sco won't never see me... like, I probably ain't good enough or something?"

Trisha looked at her friend and felt bad for her. Because even though her and Lil Will saw the good in Londa, everybody else only saw her whorish ways and only heard her slick mouth. She'd always tried to talk to Londa about *being so loose*, but her friend would not listen. Now she was stuck with the fucked up reputation that she'd made for herself.

Reaching in the car window, Trisha rubbed Londa's pretty face. "Girl, it's somebody for everybody. It's just that, a lotta times we don't know who we are, so we don't recognize that special somebody when we see 'em... you gotta stop worryin' 'bout this material shit and follow what's inside of you. It's a good person inside of you wit' a lotta love, and that person is gon' attrack somebody just as beautiful and lovin'."

Londa nodded her head. "Thanks, girl, you gon' always be my BFF."

Trisha leaned in and kissed her twice, once on the forehead and once on the lips.

"Ditto," she said and walked off into her house.

Chapter 17

It took Disco a long while to get right – straight drop eighteen ounces and chop it down to 1,600 juggler dime-rocks – but he hit the set at 5:30 like a second shift factory worker trying to get a raise in pay and promotion in work status. Everything that pulled up or walked up he was serving. He wasn't just serving jugglers to hustlers, he was slingling fat-ass working-dimes to the smokers. Six for fifty, twelve for a hundred, and all eight and nine dollar shorts were taken. By 9:45 he'd made five trips to the rental car that he had parked on the 17th Avenue side of Silver Blue to re-up, thus running through six $2,000 bombs, and he had three more left.

With his Arab tied around his head, shirtless he stepped out of the second floor hallway yelling, "Straight drop! Fat-ass green bags, right here!"

Blue followed hIm out of the cut. "Patch up, my nigga. I got that red-gold."

"My nigga, the only thang gold I want is some chains. And I ain't smokin' shit 'til I move the whole thang. You feel me?" Disco capped back.

"How much you got left, my nigga?"

"Enough to flood the block," Disco said and turned towards a blue box Chevy. "Green bag!"

The Spanish dudes that were inside the car all jumped out and walked over toward the hallway. "We got three-fifty, poppa."

Ziggy ran over and pulled out his bomb. "Right here, amigo," he said and snatched the money.

The Spanish dude saw the clear bags that Ziggy had and bucked. "No, no clear bag. I want green, poppa."

"Nah, chico, that's yo' shit now," Ziggy said.

"Ziggy, my nigga, give the man his shit, dog."

Ziggy looked at Disco like he was crazy. "I ain't givin' that cracka shit! My nigga, fuck you and that cracka!"

Whop! The straight right sent Ziggy flying to the wall. *Whop! Whop!* The left hook and right upper-cut laid Ziggy out like a rug.

Shelton stepped up but Blue upped his .38. "Fall back, Shelt. If you wanna fade, you can fade, but y'all ain't 'bout to jump."

Disco looked at Shelton and sucked his teeth, knowing that the soft-body red nigga didn't really want no pressure. He then leaned over Ziggy, who was out cold, and took the $350 that the Spanish dude had handed him and the rest of his bomb.

"Y'all fuck-niggas can't serve 'round here no more!" he said to Shelton. "Here, poppy, lemme get that other shit back."

Disco gave the Spanish dude thirty-eight double-ups and dropped all of Shelton's clear bags in the bomb with his own.

"Aye, Disco, my nigga, it ain't gotta-" Shelton started.

Disco cut him off. "Get this fuck-nigga up and don't let me catch y'all niggas out her *ann* other day... now play wit' it if you wanna."

Shelton helped Ziggy to his feet and the two stumbled off to the Delta and cleared it.

$$$

For the next two hours customers continued to cop and go. Disco had crumbled up bills in both pockets, his socks, and in his briefs. He'd made two more trips to the car and was now finishing off his last $2,000 bomb.

"Man, you ready to patch up?" Blue asked. "You done got all the money."

Disco folded another stack and pocketed it. "Here, my nigga. I got ten dollars."

Blue gave the $10 bill to Jit along with two nickel-bags of weed. As the three sat in the shadows of the hallway preparing to blaze the lace-blunt, a familiar voice called out.

"Sco! Aye, Disco!"

Disco walked out and saw Londa. She had a big Miami Sub's bag in her hand.

"You hungry?" she asked.

"Umm, yeah, kinda," he answered, wondering what was good with her being so nice to him when she had to know that he hated her *roxy* ass.

"Well, here." Londa handed him the bag. "Make sure you get *everything* outta the bag."

"Aiight."

"Well, aiight... and my number still the same," she said and walked back to her apartment.

This bitch crazy, he thought and re-entered the cut.

"Boy, what we got?!" Blue asked.

"We ain't got shit," Disco said, squatting on the steps to eat. "I got some Miami Subs, you heard me?!"

"My nigga, you must be guttin' Londa, 'cause shawty don't give a nigga shit! I been tryna holla at her fine-ass for the longest," Jit stated, putting the finishing touches on the blunt.

"Nah, I ain't fuckin' that bitch," Disco said, tearing into the wings and fries.

"Dog, you gon' break bread," Blue entoned, grabbing a wing and a handful of fries. "'Specially after a nigga kept them boys from fuckin' yo' ass up today."

"Nigga?!" Disco yelled and they all bussed out laughing.

For the next five to ten minutes they just smoked and ate. Every few minutes a smoker would venture into the hallway to be served. With all of the fries and wings gone, Disco searched the bag for a napkin, but instead came up with a white envelope. Pulling it from the bag he looked at it crazy-like. *What the fuck is this?* he asked himself before ripping it open. *What the fuck?!* his mind screamed upon seeing the crispy bank notes.

"Boy, what's that?" Blue asked.

"Whatever it is, it ain't yours!" Disco fired back and hopped up.

I wonder if that bitch left this money in the bag by accident, he wondered. Of course he knew that money hungry bitches like Londa didn't forget money. *But what if she did?* Disco was a lot of things, but a thief he was not. So he walked off towards Londa's apartment.

"Disco, where you goin', boy?" Blue yelled out.

"To chase my dreams," Disco answered, never breaking his stride.

... don't go chasing waterfalls/ just stick to the rivers and the lakes that you're use to/ I know that you're gonna have it your way or nothing at all/ but I think you're moving to fast...

TLC's *WATERFALLS* played softly as Londa lay naked between her sheets. After taking Disco the food she'd simply showered and slipped into bed. She hoped that he enjoyed his food. More so, she prayed that he saw the sincerity in her actions. *God, let him see me and not the fucked up shit I done done befo' this,* she continued to verbally petition a Higher Power with whom she had no prior relationship. However, she was desperate for something new in her life... change... love... some kind of devotion... perhaps, they, her and Disco, could share what Trisha and Lil Will shared... a smile bright enough to light up her dark bedroom eased its way onto her face as she pictured Disco doing more than just *fucking her.* Somehow in her mind she'd made Disco love her. A tingle started in her belly and traveled south to her *center-of-pleasure.* Her delicate fingers followed, but was interrupted by a rapping on her front door.

God, please, she thought as her heart rate suddenly increased. She jumped out of bed and eased into her long silk robe. With her heart fluttering, Londa shuffled off to the front door. Knowing exactly who it was, she unlocked and pulled the door open. Disco stood there before her. For what seemed like forever they just stood there eyeing each other. Londa broke the pregnant silence that threatened to derail the beginning of what she so desperately yearned.

"What's up, Disco?" she damn near whispered.

"Ain't really shit," he answered, shrugging his shoulders as he spoke.

Another moment of silence ensued as the two began a new stare off. It was as if they'd just met. Whereas Disco was confused with her recent actions and trying his damnest to continue hating her, she was nervous and trying her damnest to continue showing him the absolute best side of her.

Looking at his handsome face and into those sexy slanted eyes of his, she wanted to hug him and pull him off to her bedroom for what she figured was her truest expression of love. Yet she knew that he wasn't there for that.

"Is you gon' come in, Sco, or you just gon' stand there?" she asked jokingly and cracked that bright smile of hers.

Without returning her smile he walked into the well decorated one bedroom apartment and found himself a spot on the large over-stuffed sectional that hogged up much of the apartment's space.

Londa closed and locked the door before seating herself, with one leg folded beneath her soft round ass, right beside him. Her robe was loosely tied so beautiful aspects of her smooth light-honey colored composition was on display. With wanton eyes she watched him sleepishly steal glances of her exposed anatomy.

"Sssooo," she began, smile still in place. "You gon' wait all this time to drop in on ya girl, and now that you here, you just gon' sit there and look. You ain't doin' or sayin' nothin'?"

Disco looked up from between her smooth shapely thighs into her pretty face before standing up. Her eyes widened in a sudden moment of fear, for she felt that her question had caused him to leave. But to her relief, he went into his back pocket and removed the white bank envelope containing her $7,000. Tossing it in her lap, he reseated himself.

"What's up wit' that?" he asked, pointing at the envelope. "It was in the Miami Subs' bag."

"I know," she answered curtly, a faint scowl on her face. "I put it in there."

"Why?" he just had to ask. Having known Londa for so many years, and knowing that she was self-centered, greedy, and never the one to give anybody shit – especially a nigga. Her actions had him *throwed*.

Londa simply shrugged her narrow shoulders and said, "because I wanted you to have it."

"What make you think I want or need yo' money, Londa?"

The boldness of his inquiry kind of crushed her spirits. Nevertheless, she'd come too far to tuck her tail and run. So she steadied herself and expressed the affinities of her heart.

"I was actually hopin' that you'd want the money, 'cause even though it ain't a lot, it's all that I have. And I promise, ain't no strings on it," she explained before dropping her head, unable to look him in his piercing eyes. "As far as you needin' the money, well, I ain't never seen you out there sellin' yo' own stuff befo'... and I know you probably helped Jay's people out wit' the funeral and all, so I was just tryna help you out, 'cause I felt like you've always kinda helped me wit' a lil' bet or whatever if I caught you right," she finished and looked up at him.

Disco had a little smile on his face. He also had a little more respect for the bitch that sat before him.

Seeing his facial expression, Londa felt a *tad-bit* more confident on her position. "Besides, nigga, you ain't even got no hair cut." Laughter followed her words.

Disco couldn't help but to laugh himself. "I do need a cut, huh?"

"Do you?!" she said, still laughing. "Yo' butt need to hit that water too."

"Oh, you illustratin' now!" he said, laughing along with her. "You a trip, shawty."

"So you want it?" she asked, then drew his attention to her lap where the envelope still sat.

"The money?" he asked, his eyebrow raised.

She smiled seductively and replied, "Sco, you can have *anythin'* in this apartment, boy, wit' no pressure... and it ain't no strings."

"Well, how 'bout you just gimme what you want me to have."

Londa took the envelope of money out of her lap and handed it to him. Londa then unzipped his shorts and removed his semi-erect penis, covering it with wet kisses and long laps of her tongue.

Disco shifted his position and crowned the back of her bobbing head. His eyes closed and his hips began to grind on their own. *Damn Londa*, he thought, not knowing if it was the *money,* her *change in attitude* or if she'd just become a *better dick sucker*. Either way, his dick was at full mass and about to shoot off.

With her free hand, Londa pulled her robe off. She was now ass-naked and putting on the performance of her life. Loud slurping sounds and deep moans resonated from her throat.

Disco moaned involuntarily and filled Londa's mouth with a load of hot, thick nut.

"Mmmmm!" Londa groaned and swallowed. "Wait a minute, bay," she said, standing as she wiped sperm from her chin.

Disco watched Londa's ass jiggle as she sashayed off to the bedroom.

After gargling and brushing her teeth, Londa soaped up a rag and returned to the couch in the living room; where she found Disco knocked out and snoring.

No this nigga didn't, she said to herself as she walked in her bedroom and pulled the big comforter off of her king-size bed. She then walked back over to her sleeping *dream lover* and stared lovingly at him as he slept. Londa found a spot on the big couch beside him; resting her head on his chest, she pulled the soft comforter over them. A big smile played across her face as she felt his strong arms encircle her. *This can't be real,* she thought and rushed off to sleep in the event that it was only a dream.

Chapter 19

Lil Will and Maine sat across the street from the stripper chick's crib for the fourth consecutive day. Both men were bored and growing tired of the waiting and watching. Riding was one thing, but this shit was altogether different. Growing up and beefing with other neighborhoods had shown them both plenty of bloodshed. And a rule of *thuggin'* had always been, if a nigga *killed your homeboy you had to kill everybody that was with the move before your homeboy's funeral.* Yet Jay had been dead and buried and not one shot had been let off. The whole situation had Lil Will *super-hot.*

"Aye, look here, Maine, this shit really been draggin' on, my nigga."

"Fool, who you tellin'?! We just need to ride four blocks over and let these choppas dance. Once we start heatin' this shit up 'round here, niggas gon' respect our mind," Maine stated. The robbery had really damaged his ego. He couldn't believe that niggas had the nuts to lay on him.

"Nah, we ain't 'bout to do that. Shit like that have niggas in full-scale wars. And when you warrin' you can't eat."

"Said who? I'm 'bout that life for real, my nigga. I do this trappin' shit 'cause I'm tryna slow down and not end up wit' one-hunnid years for them banks, or three-hunnid years for paintin' a nigga's ass 'bout his own shit. But, bruh, I ain't wit' this hoe-ass-shit!"

"So whatchu sayin'?" Lil Will questioned his main man.

"I'm sayin' we need to do what we do! Jay gone, Sco down bad, and ain't no money movin'. And, my nigga, I needs that money. Feel me?!"

Lil Will digested his homeboy's words and said, "Aiight, let's get a handle on this shit. At least find out where these fuck-niggas be. Once we do that, we'll get down to business. Feel me?!"

"Yeah, I feel you, but what if we don't get no handle on this shit...my nigga, them fuck-ass niggas licked for a quarter! They could be livin' in Atlanta right now."

That is true, Lil Will thought. "Aiight, check this out, soon as this bitch clear it we gon' break in this bitch. It gotta be somethin' in there to tell a nigga somethin'."

"And if it ain't?"

"Then it's all on you. We gon' get back to business."

Maine smiled. "That's what the fuck I'm talkin' 'bout! 'Cause it's money to be got and I got to get that shit."

"Fuck it! We on one!" Lil Will yelled and racked his .40 caliber.

$$$

"My nigga! What's up wit' this soft-ass-nigga, Jack, my nigga? Gotta nigga 'round here hungry as fuck. My nigga, call that nigga," Mac-90 complained to Varray. Being stuck in that little ass apartment was driving him crazier than he already was. Which in turn was driving Varray crazy.

"Mac, stop cryin'. Fool gon' be through here. Niggas can't just move when you want 'em to all the time."

"That nigga don't have no problem movin' when he gettin' my muthafuckin' money!" Mac-90 checked the situation. "And for real, fuck that pussy-nigga! I'ma call my muthafuckin' sista. She should be home."

Yeah, I hope the animal-ass-bitch is home, 'cause I ain't had no pussy in three days, Varray thought to himself. "Do that, my nigga. And tell her to brang me somethin' too."

"Aiight," Mac-90 said, lifting the phone and punching in numbers. The phone rung about thirty times before a sleepy voice finally came across. "Sis?!... I need you... Mmaann, getcho ass up! I need you to make a lil' run for me... I know you strip and I know yo' ass need money too... yeah, I'ma break you off... yeah, I need you to run by Artoria's and get me and Varray two big breakfast plates, and then go by Drew-Dog spot and get me three raw-fifties of that clean and two dimes of that zona... yeah! I got the muthafuckin' money!... aiight, and hurry yo' ass up!"

"She comin'?" Varray asked, his dick already hard at the thought of *her eating that dick* and throwing all that pussy at him.

"Yeah, she comin'," Mac-90 shot back. "And since you fuckin' her, you gon' pay her."

"What?!"

"Nigga, you ain't slick."

Varray couldn't help but laugh. Mac-90 wasn't that slow after all.

$$$

"You tryna hit this, my nigga?" Maine asked Lil Will as he puffed on the big lace-spliff.

"Nah," Lil Will replied, fanning the blue smoke out of his face. "How you gon' smoke when we workin'?"

"Fool, this ain't work. We ain't doin' shit but eye-spyin' a hoe and probably breakin' in a crib. That ain't no pressure."

"I hope not, 'cause there she go."

Maine looked up and saw the chick locking her front door. She had on some little nasty-ass cut off jean shorts and a baby-T. "Damn, my nigga, hope we don't have to end up killin' this hoe, my nigga, I gotta fuck her. Looka that bitch lips!"

"Huh, man?! That lil' bitch *bad-to-death.*"

"And I know the head on fi'," Maine commented as he put out the lace-blunt and got ready to jump out.

"Hold up!" Lil Will stopped him.

"Fuck you mean?!"

"Man, we should probably follow this hoe."

"For what?! We been followin' the hoe for three days... now you wanted to go in the hoe shit so let's go in the hoe shit."

Something inside of Lil Will was telling him to ignore Maine and follow the hoe. But going against his better judgment, he simply jumped out and followed Maine across the street. The two entered the gate and walked straight to the back, where they saw the black 300C parked and covered. This was their element: breaking in people's shit, hitting banks and running up in spots.

"There we go right there," Lil Will said, pointing at an AC-unit mounted in a window.

"Yeah, come on! This definitely the spot or that fuckin' car wouldn't be here!"

Within five minutes the AC-unit was laying on the ground and Lil Will was pushing Maine through the window.

"I'ma open the back door," Maine said after falling inside the cluttered bedroom. There were panties, bras; all sorts of designer jeans, blouses, and dresses scattered everywhere. Maine shot straight to the back door and opened it for Lil Will.

"Come on, fool. Let's search this bitch and get the fuck on!"

Maine nodded and the two split up to ramsack the house.

Chapter 20

Londa woke up with a subdued stir. Slowly she opened her eyes, fearing that last night might have been a dream or figment of her fiendish imagination. However, when her glance landed on Disco's handsome face she knew that it had all been true. God had made her dream a reality. The two of them lay *body-to-body*, their legs intertwined. She could feel his early morning hard-on pressed against her thigh. It made her mouth water and her pussy tingle. Londa began massaging his dick through his shorts. The more she fondled him the hornier she got. Unable to resist the dick any longer, Londa slipped down beneath the comforter that covered them and freed his erection. Slowly, but forcefully, she began administering *super-head*. Up and down she bobbed her head, taking him balls-deep into her throat. And it seemed the more pressure that she applied with her big soft lips, the bigger and harder his dick got in her mouth.

With his sleepy eyes still closed and his tired mind spinning, Disco cupped the back of her bobbing head and started fucking her face. "Damn, Shoniece!" he moaned out loud.

Londa's bobbing head stopped mid-bob. *No the fuck this bitch didn't just call me his other bitch's name*, she thought, spitting his stiff dick out of her wet mouth. Clearing her throat, Londa said, "Umm, excuse me?! But what did you just call me?"

Disco's eyes popped open. He looked around the room he was in and then down at Londa, who was still holding his dick, and wondered *what the fuck was going on?!*

"Sco, don't ignore me, boy." Londa was staring in his confused eyes.

"Londa, what is you doin'?"

"Umm," she said, looking at him like he was super-stupid. "Suckin' yo' dick, *duuhhh*."

"Smart-ass! I know you suckin' my dick. I wanna know why you suckin' my dick."

"'Cause it was hard, nigga," she said, laughing.

Before he could say another word she started back blessing him. As she devoured his throbbing manhood he wrecked his brain trying to remember how he'd ended up on her couch. He scanned the room and spotted the white envelope. *Okay!* he said inwardly. Remembering that the new Londa had broke bread with him. Then, looking at the window and seeing sunlight shining through the edges of the blinds, he realized that that had been last night. *Fuck! This bitch Shoniece gon' be trippin',* he thought.

"Umm, Londa."

"What?" she answered and kept sucking.

"What time it is?"

Londa stopped, rolled her eyes and said, "'bout eleven or twelve." And went back to serving his member.

Disco sighed. He knew that only one thing could get her mouth off of his dick, and that was to fuck her and that was something he *did not want to do!* Because he had shit to do and he couldn't get them done with his dick in her mouth. He had to buss a nut to satisfy her and hope like hell that she nutted in the process. So with much reluctance he pushed her off of his dick and forced her onto her back. Grabbing both legs, he threw them on his shoulders and plunged into her.

"Ooooh, Sco, baby, oooooh!" Londa moaned.

Disco bit his lower lip and dug deep, banging her with all that he had.

"Oh, Sco! Oh, Sco! Un'huh! Un'huh! Fuck this pussy, Sco!"

After about ten strokes it felt as if the elastic had stretched out of Londa's big pussy. He was balls-deep in her and his entire abdomen was all wet up. *Damn, bitch!* he thought and pushed her legs further back.

"Oooh, Sco, damn... baby!"

He angled his dick to the left and beat until sweat began to cover his face. Londa moaned and threw it back as best she could. Disco looked down at his dick disappearing into her meaty pussy. Everytime it came back out it was covered in more of her lady-nut.

"Ssscccooo! I'm cummin' again, baby!" she yelled.

He couldn't understand how, because he couldn't feel shit. *Lil Will, my nigga, forgive me!* he said almost in a prayer. Because everybody knew that forbidden pussy was the best pussy, and being that Londa and Trisha looked just alike – Londa was just lighter in complexion, two inches shorter and five pounds thicker – Disco closed his eyes and imagined Trisha being beneath him.

"You like this dick? Huh? This dick good to you?" he asked, slamming into her.

"Yeah, Sco! Yeah, baby! I love this dick! Give it to me!"

Disco fucked her faster, feeling his nut building. Londa's pussy started smacking and sloshing. Disco leaned forward and started sucking her neck as he fucked.

"Oh, Sco!"

"I'm cummin', girl!"

"Cum on!" she yelled.

And Disco exploded inside of her. "Damn," he moaned and released her legs.

She held him. His breathing was heavy. She was in heaven. Disco slowly rolled off of her. Londa got up and came back with a soapy rag. After cleaning him up she went and jumped in the shower.

When she returned twenty minutes later, she found him counting money. There were stacks all over her coffee table. She just sat down beside him and watched for a minute.

"Them two-grand stacks?" she asked.

"Yeah."

Without saying anything else she picked up some of the crumbled bills and helped him count. When they were finished it was $22,800 on the table [that included the $7,000 that she'd given him and the money he'd made off of the rocks he'd taken from Ziggy].

Picking up his cell phone he called Chico.

"Yeah-yeah?" he answered.

"Where you at?"

"To the crib. Why, what's good?"

"You still got that big Kawasaki for sale?"

"What Kawasaki?"

"That white 1,000?"

"Yeah."

"I'm comin' to get that bitch right now!" Disco said excitedly.

"Aiight, come on."

Disco hung up and turned to Londa. "You gotta bag to put this money in?"

"Yeah," she said and looked at him funny. "But, umm, is you finna buy a motorcycle?"

"Hell nah!" he laughed at her. "Stop bein' nosey and listenin' to people's conversations."

"I ain't nosey, boy!" she punched him on the arm. "I was just sayin'."

"You wasn't sayin' shit, you was bein' nosey. Now get the bag so we can go!"

She wanted to be mad because he'd called her nosey, but he'd also just said 'we', which meant that she was going with him. *I can't be mad at that! Especially after he done gave a bitch that good as dick*, she thought and walked off smiling.

Chapter 21

"So hold up, my nigga. You tryna tell me that it ain't no heaven?! That when a nigga die he just dead and worms and shit come out 'im?" Mac-90 squealed in his squeaky voice before hitting the raw-square he'd just built. "'Cause, my nigga, that shit sound crazy."

"Mac, the crackas just teach us 'bout heaven and hell to make us be good. Just like when we was lil' they taught us 'bout that Santa Clause shit."

Mac-90 jumped up. "Now I know you trippin'! You tryna say it ain't no Santa Clause?!"

Before Varray could answer a knock sounded at the door. *Boom! Boom! Boom! Boom!*

"Get the door, man."

Sucking his teeth, Mac-90 walked over to the door with his pistol cocked and ready to rock. "Who is it?"

"Who the fuck you think it is?"

Hearing his sister's voice, Mac-90 snatched the door open.

"Gotdamn! What took you -" Mac-90 began *going off* on his sister but stopped short at seeing her stank little outfit. "Bitch, what the fuck you got on?"

She sucked her teeth and pushed past him. "Boy, I *scrip*, remember?"

"Yeah, but this ain't no fuckin' *scrip* club. So you shouldn't be 'round here showin' all ya pussy and shit, bitch."

"No! You got me fucked up. I ain't no bitch, Mac-"

"Y'all two chill out, damn!" Varray stepped up, squashing the sibling beef.

"You got the weed and coc'," Mac-90 asked, already having seen the bags of food.

"Yeah, you got my money?"

"Don't play wit' me, Joy... gemme my shit." He held his hand out.

"Here, boy!" Joy forced her small hand into her pocket and came out with the three bags of cocaine. She then squeezed her other hand into her other pocket and pulled out two bags of weed.

Mac-90 snatched the weed and cocaine and said, "Ya man gon' pay you."

"Ut'un, no bitch! See, that's why I ain't wanna be fucked up witcha petty ass. You gon-"

Varray stepped over and pulled her to him. He then leaned in and pulled her tongue. Joy responded by sucking his lips and hugging him tight around the neck. With both hands palming her soft round ass, Varray slipped one of his fingers underneath the bottom of her little shorts and worked it into her pussy. Joy moaned and really started sucking on his lips.

"Aye! Y'all on some bullshit, now!" Mac-90 yelled and snatched his sister back. "My nigga, that's some disrespectful shit, my nigga. You tryin' me like my sista a animal or some shit."

Nigga, she is! Varray wanted to yell, but instead he respected his lil' partner's mind. "You right, fool. My bad."

"Tryin' the Mac-man. Y'all take that shit back there somewhere."

Being the true animal that she was, Joy rolled her eyes at Mac-90 and pulled Varray in the back room to get her back *beat out*.

$$$

Maine had gone through every drawer, shoe box and bag in Joy's cluttered room. In the process he'd found $673 and smelt every pair of panties that she owned – both dirty and clean. And to his surprise they all smelt like some sort of fruit or potpourri. Right then and there he decided that he had to have the cute little raunchy female with the provocative body. With the money he'd found in pocket, he walked back over to the dresser and was about to rummage through an old looking jewelry box when Lil Will walked into the room.

"My nigga, check this out!" Lil Will said excitedly, placing a large photo album on the bed. "Look!"

"Dog, that's that bitch-ass nigga from Laguna's!" Maine pointed to the photo of Jack and Varray posted up next to the black Chrysler 300C.

"And look at this," Lil Will said, flipping the page.

There were pictures of Joy and Mac-90 dating from childhood to the present.

"That nigga there must be the nigga that shot Jay... the hoe is his sista, look like."

"Yeah," Lil Will agreed with a nod of his head. He then pulled out his cell phone and snapped a picture of the photos. "Her name Joy."

"How you know?"

"Bills on the table."

Maine nodded and walked back over to the jewelry box. Inside were a few rings and a nice tennis bracelet. Maine put them all in his pocket.

"My nigga, I know you ain't stealin' the hoe jewelry."

"Her brutha stole my money!" he stated and walked out.

Lil Will shook his head and followed, pleased that they were one step closer to killing the nigga that robbed them and killed their big partner.

$$$

"Oh shit, Var! Baby, ease up! Please! Oooh shit, Var! Please, let, let me turn around! You in my stomach!" Mac-90 heard his sister yelling from the bedroom.

"Maaann, this shit crazy! A nigga don't wanna hear that fuck-shit... I ain't had no pussy in four days 'round this bitch!" Mac-90 complained.

Firing up his eighth raw-square, he thought about the position he was in. He'd been hiding in the apartment ever since he'd killed Jay, holed up like a rat in a hole. No pussy, no real gambling, and no money coming in. Mac-90, in his own mind, considered himself a real 'G'. So he couldn't understand how Varray could just lay back and do nothing about the situation. *'Cause ain't no muthafuckin' reason to have no money if you can't ball-out! I ain't do all that robbin' to hide in no muthafuckin' 'partment!* Mac-90 surmised and picked up his .45. His sister's car keys were laying on the table. Just as he was picking them up the phone rung. He should've just ignored it, however, he didn't.

"Hello?!"

"Mac."

"Nigga, where the fuck you at?" he asked Jack.

"At my apartment."

"My nigga, you tried a nigga!"

"Nah, dog. My hoe took the rental. They havin' somethin' at the park."

"They jammin'?"

"Yeah, Ghetto Style and BDC Express out there."

Mac-90 knew it was going to be some hoes out there and he damn sure needed one. "I'm 'bout to come through."

"You got wheels?" Jack asked.

"Yeah, nigga, my sista shit."

"Aiight."

Mac-90 hung up and bolted for the door before Joy or Varray came out and fucked up his plans.

$$$

Leaving the house that they had just broke in, Lil Will and Maine got out into traffic. As he drove along, Lil Will thought about his next move – the best way to use the new information that they now had. Maine, on the other hand, was consumed with provocative thoughts of him and Joy.

Lil Will continued cruising until he came to the light on 12ᵗʰ Street. Beside him sat a gold Honda Accord. *What the fuck?!* he thought, tapping Maine on the arm.

"What's up?"

Lil Will pointed at Joy's car, only Joy wasn't driving.

"Bitch-ass-nigga!" Maine said and tried to hop out, but Lil Will grabbled him.

"Nah, let's see where they go. They might be goin' to meet the other nigga, Varray."

$$$

Pulling into Gibson Park on 12ᵗʰ Street and 3ʳᵈ Avenue, Mac-90 and Jack jumped out high as a muthafucka. Niggas, bitches, and little children were everywhere.

"Jack, my nigga, this bitch jam packed!" Mac-90 said, slapping five with Jack.

"No bullshit," Jack replied and scanned the area for his baby-momma.

"Aye, Jack, ain't that that animal-ass-bitch Felicia?"

"Where?"

"Right there!"

And sure enough, Felicia was posted up next to her BMW with Apple and Tawanna. All three of them were known *off-the-chainers* and they were definitely dressed the part in their bathing suits with sheer wrap-around skirts and heels.

"Aye, Felicia, check this out, girl!" Mac-90 holla'd like he was a big-boy.

Felicia looked, saw that it was Mac-90 and waved him off. Apple and Tawanna laughed.

Firing up the fat-ass lace-blunt that he'd just perfected, Jack laughed and blew big lace-smoke. "That hoe tried you, my nigga!"

"Nah," Mac-90 said and gulped the 40 ounce of Old English. "That bitch tried herself, 'cause I'm Mac-90, the money magnet... and I'm 'bout to go straighten this hoe, tryna act like she don't swallow dick."

Mac-90 turned to get the blunt from Jack and almost shitted on himself. "Jack!"

Boom! Boom! Boom! Boom! Boom! Boom! Boom! Boom! The nigga with the big gun and the scarf over his nose and mouth let off. *Boom! Boom! Boom! Boom!*

Jack never stood a chance. It's as if his body was a magnet for the hot lead, because several shots landed in his head and chest area, sending his lifeless body crashing to the pavement.

Mac-90 quickly upped his .45 and sent all eight of his shots in the direction of the shooter. *Doom! Doom! Doom! Doom! Doom! Doom! Doom! Doom! Click!* The big gun locked up. *Oh shit!* he cursed himself and broke out running.

Yyyyyaaaaaaaaaaaaaaaakkkkkkkkk!!! Maine let loose with the AK-47 and gave chase, but a F-14 Tomcat Plus figher with .50 caliber cannons and Tomahawk missiles wouldn't have caught Mac-90.

Lil Will stood over the already dead Jack and *Boom! Boom! Boom!* Sent three more Into his face. He then jumped into the splack and peeled off in the direction that Maine had ran. Spotting his man he quickly skidded to a halt.

"Nigga, come on!"

Maine jumped in and they peeled off, leaving Jack dead and three bystanders severely wounded.

Chapter 22

...Puusshhh/ I'm pushin' it / Puuusshhh/ I'm pushin' It/ Puusshhh/ I'm pushin' it/ Puussh/ I'ma push it to the limit...I push and I push/ I ride and I ride/ Tryna survive on 95/ I push it to the limit...I be pushin' it hard/ I be pushin' it soft/ If you pushin' a lot/ Then you pushin' for Ross...

Ricky Rozay's PUSH IT TO THE LIMIT boomed from Londa's home entertainment center as she and Disco sat at the dining room table chopping and bagging work. After leaving Chico's house with his first *block* since Jay's murder, the two had driven to the flea market on 27th Avenue and 79th Street to cop a scale, bags, baking soda, a sealer, razors and a new set of Vision Ware pots. With everything in place, and Londa doing *everything* she could to help, Disco quickly whipped up twenty-seven ounces into thirty-six [dropping 84's and bringing back 103's]. So he still had nine zones of soft left and he planned to sack them all up in raw-halves and let Jit *tear the block apart*.

Everything was moving as he wished. Smiling to himself he watched Londa out of the corner of his eye. She had a three-ounce pile of cocaine in front of her and she was steadily knocking it down, raw-half by raw-half. She'd started out slow, complaining and bitching, but by the time they'd cut up and bagged up all of the hard she was working like a vet table-worker, so she'd gained a few more *browny-points* in his book. *Yeah, this bitch gon' fuck 'round and make me stop hatin' her dog-ass*, Disco thought, *'cause she startin' to look like a real asset.*

105

Calculating the work and its return in his mind, he saw an easy $19,999 today because he planned to bleed the block his self with a 1,440 rock bomb [half a block], and he'd already called Boe and Cuz from Broward to come get a nine-ounce bomb [720 double-up rocks]. If that went smooth with them and he *bammed* the last nine-ounces tomorrow before dark, he could cop a brick-and-a-half for $33,000, shoot Lil Will and Maine $5,000 to buss-down, and the money from the nine ounces of soft would be free money. Still, at this rate, there was no way that he'd hustle up $255,000 in three more days. His little smile disappeared as he realized that he'd definitely have to sell his Vert.

The ringing of his cell phone interrupted his calculating. Looking at the phone's screen he saw that is was Shoniece. She'd been calling him and leaving *slick-ass-messages* all day. *Fuck Shoniece*, he thought. He had bigger problems to deal with and other more important shit that he could be doing besides arguing with her selfish ass. *Bitch don't want nothin' but some money or to talk shit*, were his conclusions.

Looking over at the living room window he saw that the sun was going down, which meant that he'd missed some money, but that the real money was about to start coming.

I gotta get out there and get this money, he thought as he peeked over at Londa.

"Boy, what is you lookin' at?" she asked, faking like she was mad.

"Nothin', for real," Disco said and started laughing.

"Whatever, nigga!" she shot back and stood up. After a long stretch and a yawn she sat back down. "That's it for me, Sco. This shit got my fingers hurtin'."

"Well, yo' ass gon' be hurtin' if you don't finish baggin' them halves."

"Oh," she replied, her index-finger in her mouth. "You gon' beat me?"

Disco laughed at her play on innocence. "Yeah, I'ma beat you, but not like you think."

She sucked her teeth. "You ain't no fun."

"Not all the time, 'cause all times ain't s'posed to be fun. You just do what a nigga tell you and I promise you'll have yo' share of good times, and it'll be way more realer and way more better than what you experienced wit' them fuck-niggas."

Londa smiled brightly, because his *thug-nature* had her insides on fire. Right then and there she wanted to get under the table and suck the hell out of his dick. But she didn't, she picked up the card and got back to bagging up the cocaine.

Disco stood up and put two $2,000 bombs in his briefs. "Londa, this here is for Boe, he gon' call my phone. When he calls it's gon' say Boe on the screen. Don't answer no calls but Boe! Tell the nigga to meet you at Block Buster and give him this work. Tell him it's whatever and to hit me up when he finish."

Londa nodded okay. Disco leaned over and kissed her forehead before leaving to beat the block.

$$$

After meeting up with Disco's partners, Boe and Cuz, and giving them the quarter-kilo of chopped down dime-jugglers, she'd decided to do a little grocery shopping while at the neighborhood strip mall. Now, with all of her purchases sitting neatly on her passenger seat, Londa pulled out into the flow of traffic on 103rd Street.

...long as it's love we're making/ there's going to be some pain/ but as long as I know... Our love will show/ Our love will grooow/ and I know love will be right here... be right here/ no fear/ love is here... love's going to be right here...

SWV's hit BE RIGHT HERE played at a whisper. Londa bobbed her head to the Michael Jackson sample, she'd always liked the song. However, today it felt better. Hearing the song was now like living the song. Because she'd found love. *I gotta tell my girl*, she thought as she drove along. Picking up Disco's cell phone, she called Trisha.

"What's up, Sco?" her best friend answered.

"Bitch, this ain't no Sco!" Londa fired back.

"I got yo' bitch! Who the fuck is this?" she asked, because even though the voice sounded like Londa's she knew that Disco hated Londa, so there was absolutely no way that Londa would be calling her from his phone.

"Bitch! This Londa!" Londa screamed into the phone.

Trisha could not believe her ears. "Hoe, Disco gon' kill you! Whatchu doin' wit' his phone?"

Londa laughed. "Chick, you crazy..." She laughed some more. "He gave me the phone to make a lil' run for him. I'm on my way home to cook 'us' somethin' now."

"Us?! Whatchu mean, Disco at yo' house?!" Trisha almost yelled, knowing Londa couldn't cook.

"Yeah, you act like that's hard to believe."

"Bitch, that's 'cause it is! When Disco got friendly?"

"Hoe, yo' sista out here snatchin', I tell you, I promise." Londa laughed, very pleased with what she'd accomplished. "I sucked that dick last night and woke up to the dick this morning."

"Sco spent the night atcho house?!"

"Holla!"

"Bitch, how you did that?" Trisha was seriously throwed.

Londa inhaled and then let it all out. She told Trisha how she'd been seeing Disco in Silver Blue every day hustling his own work and how she'd made it her business to bring him food every night. She then added the fact that she'd given him $7,000.

"You did what?!" Trisha screamed, knowing that Londa didn't do nothing for nobody, especially niggas.

"I gave him seven stacks, girl. He was fucked up," Londa said sincerely.

"And who you fucked to get seven bands, hoe?" Trisha asked, knowing her best friend.

"Bitch, nobody!" Londa replied, then got quiet for a minute. "I emptied my bank account and pawned the rest of Dave's jewelry."

"Girl, Dave gon-"

"Fuck Dave!" Londa said, cutting Trisha off.

Trisha sighed. "I hope you know whatchu doin', girl."

"I'm good."

"Nah, my big bruh good! He got yo' tight-ass wide open! He got the money, the head and the pussy. Sco a pimp-pimp!" Trisha said laughing.

"For real, Trisha, it ain't even 'bout no pimpin'. Disco ain't even gotta put his mac on, he just gotta gimme that look, when he gimme that look, these panties comin' off-off."

"Whatever, Nicki!" Trisha laughed her ass off! "Yo' ass crazy!"

The two talked and laughed for a while longer, Trisha giving Londa the latest in street gossip. Their conversation then ended when Londa pulled up in front of her apartment building.

Chapter 23

Varray laid on his back, ass-naked, moaning with his eyes closed. Joy was on her knees, ass-naked, with Varray's dick firmly pressed between her sensual lips. The two had been fucking off and on for the past four hours, neither leaving the small musky room. Only taking occasional breaks to snort a few lines or smoke a lace-blunt.

"Damn, Joy! Hold up..." Varray pushed Joy's bobble-head off of his swollen dick and got on his knees. "Turn around."

Joy frowned and sucked her teeth. "Ut'un, Varray, my pussy sore, boy."

"Damn, Joy, come on! I'ma break you off," Varray begged, because even though Joy was a certified animal with Harvard-head, her tight little black pussy was the best in the world.

Joy held her hand out. "Gemme mines now."

Varray sighed and reached for his pants. Removing a wad of money, he passed Joy $250.

Joy bucked her eyes and rolled her neck. "Ut'un, nigga. This just for the drugs and food I bought y'all. Now where mines?!"

I'ma fuck blood out this lil' bitch, Varray thought as he peeled off another $300. "You straight?"

"Yeah, I guess," Joy replied, faking like hell, because she was more than straight with the $300. Even though she was cute and *fine-as-hell,* she was so *shoned-out* that niggas only gave her $80 to $100 for the head and pussy.

After placing her money in her little-tiny shorts pocket, she turned around on all four and prepared for the penetration.

Boom! Boom! Boom! Boom! Boom! Sounded from the front door just as Varray was easing the head in.

Joy jumped. "Who is that?!"

"Bitch, I'on know." Varray pushed the dick in and started long dicking her. "Mac gon' answer it."

Varray dug deep into her pussy, trying to push his dick up into her lower-intestine.

"Sssssslllllll! Daaaammmmnnnnnm, Var!" Joy cried out.

Boom! Boom! Boom! Boom! Boom! The front door sounded again.

"Fuck!" Varray said and pulled out. "Mac! Aye, Mac!"

There was no answer.

Varray jumped up and put half of his clothes on. Joy, somewhat worried, did the same. Together they walked into the living room expecting to see Mac-90 either stuck-on-cocaine or fast asleep; they saw neither, the apartment was completely empty.

Boom! Boom! Boom! Boom! Boom! Boom! Boom! The loud knocking continued.

"Fuck is this nigga Mac at?" Varray asked out loud.

He then grabbed his gun and approached the door.

"Who is it?!"

Boom! Boom! Boom! More knocks came.

"I said, who is it?"

"My, my nigga! It's Mac! Open, open the door, my nigga!"

Hearing his partner's high-pitched voice, Varray snatched the door open and Mac-90 damn near ran his ass over. Varray closed and locked the door before turning to Mac-90. He was bent over with his hands on his knees, throwing up and gagging. His clothes were sweated through.

"Mac, what's up? What happened?" Joy asked, concerned for her little brother. She'd never seen him so scared.

"Jack... the park... niggas... sticks... ambush... a nigga," he mumbled between gags and heaves of air.

Varray brought a cold Miller Draft over to his partner. Mac-90 took it to the head, nearly draining half of it. But before he could down it all he threw up again.

"Damn, boy!" Varray shouted, taking a step back.

Mac-90 wiped his mouth and fought to catch his breath. He'd just ran nonstop, at full speed, from Gibson Park. Seating himself on the couch, Mac-90 stared off into space.

"Mac, my nigga, what happen?" Varray asked, patting his homie on the back.

"My nigga, Jack dead."

"When?! How you know?!"

"Niggas killed him," Mac-90 whispered.

"When, my nigga?"

"On Gibson Park. Me and him was holla'n at some hoes and 'bout twenty niggas jumped out wit' K's... I upped and bussed 'bout four of 'em, but Jack got it, my nigga," he greatly exaggerated.

"Damn!" Varray said and looked over at Joy. "Let me use yo' car right quick."

"Go 'head."

"Where yo' keys?"

"Over-" Joy began, seeing that her keys were not where she'd left them.

"They on the park," Mac-90 whispered. "I left 'em in the car."

Joy wanted to curse his scary-ass out, but seeing the mental state that he was already in, she just held her tongue and called her partner Lisa to come get her.

Chapter 24

Disco and Blue sat in the cover of the hallway smoking a lace-blunt and talking neighborhood politics as customers came and went. They'd both been out there since the declining of the sun some four-to-five hours ago and Disco had moved five $2,000 bombs, most of which was bought by his three Puerto Rican partners out of Carol City. They'd each came through and spent $2,500 for 280 jugglers, which was a real lick for all parties involved.

"Man, where this nigga Jit at, my nigga?" Disco asked.

"I'on know where lil' fool at. He normally be out here already." Blue hit the blunt again and passed it to Disco. "But Shelton and Ziggy came through earlier though."

Disco frowned. "I wish I woulda caught them fuck-niggas 'round here."

"Maann, them boys don't want no problems. They asked me to holla atchu."

"Well, you done holla'd and them two fuck-niggas can't come 'round here no more 'gin."

Blue nodded and got the blunt back from Disco. "Well, is you gon' straighten 'em 'bout the work?"

"What work?"

"The work you took," Blue stated, passing the blunt back.

"You said it, my nigga, took! That's dead. Pussy-niggas shouldn't have tried me," Disco said as a thick little broad in a BSO uniform came up the stair. Her hair was cut short and whipped, and she had ass for days.

"What's up witcho brutha, Sco? You talked to him lately?" Kawannah asked, because she hadn't heard from Pretty Pulla in almost a month.

"Yeah, he said holla atchu. He want some exclusive freak-shots, so I s'pose to get up witchu and make that happen."

"Sshhiiddd, getcho camera or whatever and set the time," Kawannah popped back, always 'bout it when it came to Pretty Pulla.

"Aiight, I'ma let you know. Probably this weekend."

"That's straight, 'cause I'm off Friday and Saturday."

Before Disco could respond Londa walked into the hallway. She looked at him and then at Kawannah. A nasty scowl covered her pretty face.

"What's up, Blue?... Umm, Disco, is you comin' to eat?" she said and looked past Kawannah.

Kawannah peeped the 'L' and laughed. "Disco, holla when you ready," she said and walked off slinging major ass.

"You a trip," Disco told Londa and laughed.

However, Londa didn't see shit funny. Without saying anything she followed Disco to the apartment.

When Disco walked through the door he was floored by the scenery. The entire space was dim. An array of scented candles flickered from spacings throughout the living and dining area. Londa closed the door and hugged him from behind.

"You like?" she asked.

Smiling, he shot back, "You did aiight."

They walked, still holding one another, over to the table and seated themselves. Londa had a bottle of chilled red wine in an ice bucket and two dozen roses sat on the table. Salad and garlic rolls colored the table as well.

Disco went to lift the silver plate cover but Londa stopped him.

"Ut'un, Sco, you ain't gon' say yo' prayers?"

"I said 'em this morning, 'God letta nigga live to thug anotha day.' Feel me?!" he retorted and lifted the cover. "Girl, you a trip!"

"What?" Londa said, laughing as she lifted her own. "Boy, that's Italian," she said of the seasoned can ravioli with the melted sliced cheese on top.

Disco shook his head and dug into Londa's cuisine. The two laughed and enjoyed small talk while they ate. He was truly surprised that Londa was so cool and enjoyable. Downing the very last glass of red wine, Londa stood and struck a seductive pose.

"You ready for dessert?"

Disco could see that she was tipsy. "And what's that?"

"Boy, don't play!" She started taking her shirt off just as his cell phone started ringing.

Thank muthafuckin' God! his mind screamed as he answered. "Yeah-yeah?!"

"Boy, you comin' back out? This shit still jumpin'. You done missed 'bout a stack."

"Damn, here I come."

"And that boy Jit out here too," Blue finished and hung up.

Shaking his head, Disco stood. "I gotta hit the block, ma... where you put that powder?"

Londa sucked her teeth and stormed off. She came back seconds later with the work in a big zip-lock bag. Disco took the zip-lock and cuffed it in his briefs.

"You comin' back...tonight?" Londa almost begged.

"I'ma try too." He stepped closer and kissed her on those full lips of hers. "Thanks for the good time."

Londa smiled and held herself as she watched him leave.

$$$

As soon as Disco walked off in the hallway two chicos walked up looking for powder. Jit got up to serve them but Disco cut him off, pulling the big *powder-bomb* out of his brief.

"Right here, chico, *dumb-raw-halves*, green bags," he pitched, serving them both a $20 sack a piece.

When the chicos left Disco turned to Jit and gave him the big powder-bomb with the $40 in it. Jit looked at Disco and the bomb crazy.

"Fool, I got sack," Jit stated.

"Yeah, but that re-rock ain't no clean... you fakin' wit' that shit! You might as well move them nine and gimme seventy-five-*hunnid* back. Then I'ma give you ounces of that same raw for eight a zone, but you gotta use green bags and you can't cop from *nann* nother nigga."

Jit did the math right quick and said, "hell yeah!"

Blue laughed and said, "Boy, you a muthafucka! Just like yo' wild-ass brutha."

"Here, man." Disco ignored Blue's comment. "This fifteen dollars, y'all niggas build that shit."

$$\$\$\$$$

The next moring Disco woke up on Londa's couch again with Londa's hot mouth on his early morning piss-dick. Shaking his tired head, he gently pushed her head away. Londa looked up at him with confused eyes. No one had ever refused her head before.

"What's wrong?" she asked sadly.

You really don't wanna know, he thought but simply said, "*shawty*, we gotta lotta shit to do today. Feel me?!"

Slipping his dick out of her hand and back into his shorts, he checked his phone. He had damn near 100 missed calls. 85 were from his crazy-ass wifey, Shoniece. *Damn! This crazy bitch gon' kill me*, he mused. He hadn't been home or talked to her in two days. His plan was to go home last night, but shit started jumping so hard that he decided to hang out until his bomb was gone. He ended up jumping all of the work that he had and there was $24,000 on Londa's coffee table to show for it.

The other fifteen calls were from Lil Will, Maine, and Boe. He hoped that everything was all right with his homeboys. He decided to call Lil Will and Maine back first because he figured that they might need some bread, after all, they'd been out beating the streets for Jay's killers and he hadn't shot them a bet in a minute. Lil Will's phone went straight to voice-mail. He hung up and tried Maine, it did the same thing. *Fuck these niggas doin'?* he wondered, calling Trisha's phone. Her phone shot him straight to voice-mail as well. He didn't want to think the worst so he simply called back. Still no answer. He sighed and called Boe.

"Yeah?"

"What they do, boy?"

"Damn, boy! Where you been?" Boe asked excitedly.

"I just got up."

"Well, I need to see you, my nigga! Bitches love that lil' food you cooked and blowin' me up 'bout some more! When I can see you?"

"Shiid, gimme 'bout two hours."

"Aiight, one!"

"*Hunnid,*" Disco capped and hung up.

After quickly getting cleaned up Disco put back on the same clothes and he and Londa cleared it. Shit was picking up and he felt naked without his pistol, so he had Londa to stop over on the 17th side of Silver Blue – his gun was in the rental car where he'd left it two days ago.

When they pulled up he saw that the driver side window was bussed.

"What the fuck?!" he yelled and jumped out.

Shit was scattered everywhere throughout the car, so he knew that the pistol was gone. *Bitch-ass-niggas!* he fumed inwardly. Londa walked over and started picking up the many DVD's and placed them back in the bag. Disco just shook his head, feeling like he knew exactly who had tried him. *Good thang I been fuckin' wit' Londa, or them niggas woulda hit me big*, he thought, knowing that he usually kept his bombs in the car until he ran out.

It had to be that fuck-nigga Shelton or that pussy-nigga Ziggy. And even if it wasn't, they gon' pay for it.

"Look, Londa, just leave that shit. I gotta get this work befo' Chico dip."

"You go 'head and take my car. I'ma straighten this nasty car out, take it to the window place and then go by Trisha's house. I ain't seen her in two days."

"Bet, give this money to Lil Will for me. It's five-stacks for him and Maine to buss-down."

Londa took the money and Disco cleared it.

BOOK 3HREE
THE COUP

...a bunch of niggas and they all troops... wit' big guns so hollow points what a nigga shootin'...I'm throwin' a party everybody come and fall through... I got sinse and duss and fonton too... a bunch of hoes and they all freaks... here's the keys to the 'tel use my suite... I'm throwin' a big-time 'cause I'm the big-boy now...and 'cause I sell dope don't make me no bad guy... I had bills to pay wit' no damn job... two ways to get paid sell dope or rob ...

-Trick Daddy [Off Based On A True Story]

Chapter 25

The metallic-blue 2010 VW Routan SE pulled up into the parking lot of Hialeah's Bank of America. It was early, so very few cars were in the parking lot, which also meant that there were very few customers inside. The passenger of the mini-van jacked a round into the chamber of his AR-15.

"Keep this bitch runnin'! If you see 'Tro, hit me on the chirp!" he told the driver and then turned around to his partner on the van's first row of seats. "Hold the floor! Buss *ann* bitch that move! I'm jumpin' the counter... you ready?!"

His partner chambered his AR-15. "Game time, my nigga. Let's get it!"

They both pulled on Presidents masks, one wore George H. Bush and the other wore George W. Bush. With the AR-15's tucked neatly behind the full-length coats, the two gangstas entered the bank without drawing any tips. However, once inside the gangsta party began.

Yyyyyyyyyyyaaaaaaaaaaakkkkkkkk!!!!!   The   floor-man released about twenty rounds as he saw his partner leap and go over the counter.

"Everybody! On the floor! Now! I gotta *hunnid* more rounds and I don't care who get 'em! Now move! On the ground!"

The security guard was the very first one to lay down. The floor-man quickly walked over and kicked him twice in the face and ribs before bending down to relieve the muscle-bound Spanish man of his service revolver.

$$$

After clearing the counter, the vault-man cracked the attractive young Spanish teller in the face with his assault rifle. Blood gushed everywhere as she fell to the floor like a dead log.

"My partner said get down! You bitches don't speak English? *Tirence en el fuckin' piso antes que les pege un tiro a una de estas peras!* Now play wit' it!" the vault-man threatened them in both English and Spanish. "Where the manager?" he asked but already knew. He'd been watching the lick already.

"Here, I am the manager," a little Spanish man whispered.

The vault-man unlatched and tossed the big sturdy duffle bag to the bank manager. "Fill it up! I want all the big-face *hundones!*"

The manager turned towards the cashcow but the gun toting vault-man stopped him. "Gemme yo' wallet, chico!"

"No, me-"

The vault-man spun around with lightning efficiency, the AR-15 shouldered, and let off. *Yak! Yak! Yak!* The assault rifle sounded, sending two of the three .223 projectiles into the back of the knee of a large Spanish woman that laid on the floor, nearly amputating it.

"Ay dios! Me resento la pierna con un tiro!" she yelled out.

"Callate pera! Befo' I shoot yo' head off, bitch!" the vault-man retorted.

The scared woman stifled her cries by covering her mouth with both hands. Tears ran freely from her wild eyes. Big globs of spit and snot ran between her fat fingers.

When the vault-man spun back around to face the bank manager, the wallet was in his shaking hand. He extended it for the vault-man to take.

Placing it in the inside pocket of his trench coat, the vault-man said, "If I walk outta that door and a dye pack blow up I'ma

121

go straight to yo' house and rape and kill every thang in there! Now fill it up!"

The scared manager filled the bag up and drug it over to the vault-man who quickly snatched it up and ran towards the counter.

$$$

"Ten seconds, fool!" the floor-man yelled just as his man cleared the counter.

The floor-man quickly chirped, "We clear?"

"Clear!" the chirp came back.

The vault-man ran past him and out of the door.

The floor-man backed out, watching the people inside the bank as he made his exit.

$$$

'Bout damn time! the driver thought as the chirp was ended.

Now seeing the first black suit emerge from the bank, the driver slammed the mini-van in gear and sped over to the bank's entrance. Both men jumped in and the driver sped off, leaving three injured, but not a trace as to who'd done it...

Chapter 26

After seeing Chico earlier that morning, Disco had gone back to Londa's apartment and made *dopeboy-magic* [whipping three-quarters of a kilo into a whole-thang and leaving himself a free nine-piece of *clean* to front Jit]. Now, sitting in the parking lot of Winn Dixie on 7th Avenue and 151st, he hoped that Boe would hurry up so he could get back to the trap, because he had dope to move.

Seeing a gray Dodge Charger enter the far side of the parking lot, Disco flashed his high beams. The Charger circled in his direction and parked beside him. Boe jumped out on the passenger side.

"What they do, boy?!" Boe greeted.

"Ain't shit, my nigga."

Boe passed Disco a brown paper bag.

"What's this, yo?" Disco asked, looking into the bag.

"That's ten stacks."

"Ten?!" Disco repeated, eyeing the money and then Boe. "Dog, them was jugglers."

"Yeah, I served a few nigga. But, boy, the smokers was hittin' all night for quarters. That shit was straight gate!" Boe said and continued. "I told you I was gon' hit the block for you, my nigga."

Disco nodded his head, Boe was a real nigga. "Thanks, dog."

"Man, ain't no pressure. You got some more?"

"Yeah," Disco answered and passed him 720 more dime-jugglers. "That's the last bomb I'ma give you like that. After today, y'all gon' get zones and just gimme back eight-*hunnid* each."

"That's a bet, boy. Bet that up!"

"No pressure, dog... y'all be safe."

Boe dapped him up and jumped out.

Once the Charger cleared the parking lot Disco exited in the opposite direction.

$$\$\$\$$$

The ride from Winn Dixie to his four bedroom, two and a half bathroom, two car garage suburban home seemed to take hours; while in actuality it was only a 40 minute drive. So much shit swam through his young troubled mind. His body was tired, however he could not afford to sleep, for his whole future was at hand. He really needed that connect with Bertto, but his deadline was tomorrow and he didn't even have half of the money. Of course, losing the connect was only a fraction of the problem. *What if this faggot-ass Cuban try to bring a nigga a move behind that money?* Disco thought as he drove, because Bertto hadn't exactly *asked for the money*. The Cuban big-boy had more so *demanded the money*.

With his mind steadily scanning for answers to his problems, Disco picked up his cell phone and called Lil Will... *no answer*. He then called Maine's phone only to get the very same results... *voice-mail*. Disco tossed his cell phone onto the passenger seat of Londa's sleek Volvo convertible and wondered, *where the fuck these niggas at?!*

$$\$\$\$$$

"Oooh, Pulla! Baby, you got this pussy toooo wet! Damn, baby, I wish you was here to air this thang out!" Shoniece moaned into the phone.

"How many fingers you got in that pussy?" Pretty Pulla asked from Coleman USP 2.

"Three... and, baby, it's cum all over 'em!"

"Well pull 'em out and stick 'em in yo' ass."

"Okay, baby... ssssssssslllll!!!!"

Pulla had called the house for Disco, but Shoniece answered and one thing had led to another. Of course, this wasn't their first sexual encounter. They'd met up a few times in the distant past, back in Anniston, before her and Disco had gotten serious.

"Put the phone down there and let me hear that ass smack," Pretty Pulla instructed her.

"Okay, listen."

Shoniece's asshole gushed and sloshed like a pussy through the line. "You heard it, bay?"

"Hell yeah!"

Shoniece was about to really lose her mind for Pulla but she heard a car pull up. *Oh shit!* she thought and jumped out of the bed. Running over to the window she saw Disco getting out of a convertible Volvo. *Damn!* her horny mind screamed. "Pulla, here come Sco, call back later."

"For what? I need to-"

Shoniece hung up on his ass and ran into the bathroom. Quickly soaping up her wash rag, she cleaned herself and dried off. Now with all bases covered, she set her mind *to read his muthafuckin' ass the riot act*. She was seriously *pissed the fuck off*! Disco hadn't been home or answered his phone in two days. *Oooh, I'ma cuss this bitch out!* she told herself. Still ass-naked, Shoniece stormed into the living room to confront him. As soon as he walked in the door she went off.

"Bitch! Where you been? And don't lie! I already done talked to Candi and Mrs. Jones!"

125

Disco simply walked right past her.

"Ut'un, bitch! You ain't gon' try me! Where the fuck-"

"Shoniece!" Disco spun around with murder in his eyes. "Shut the fuck up! Stupid bitch! I been in jail. Now leave me the fuck alone!"

There was silence for a while. Disco wondered why he'd even came home.

Walking over to his nightstand, he opened the drawer where he kept his money. Something told him to count the stacks. He was two bands short.

"Shoniece, you been in my muthafuckin' money again?!"

"Umm, yeah... I umm, I only took a few dollars," she whined.

Disco mean mugged her. "You took two-grand... can't you see a nigga fucked up?! I got on the same clothes I had on three days ago. Look at my head and my face! I ain't been to the barber shop in a week. And all you can thank to do is steal money?"

"Ut'un, Sco, I wasn't stealin'. I was just-"

"Thankin' 'bout Shoniece! You been wit' a nigga all these years, a nigga takin' care of you, yo' momma and all yo' children, and you can't see I'm fucked up? Or you just don't care?" Disco finished and thought about Londa. As money hungry and *shoned-out* as she was, she'd still cared enough to notice and help out — by giving him her last $7,000.

"Sco, I'm sorry. I'll get the money-"

"Don't worry 'bout it. You goin' home tomorrow."

"Noooo, baby, I'm not ready to go." She ran over and hugged him. "Don't make me go. Not like this. Let's make things right befo' I go... please, baby," Shoniece whined as she slithered down his body onto her knees.

Disco tried to push her away but Shoniece was too determined. She worked his dick out of his shorts and

126

into her hot mouth. With soft lips and extreme pressure, Shoniece worked the full-length of his dick.

"Hold, hold up, girl." Disco grabbed her head for balance, because his knees almost buckled. Compared to the head he'd been getting from Londa, Shoniece had that Strawberry Cush and Londa was working with B-grade Zonia.

With Disco's dick deep in her throat, Shoniece licked her tongue out and started stroking his balls with it. The feeling was incredible. Disco pulled back and got on the floor. Turning Shoniece around, he entered her sloppy-wet pussy from behind. In three stokes he had her sex juices running down his legs.

"Ooooh, Sco! Damn, baby! Fuck yo' pussy, baby! Yyyeeesss!"

Shoniece's pussy was so good to him. Besides her fire-head and dime-looks, her pussy was her best attribute. Sliding in and out of her, her pussy smacking and gripping his long stiff dick, he realized how much he really missed fucking her.

"Baby! Baby! Pu-put it in my ass, bay!" Shoniece asked.

"What?!"

"Put it in my ass, Sco. Please, I want you to fuck me in everyway!" she begged.

This bitch nasty as fuck! he thought, pulling his dick out of her wet pussy and pushing it into her tight ass.

"Ooooh, Sco! Damn!" she yelled.

Disco continued to work himself inside of her. "Damn, th-this shit feel good," he moaned.

"Come on, fuck me, baby."

With half of his dick up her big ass, Disco found his pace. Slowly sliding in and out. He'd never felt anything that felt so good.

"Baby, I'm cummin'! You got me cummin', baby!" Shoniece yelled, feeling her inside tremble.

"Me too, baby. I'm 'bout to nut!"

Shoniece began gyrating her hips and pushing back into him. This was the first time she'd been fucked in the ass since Pretty Pulla had been in jail and she missed it. Her head was now buried in the carpet and her groans were deep.

"Aaaaaaahhhhhh!" she cried as her cum released.

Disco shivered and fell on top of her.

$ $ $

After laying there breathing heavy and holding each other for a while, the two shared a long steamy shower and dressed. Shoniece then fixed a nice lunch. As they sat enjoying their food and each other, Shoniece let Disco know that his brother had called.

"Did you give him some phone-sex?" Disco asked.

"What?!"

"You heard me."

"Boy, me and Pulla is not even like that. So don't play wit' me," she lied, wondering why he would ask such a thing.

"You thank I'm stupid? I know my brutha. Plus I done been heard 'bout the lil' trip to Atlanta," Disco shot back. He was fishing, because he didn't know, yet he'd always felt that Shoniece had fucked his big brother.

"Boy, you trippin'! I don't know what you done heard, 'cause bitches always hatin', tryna fuck up my happy home... but anyway, yeah, Pulla went to Atlanta, and yeah, I was there, but yo' brutha ain't never had none of this pussy!" Shoniece said and continued. "I swear on my children, Sco. Yo' brutha ain't never touched my pussy in no kinda way," she finished, telling the God-honest truth. Because Pretty Pulla had never fucked her in the pussy, all of their intercourse had been in her mouth and asshole.

"Whatever," Disco replied, truly wanting to believe what he'd just heard. "When fool call back, tell him I'ma put that money on the wire tomorrow."

"Aiight," Shoniece whispered. "Whatchu 'bout to do?"

"Go get it," he said and left the house.

Chapter 27

...we count hundreds on the table/ twenties on the floor/ fresh outta work and on the way wit' some more/ and I love it [Yeah!] I love it [yeah!]... got gangstas in crowd/ mad broads at my shows/ Chevy parked outside and its sittin' on fours/ and I love it [Yeah!] and I love it [Yeah!]...

Young Jezzy's get money anthem boomed from Lil Will's bedroom stereo as Maine counted the last $10,000 stack of crispy bank money and hurled it to the ceiling, causing money to rain down over Lil Will, Trisha, and himself.

"We rich, my nigga! We rich!" Maine yelled, feeling too good about life and what laid ahead. This was their biggest lick and the most he'd ever seen at one time.

Lil Will just laughed at his partner and pulled Trisha close to him, placing a super-wet kiss on her juicy lips. $650,000 in *cold-tax-free* cash had a way of making everybody feel better.

"I told you the lick was sweet, my nigga. Timin' is everythang! And our shit was right on time," Lil Will commented.

"True that, my nigga, you did yo' thang-thang, and we rich 'cause of it."

"We ain't rich yet, but we gon' be. Believe that!"

Trisha sat smiling until loud knocks sounded from the window, *Boom! Boom! Boom! Boom!*

Everybody jumped and grabbed guns. Lil Will signaled for Trisha to check it out. She slowly walked over and peeped through the curtains.

"Bitch! Whatchall havin' a damn party? Open the door!" Londa yelled and walked back to the front door, leaving Trisha at the window.

"Chile, that Londa's ass," Trisha told Lil Will and Maine as she exited the bedroom.

$ $ $

Londa stood at the front door of Trisha's house anxious to see her best friend. She hadn't seen Trisha since they'd been shopping with Shoniece, and even though that was only like four or five days ago it seemed like forever. So much had changed with her, *all of it concerning Disco and their new love life*, and she couldn't wait to share it all with Trisha.

When the door opened Trisha surprised her with a big bear hug. Londa hugged her back, wondering what had the usually super-cool Trisha so happy and excited.

"Bitch, where you been? You just done kicked yo' sista to the curb, huh?" Trisha said, smiling brightly.

"Don't even try it, chick. You know where I stay, so you wasn't tryna see me, so stop playin'...besides, you know how it is when you gotta man, chile."

Trisha's eyebrows furrowed and her hands went to her shapely hips. "When Dave got out?"

"Bitch! Fuck Dave, okay!? You lookin' at the new Mrs. Jones, baby." Londa did a half circle and struck a pose.

Trisha fell the fuck out laughing at Londa's crazy ass. "Hoe, you a mess. Where you just comin' from?"

"Chile, somebody must be tried to steal Disco's rental last night while we was sleep, so I had to take it to get the window fixed, then go to the tint place to get the damn window re-tinted and I got that nasty bitch washed. I just left from 22nd Avenue Car Wash."

"Damn, y'all changin' cars and sleepin' together now?"

"Girl I told yo' ass that I'm snatchin' out here, I tell you, I promise!" Londa retorted, laughing but *dead-ass-serious*. She just knew her head and pussy was on fire. "Trisha, I put this fi' top on his ass and he ain't left my house yet."

Trisha fell out laughing again. Londa was so funny to her. Before they could resume their silly girl-talk Lil Will yelled for Trisha to come back to the room.

$ $ $

Lil Will and Maine had put up the majority of the money, but there were plenty of stacks still laying out when Trisha and Londa entered the bedroom. Londa's gold-digging eyes automatically locked in on the cash and her mouth began to salivate.

"Daaammmnnn, ain't we gettin' it-gettin' it! Y'all niggas break a bitch off!" she quipped like a true hoodrat.

"Shiid," Maine said, getting up with about $2,000 in his hand. "We can trade out, 'cause a swop ain't no swindle, Londa."

"Maine, puleez, boy. I don't trick," Londa shot back.

"Good, 'cause it ain't trickin' when you got it, and I got it, this chump-change momma," Maine popped his game.

Londa rolled her eyes and neck as she said, "That was cute, but I don't fuck wit' the help... sorry, baby." Londa rubbed Maine's face and laughed.

Maine snatched his face away from her soft hand. He'd always wanted to fuck Londa's fine-ass. It was something about a *dog-ass-bitch* that really turned him on. He absolutely loved them.

"Help? You got Maine fucked up!" he bassed.

"Boy, you ain't know!? That's Mrs. Jones right there!" Trisha informed him.

"Trisha, get the fuck outta here!" Lil Will and Maine said in unison.

Londa stepped up for her friend. "You ain't gotta tell 'em nothin', Trisha... y'all just ask yo' boy. He probably at my house now. Lil Will, you know the number."

"Damn, you for real? You for Sco now?!" Maine asked, surprised at the news but also disappointed because he really wanted to fuck Londa too bad. But if she was Disco's hoe that was now out.

"Boy, whatchu thank?!" Londa popped too slick. "And befo' I forget... here, he told me to give y'all this money. It's five-grand, but it don't look like y'all need it."

"It's all good," Lil Will replied, taking the money from Londa. "We got somethin' big goin' down and I need you to make it all happen."

"I ain't fuckin' nobody and I ain't puttin' nothin' in nobody's drink."

Lil Will sucked his teeth. "Hoe! Stop actin' stupid. It's simple, this all a nigga need yo' ass to do..."

Chapter 28

Disco walked down the hallway eating a grilled cheese sandwich. Shit had been slow, still he'd managed to boom $1,000 worth of jugglers. But shit was always slow when the sun was out, the exception being on the first, third and the fifteenth.

Rounding the corner near the cut, he found Blue posted up just where he'd left him.

"Piece me, my nigga," Blue said, reaching for the half eaten grilled cheese.

"Where Jit?" Disco asked, passing his dog the sandwich.

"Over in the empty 'partment, the end one, fuckin' Fannie Mae."

"Crackhead Fannie Mae?"

"Yep."

"This nigga still fuckin' bassers, my nigga?"

"I'on know what's up wit' that wild-ass young nigga."

Blue finished the half-a-sandwich and fired up a lace-blunt. It wasn't in the air a hot ten seconds before the door to the end apartment swung open and out walked Jit and Fannie Mae. She wore a hot-pink *move-something-skirt* with some dirty-white Pro Keds. Her hair was in a simple ponytail, as always. Fannie Mae had to have been in her 40's, but aside from a small gut she was fine-ass-hell. She looked in Blue's direction and rolled her eyes before sashaying off. Her big juicy ass bounced and rolled as she walked.

Disco caught the look and turned to Blue. "Boy, what that be 'bout?"

Before Blue could formulate his lie Jit bussed him out. "My nigga, Fannie Mae hot 'bout them five dollars, boy. But I straightened her."

"What? Blue, you fucked too?" Disco asked, laughing.

"Hell nah, my nigga. Fuck Fannie Mae's stank ass," he retorted. "I just got some dome."

Jit took the blunt from Disco. "I got half that bread for you."

"Aiight, bet."

By the time Jit and Disco had counted out the $3,750 in small bills, Londa bent the corner walking like a hoe. Her pants were so tight and crammed up in her pussy lips that they looked painted on. Coming to a stop right in front of *her man,* her pussy eye-level with his face as he sat on the bottom step.

"Sco, baby, lemme holla atchu right quick," she spoke like a hoodrat.

"I'll be back," he told his partners and stepped off with Londa.

"Sco, you still tryna sell yo' car?"

Disco looked at her, wondering where she was going with this. "Why?"

"'Cause I know somebody, that's why."

"Who?"

"Do it matter?"

"Hell yeah, it matter! Bitch, I ain't no sucka! And I ain't sellin' my car to no sucka," Disco snapped.

"Well, he a rapper. He be wit' them Triple C's niggas."

Disco thought for a minute. "Londa, this bet' not be one of Dave's people or no nigga you 'round her shonin' wit'.... And anyway, how the nigga know I wanna sell my shit?"

Londa sighed. Here she was trying to help his ass and all he could think to do was be a damn asshole about the whole ordeal.

"Look, Disco, I respect yo' mind, boy. So I wouldn't dare play you like that wit' Dave or no other nigga. Fuck Dave, okay?!" she stated, standing her ground. "Now, I was at the tint place talkin' to the man that did yo' windows. Yo' name came up and I told him 'bout you sellin' the car. He called the dude and I talked to him."

Disco rubbed the small patch of hair on his chin. "How much he say he tryna pay?"

"Two-hunnid-fifty-five-thousand," she said with a smile.

"What?!" Disco asked, frowning at her.

"That ain't enough?"

"You sho' that's what he said?" Disco asked, because that was music to his ears. Even thought it was too hard to believe. Nobody in their right mind would pay that much for his Vert - or no other Chevy Vert.

"Yeah, that's exactly what he said."

"When?"

"He said tonight at KOD. Just bring the car and title."

"Aiight," Disco said. "But this bet' not be no bullshit, Londa."

She sucked her teeth and walked off slinging ass.

Chapter 29

Dressed simply in a brown Dickie, black One's and a black Miami Heat fitted, Disco pulled up into the parking lot of King of Diamonds. And even though he knew that there was no way he'd be able to get his .9mm in the club, he brought that bitch anyway.

The parking lot was packed! It was *duffle bag* night and all *stuntas* seemed to be on deck. He circled the parking lot twice before he spotted Londa's Volvo parked beside a cream Lincoln Navigator and a black Lexus ES 350, both rimmed up with paper-plates. Disco parked the Vert and called Londa's cell phone.

"Londa!" he yelled into the phone over the loud music. "I'm outside, you straight?... look, I can't hear ya! So just come out!" he said and hung up.

With the car's title in his pocket and plenty of regret in his heart, Disco made his way towards the club's entrance. He truly did not want to part with his Vert. Not only was it his pride and joy, but Pretty Pulla had copped it for him; it was his first car. *I swear God, let me get right and be able to get my car back...help me through this shit so I can make my big brutha proud of a nigga... let me get this cake for my team, Lil Will, Maine, Trisha, Boe, Cuz, Jit, Blue and Londa... God, help me to set my ole girl and my sista straight... and I promise, God, I'm through wit' all that flossin' and stuntin' shit. I'm finish wit' these raggedy-ass-hoes and trickin' off stacks. That's on stacks, God! Just help a nigga this one last time*, Disco prayed as he walked.

When he got to the entrance Londa was standing there in a yellow loose fitting Nadia Terrell one-piece jumpsuit with a pair of white and yellow shell-toe Adidas. Her short hair style was whipped to perfection and her ring finger and wrist blinged like the sun.

"What's up?"

"You," Londa responded with a smile.

"You seen the money?"

Londa hugged him tight to her body. He felt so good in her embrace. And the scent of weed and lace on his person added something to his appeal that she just loved.

Finally pulling herself away from him she anwered, "yeah, I seen it. They in the VIP and they got it roped off. Bottles, big duffle bags and they stuntin'."

"You sho' is on they dicks," he said sarcastically.

"You the one that asked me... you know what, come on, let's get this over wit' 'cause I'm not 'bout to be arguin' wit' you 'bout no other niggas," she said and walked off.

Disco followed behind her. And even though her jumpsuit was loose fitting, her ass was doing everything that it was supposed to do – bouncing and jiggling.

They made their way through the sea of naked women and money throwing dudes. Disco couldn't wait to get his money and get the fuck on. He was a Club Lexxx type of nigga anyway. *Fuck King of Diamond and all these suckas in it!* he thought.

As he and Londa came to the VIP's entrance the sea of people parted all ot a sudden and before him stood Trisha, Maine and Lil Will. Maine lifted and dumped a duffle bag full of money onto the table.

"And you can keep yo' titles, nigga! 'Cause we fucks witchu, fool!" Lil Will said and walked around the table to hug his homeboy.

Disco couldn't believe it. He looked around at Londa, Trisha, and Maine. They were all smiling and lifting champagne glasses. When he and Lil Will broke their embrace, Trisha and Maine stepped over and hugged him.

"We all we got, bruh!" Maine said.

"Mmaann, I love y'all niggas!" Disco replied.

"Well," Londa cleared her throat. "What about the chicks? You don't love us?"

Disco laughed and hugged her super-tight. "You a trip... you knew 'bout this shit and yo' ass stood right in my face and lied 'bout some *Triple C's niggas wanna buy my car.*"

Londa laughed and snuck a quick kiss on the lips. "You gon' beat me for bein' bad and lyin' to you, Daddy," she whined in a little girl's voice.

"If that's whatchu want... you want Daddy to beat that ass?" he asked, softly spanking her soft round ass before gripping a handful of it.

"Oooh, and you know I do!" Londa shot back, her pussy dripping already.

"Aye, y'all fuck that shit for right now!" Lil Will stated, breaking Londa and Disco apart. "Y'all got all morning and all day tomorrow for that shit. But right now, we 'bout to party and get *off-da-chain!*"

He popped a fresh bottle of bubbles and took it to the head. When he brought it back down he passed it to Disco.

Disco held it up, "To Jay, my brutha, and all our niggas that didn't make it... it's thug life again!" he yelled and took the bottle to the head.

"Thug life again!" everybody repeated and turned their glasses up also.

$$$

The celebration was in full swing! Bottles were popping at every booth and table, and naked hoes were popping pussy and ass. Heavy-lace was in rotation, while niggas and females that snorted cocaine did their thing as well.

Maine was eye-level with a pretty pink pussy when Lil Will nudged him.

"What up?"

139

Lil Will pointed over towards a group of people in the common area. "Ain't that that hoe?"

"Yep!" Maine cut him off and rushed out of the VIP.

Q-Tip's, *a vibrant thang/ a vibrant thang/ a vibrant thang...* Boomed through the large strip clug as Maine closed the space between himself and her. It was as if time stood still, everything except her seemed to blur, her body was the only thing that stayed in beat with the music. Their eyes locked briefly, she smiled but it seemed to go right past him, causing him to question whether she'd really seen him or not.

Fool, you trippin! You don't need to be fuckin' wit' this bitch! The VIP fulla bad hoes! one side of his brain yelled. *My nigga, don't listen to that shit! If you want the hoe, go get the hoe. You young and you thuggin, my nigga. The world is yours!* something else inside of him countered.

When he made it over to her the song had just ended and she was collecting her little itty-bitty pieces of bathing suit and her money. Maine sat down at the empty table beside the table of the dude that had just been dancing her.

"Aye!" he called out, seeing that she was about to walk off.

"You see a horse?" she popped back.

Nah, I see a dog, bitch! he wanted to tell her since she'd gotten all smart out of the mouth, but he checked his tongue. "Nah, lil' momma, I see the future... so why don't you come over here and let me tell you 'bout it."

That was cute, she thought and popped back. "If you know the future then you know the time, baby. And time is money." A smile followed her slick statement.

"Shawty, you ain't gotta 'nough time in a day to get all this money," Maine said, dropping about $50,000 on the table — all big face hundreds. "Not at five dollars a dance... so I'ma start out by givin' you three-hunnid to go get us two bottles. We'll work on the other forty-nine thousand-seven-hunnid when you get back."

Ppsstt! I ain't no muthafuckin' waitress! she thought. *He tried me, but for $100 he got that.* She took the money, put on her little two-piece thong set and shook her little bubble over to the bar. She was not the baddest bitch in the club, but she was what he wanted. Since first seeing her she'd been heavy on his mind and reappearing in his dreams. The smell of her was stuck in his memory. Jim Beam's SHE FOR EVERYBODY played as her and a bouncer returned with a silver bucket, two bottles and two glasses. When the bouncer was out of earshot, the cute, well proportioned stripper stood back on her shapely left leg and gazed into Maine's eyes. The light was dim, however, the bling of his four gold-teeth and chunky jewelry gave light to the situation at hand.

"So, umm, is that it? Whatchu want me to do now?"

Maine popped a bottle and poured a glass. After sitting the glass on the table he drank straight from the bottle. "Shiid, it's all on you, lil momma... do whatchu do best."

Boy, we cannot fuck in here, she thought, foolishly believing that sex was her best attribute. Shamelessly, she began to strip naked and wind her lovely body to the rhythm of the beat.

Maine openly stared as he drank from his bottle. Her body was so pretty and sexy. Standing at 5'3", she had to weight about 122 pounds. Guessing, Maine figured her measurements to be 36B-24-36. Her skin was light-chocolate, dark nipples, and her lips were small. Nothing turned him on more than her small slanted eyes... her pussy was shaved bare with a tattoo of the sun above it. Her perky round ass bounced everytime she dropped it, occasionally bending completely over and giving him a full view of her pretty pinkish-brown insides. His dick was *rock-ass-hard*.

After the sixth song had played, she was covered in sweat and Maine was dead-ass drunk. She sat down in the chair beside him and drunk some of the expensive bubbles.

"Is you finish wit' me?" she asked, hoping that he wasn't, because he had plenty of money, and she had bills to pay. Her rent was due, and someone had broken into her house and stolen all of her money and jewelry.

Maine ignored her question and asked his own. "What's yo' name, lil' momma?"

"It can be lil' momma if you want it to be, but it's Joy."

He nodded his head, because he'd already known. He'd just wanted to know if she'd tell him the truth or give him some stage name like Black Cinnamon, China Doll, or Sunshine.

"I thank I'll let you keep Joy.... I'm just tryna see if you really is though."

"If I'm really what?"

"A joy... like, can you make a nigga feel joy?"

Joy laughed and drunk some more of her drink. *Boy, if you only knew*, she thought. Because the truth was, Joy had been a joy to too many. Not that she was a real mutt, she'd just chosen foolishly when it came to men.

"I'on know 'bout that... besides, that's kinda personal and I'on know you," she finally answered.

"True! And that's what I'm tryna change... feel me?" Maine slurred. "Shawty, I gotta brand-new black Lexus ES 350 outside and more money than *ann* nigga in this club in my pocket."

"And?" Joy sassed, nonetheless loving what she was hearing.

"*And*? And have you ever got fucked by the nigga of yo' dreams, out in London on a bed fulla hunnids while you scream?"

"Boy, no!" Joy laughed.

If you can make her laugh you can fuck her, Maine thought before capping, "Well, baby, I can take ya there...on stacks, lil' shawty, I'm that nigga."

Joy eyed him very closely. She'd never seen him before. "Well, why I ain't never seent you befo'?"

"A lotta times we be lookin' for love in all the wrong places."

Again she laughed. "And what makes you thank I'm lookin' for love? You don't know, I might just have a man."

This time Maine laughed and took a big swallow from his bottle.

"What's so funny?" Joy asked.

"You!"

"And how you figure that?"

Maine shook his head sadly. "For real, it ain't funny. It's sad, lil' momma. You a black goddess wit' everythang that a real nigga could want in a hoe... but you in here chasin' this paper like it's gon' brang you love... shawty, this ain't nothin'," Maine said and flung a stack of $100 bills in the air.

Hoes went crazy picking up the money. Joy wanted to join them but Maine had struck a nerve. Her pride wouldn't allow her to *chase the paper that she loved so much.*

"Nigga, you don't know me!" she said with a frown.

"I know," Maine replied, grabbing her small hand. "And I'm tryna change that."

"And how you gon' do that?"

"By takin' you wit' me."

"I don't even know yo' name, boy."

"Do you wanna know it?"

Joy thought for a minute. *Girl, say yeah! This nigga cute, fine as hell, and he paid like a muthafucka!* But something else warned her. *Joy, you ain't tired of gettin' used and fucked over by these selfish-ass-niggas that don't give a fuck 'bout you? He just gon' fuck yo' stupid ass and leave you wit' a few dollars, a sore pussy, and a fucked up reputation!* Joy listened to both and considered. *Shiid, can't get no worst than it already is.*

"Yeah, I wanna know it," she finally answered.

Maine gave her five-hundred dollars. "Aiight, go getcho shit and meet me at my car."

She took the money and walked off to shower and pay her tip-out.

He walked over to the VIP to let his team know that he was out.

Chapter 30

Disco woke up with a killer headache. All of the gold-bubbles and Henny he'd consumed left him feeling like an elephant was sitting on his brain. Shoniece lay beside him, fast asleep, just as she'd been when he came in at 3:34 a.m. Firing up the half of a lace-blunt that he'd clipped when he laid down last night, he looked at his cell phone. There were missed calls from Lil Will, Londa, Boe and one from faggot-ass Bertto. *Bitch-ass-cracka!* he thought, strolling to the bathroom to relieve his bladder of some of last night's intoxicants. While in there he decided to go ahead and shit, shower and shave.

Feeling refreshed, Disco quickly jumped fresh and walked into his garage. A big-ass smile crossed his face seeing the big cream-colored Navigator parked beside his brother's powder-blue Donk. *Last night wasn't a dream after all! Boy, I'm 'bout to fuck the world!* he thought as he slid into Lil Will's brand-new big-boy SUV. The duffle bag containing the $255,000 sat on the rear seat. He fired up the engine and pulled out, speeding towards the city.

Since he was en route to Lil Will's house anyway, he decided to call Londa back first. The phone rung four times before her sexy voice picked up.

"Hello?"

"What it do, ma?"

"Nothin', just sittin' here thinkin' 'bout you."

"Whatchu thankin'?"

"'Bout suckin' that dick and givin' you some of this wet-wet," Londa purred like her pussy and head was really that good.

You shoulda said big and wet, Disco laughed to himelf. "I might just let you do that, lil' momma...keep it wet, I'ma be through there."

"When?" she asked in desperation. She'd been sorely disappointed last night when he'd decided to go home to Shoniece instead of going home with her. *I know he fucked that wannabe bougie bitch*, Londa thought.

"I can't say. I'm on my way to snatch Lil Will. We gotta few thangs to handle and then I'll be through there."

"Aiight, don't carry me, Sco," she whined.

"Bye, Londa." Disco hung up and pulled the Navigator in behind his Vert, which Lil Will had driven home and was now parked in his driveway.

Pink and white Polo down, with the pink and white low-top One's, Disco jumped out and diddy-bopped to the door. Lil Will's daughter flung the door open.

"Uncle Disco!" she yelled and jumped on him.

"Hey, lil' baby!" Disco reached and pulled her up into his arms. It had been a minute since he'd seen the pretty little girl, because she actually lived with Lil Will's mother.

Trisha came prancing out of the kitchen in some *tiny-little* North Western Bulls shorts. *Damn!* Disco mused, *I wonder if her pussy is as big as Londa's shit?* Because it was damn sure soaking up her shorts. *Maybe birds of a feather really do flock together*, he thought, remembering how he'd had to envision Trisha as he fucked Londa to buss a nut.

"Girl, come on. Leave Sco 'lone and let me fix yo' hair so we can get ready to go," Trisha said, taking Wendy from Disco's arms. "What's up, Disco? How you treatin' my girl?"

"She aiight," he shot back. *Bitches know they talk too much!*

"Yeah, let me find out." Trisha smiled knowingly and shook her little fine-ass towards the bedroom.

145

Lil Will came out of the room wearing some baggy light-blue jeans, red Clarks, green UM fitted; a red, green, and black Bob Marley shirt; and a long dread-belt. A big-ass lace-blunt was between his lips.

"What up, boy?!" Disco greeted Lil Will with a half-hug.

"You, my nigga. What we gon' do today?"

"Get our muthafuckin' money!"

"That's what's up," Lil Will said and passed Disco the blunt. Disco hit the lace hard. "You holla'd at Maine?"

"Nah. Fool probably up to his nuts in pussy."

"Well, we need to move 'round, my nigga. We'll catch him when we get finish," Disco said and headed for the door.

Lil Will grabbed his phone and his fire and followed suit.

146

Pito and Sombra sat at the opposite end of Bertto's big pool, arguing about whose outfit would attract the most women. Pito wore pea-green silk slacks with piss-colored gators and a matching piss-colored silk shirt. The shirt he wore tucked inside of his tailored pants, but unbuttoned down to the fourth button. Around his neck was about twenty little chains. At 5'2" and 140 pounds, Pito was a prototypical throw-back gangsta.

Sombra, on the other hand, was about 6'1", 200 pounds. He wore black skinny jeans, black gator slip-ins, with a leather vest - no shirt. Whereas Pito was fair-skinned, Sombra was a dark-skin Puerto Rican.

The ringing of the phone interrupted their petty dispute.

"Hola?" Sombra answered. "Quien es?"

"Yo, I don't speak that gwalla-gwalla shit, fool. Put Bertto on."

"No hablo ingles inbesil, que tu quieres!"

"Look, fool, this Disco. Where yo' boss-man?"

G, Bertto's right-hand man, heard Sombra on the phone and asked, "Quien es?"

Sombra shrugged his big shoulders. "Un inbesil en el fuckin' telefono!"

"Seguro es para Bertto, damelo a mi," G said, taking the phone. He said a few words in his broken English before walking over to Bertto, whom was ass-naked, sunbathing. *Looka this fuckin' guy!* G thought before saying, "Bertto, el telefono. Es el tipo de la funeraria el que debe el dinero."

Bertto smiled brightly. "Bien, bien!" he cheered, taking the phone from G. "Disco, how are you?"

"I'm straight, man... you ready to do this?"

"Yes, but of course... you have somethin' for me?"

"Yeah, I got that."

"Good, bien," the homosexual drug lord replied. "Where are you?"

After Disco told Bertto where exactly he was, Bertto gave him directions to a nearby Cuban café that he owned.

"Go there. Someone will meet you," Bertto finished and hung up. He then turned to his men. "Sombra, Pito, ballan con G a busca a nuestro amigo."

The three men strapped up and left.

$$$

Joy woke up to an empty bed. She was in a $450 hotel room – naked and untouched. On the table sat an empty bottle of champagne, two empty dinner trays, and two champagne glasses. The remnants of a perfect night's ending, something that was awesomely unfamiliar to her. She usually woke up in a cheap motel, hungry and sore from the penetration. A smile played at the corners of her small mouth as she replayed last night. From the time she'd danced for Maine at the club until the time he'd laid her down in the big soft hotel room bed, it had been nothing but special. Nothing short of *wonderful*. Something she knew nothing of. He'd simply held her close, conversating with her on levels in which no one had ever cared to. Because no one ever cared. At least not beyond the conclusion of a toe-curling climax.

Joy climbed out of bed; her perky young titties defying gravity, her dark nipples erect. Looking closer at the table she saw that Maine had left her a note. He really did care. Seeing him gone when she'd woke up had given rise to doubt, *will I see him again? Why did he just leave wit'out sayin' bye at least?* They hadn't even exchanged numbers, so seeing the note eased her apprehension and watered the seed of hope – the potential happiness – that Maine had planted with his thug-mannerism and kind words.

Joy floated over in a cloud and picked up the note. She read:

By the time you lay your pretty eyes on these words of mine I'll be out doing my job – thuggin in these streets. It's all good though, because I'll be thinking about you... I had fun with you, Joy. And I want to be the first nigga today to tell you that you're BEAUTIFUL... I paid for the room for another day, so you can just chill and do you. My number is 876-223-3100 in case you get lonely in that big ass bed (smile).

Holla at me,
Man

Joy smiled. *So that's his name*, she thought. He was *the man* in her eyes. But then again, all men were *the man* in the beginning – nice, caring, supportive. However, once they got what they wanted – brains and thangs – the real them, the boy that just wanted to have fun, always came out. Joy wanted to believe that Man was different. After all, he'd presented himself as different. He made her feel different – special. Joy placed the note in her stripper bag with all the money he'd given her and fell back onto the big soft bed. In no time at all she was dreaming dreams of a better day...

Chapter 32

... Mami/ el negro esta rabioso/ quiere pelear conmigo/ decircelo a mi papa... Mami/ yo me acuesto tranquila me arropo pie y cabezo y el negro me destapa/ Mami que sera lo que quiere el negro...

The loud merenque music blasted from the Cadillac's speakers as it pulled in the café's small parking lot.

Disco looked out of the café's big picture window and saw a clean-ass soft-yellow '67 Cadillac convertible. The top was down, showcasing the crazy leopard skin seats. With the exception of the twenty-inch Mirrors and Vouge tires, every piece of chrome was fresh yet original. Three Spanish dudes, two muscular six-footers and a mean looking dwarf, all hopped out. On appearance alone Disco could easily see that the driver, fresh to death in a cream linen pants set with matching leather casuals and gold sunglasses, was indeed the leader of the little three man Spanish mob. Upon entering the café he walked right over to Disco and removed his expensive gold frames, his two men beside him.

"Stand up," he ordered real calm-like. "You too, guy. Both of you. Stand up and turn around."

"What?!" Disco asked, a *unit* already covering his face.

Lil Will tried to ease his hand off of the table to get to his .9mm but was stopped short as Pito, the shortest of the trio, pulled out a gun so big and futuristic looking that it resembled a toy.

"Take it easy, man... whatchu think, we some robbers? No, man... re-lax. We pat you down, everything good, we do a good busin-a-nes," G explained.

Disco looked at Lil Will and nodded his head. They both then stood up. Pito and Sombra briskly stepped in, patted them down, each removing a gun from Lil Will and Disco, and then stepped away. G nodded his approval before speaking.

"You got thee money?" he asked in his Cuban accent.

"Yeah."

"In you car?"

"Yeah."

"Okay, give you keys to my friend. You, you." G pointed to Lil Will and Disco. "Come ride with me... that's Cad-il-lac. Top of the line style."

Without waiting for an answer he turned and walked off.

Lil Will looked at Disco. Disco shrugged his shoulders and gave Sombra the keys to Lil Will's Navigator.

$ $ $

"Aye, Boe!" Cuz called out from the house that he and Boe were trapping out of.

Boe cut his conversation with the thick young *shone* that he was trying to put the dick to and walked over to the porch where Cuz was. The block was jumping and niggas were posted up in front of different houses and crate-sitting in different cuts throughout the block. And wherever you found niggas hustling, bitches in little-ass outfits, big asses and funky attitudes were sure to follow. So the block was super-thick. The *shones* out-numbering the trappers five-to-one.

When Boe made it to the porch, Cuz handed him a smoking lace-blunt, $750 and pointed up the block. A brown box Chevy on rims was crawling up the block.

"My nigga, dog, that's the fourth time fool done rode down the block," Cuz said.

"What this is and who that is?" Boe hit the blunt and watched another nigga pull up and pull his potential dick-sucker. *Damn! Fuckin' wit' Cuz*, he cursed inwardly, because he just knew that shorty had that *throat-pressure*.

"That's seven-fifty. My books clear wit' that... but yo, that's them pussy-niggas from by the store. You know they got *smoke* wit' a nigga 'cause that *gate* we got is closin' down shop!" Cuz stated, watching the Chevy as it bent the block.

"Maann, them niggas don't want no pressure."

Cuz sighed. "Aiight, I'm tellin' you! You sleep! Them niggas on some fuck-shit!"

Ignoring Cuz's declaration, Boe hit the blunt again and passed it back. "You out?"

"Yeah, I been out... you called Sco?"

"Hell yeah, he waitin'."

"Shit crazy. We need that work!"

"We straight... go fuck yo' baby-momma or somethin'. 'Cause soon as that *gate* drop it's back to grindin'. And you know my sista don't even be playin' witcho tender-ass."

Cuz shook his head and walked off the porch. Boe looked up the block to see which way the car with his *action* had gone.

$ $ $

...En la sala de un hospital/ de una estrana enfermeda/ mi Corazon esta muriendo de pena y/ dolon porque no tiene tu amor... Victor Manuel's *Hay Anor* blasted from the Cadillac's speakers.

Lil Will and Disco rode around Miami with G, top down, eating ice cream. They'd been riding around for at least two hours. Neither of them, Disco or Lil Will, could use the phone because their cell phones were in the Navigator, which was nowhere to be seen. Pito and Sombra had simply jumped in the big SUV and hauled ass in the opposite direction.

Besides listening to the loud irritating music, which Disco nor Lil Will could vibe to; they had to listen to G's broken version of the English language, which neither of them truly understood. Disco was seriously growing tired of the riding and bullshitting.

"Aye, G, what's up?"

"The sun, but it's a handsome day... you and you want some more creamed ice? I love this stuff, man," G rambled on.

"Nah, I'm good on the ice cream... but, umm, what we doin'?" Disco quizzed. "We been ridin' 'round in this hot-ass sun and I got other shit to do-"

G held up his hand. "Re-lax. Take it e-asy... every-a-thing is handsome. We listen to some merengue, just feel the vibration," G said working his fists and shoulders in a circular motion as if doing the tango.

Disco shook his head sadly and sighed loudly. *These ponchos bet' not be playin' wit' a nigga. Or I'ma-.* Disco's thoughts were interrupted by the ringing of G's phone.

"Talk to me," G answered, sounding just like Manny from the movie Scarface. In fact, G looked just like the handsome actor. "Todo esta bien?... esperate." G turned to Disco and asked for his address. Disco gave him Lil Will's instead. With the info in his head, G got back on the phone. "Bete al 1-0-1 calle y la 25 avenida, una casa blanca... te beo en dies minutes."

$$\$\$\$$$

When the trio arrived at Lil Will's house the Navigator was parked in the yard, both Pito and Sombra were leaning against the rear of the SUV. They appeared to be in a heated debate, their faces scowled up and their hands were both gesturing aggressively.

"Estos zapatos son los mejores. Crocodilo!" Sombra yelled and pointed to his shoes.

Pito waved him off before retorting, "Ellos no valen mierda y tu traqe es para maricones! Este traq esta en ultima moda."

Sombra sighed and looked at the shorter Spanish gangsta real crazy. "Porque to hablas disparates? Esto es estilo."

"Ha!" Pito laughed. "Estilo para los maricones! Tu, tu jefe es maricon!"

"Cono! Tue lo que tiense son cellos, porque yo tengo todas la jevas!"

Disco and Lil Will looked on, not knowing what the two were arguing over, but based on their loud words and body language, they figured that the debate was ultra-serious — about that money and murder.

G stepped over to his two quarreling henchmen. "Cono! Go to thee car! Such a handsome day and you-a-two argue about-a-thee clothes! Cono, man."

The two walked over and got into the Cadillac. Disco and Lil Will walked to the Navigator and stood beside G.

"You friend, he can go. Me talke-a-thee busin-a-ness with you," G told Disco.

"I'm good, Will, my nigga. I'ma be In there in a minute."

Lil Will dapped Disco up and went inside.

"Disco, look..." G began, staring dead into Disco's eyes. His demeanor was no longer *suave and laid back*, but darkly intense. "My English is no so good looking. But I need for you to re-a-lize what I'm-a-about to say... Bertto like-a-you a lot. He tell-a-me, the other guy, T-"

Disco cut him off. "Jay."

"T, Jay, what-ever... he was-a-soft. But Bertto says you are tougher... okay, in you truck is fif-a-teen kilos of

154

some of the handsomest grade-A yayo in the world. Bertto wants two hundred-a-fifty-a-five large. That is seven-a-teen a piece... you have-a-seven days. If things are-a-good looking, we give-a-you mucho yayo... but if you do-a-not good busin-a-ness. Cono, man..." G finished, shaking his head sadly.

"I gotchu, bruh," Disco replied.

He and G shook on the deal and went about their business.

...can't nann nigga hustle more dope than me / can't nann flip more bricks than me / eighteen on the stove / tryna beat me a key... dime it all down / bricks to crumbs / dime it all down / cop me a brick, bitch!

Raw-Nitty's DIME IT ALL DOWN beat from Maine's home entertainment system as him, Disco and Lil Will did exactly as the song said, *dimed it all down*. Disco was working a set of Vision Ware in the big industrial microwave while Maine worked another set on the stove top.

Disco had decided to whip up ten kilos and move five, untouched in the wrapper, to build up his *big-money-clientele*. The first person on his list was Chico, if he could get him on his line everybody else would fall in line.

Of the ten bricks that him and Maine whipped up they brought back 10,000 grams of hard white and had 2,500 grams of soft – street valued at $392,000. Which would leave them $137,000 after they paid Bertto $255,000. Plus the five untouched kilos that he planned to sell to Chico for $92,500 - $18,500 a piece. All-in-all, the crew stood to make $229,500 without even hitting the block.

Disco smiled at the projected profits. *Damn! A nigga in-there!* he thought as he looked from the drugs to his men – Lil Will and Maine. And at that moment he truly-truly realized how blessed he really was. Maine and Will had really come through for him. If it wasn't for them he'd be least his Vert, minus the cocaine connect, and maybe even dead. However, because of them he had it all and stood to gain so much more.

With all of that heavy on his mind, Disco stood and gave his two best friends the business. He promised to give them half of the $255,000 back that they'd given him, plus a third of all profits – they'd be equal partners from then on, one-third a piece. With big smiles on their faces and even bigger money on their minds, the three of them popped a bottle and toast to their new agreement. It was all laughs and jokes as they drank. This was something that had been absent in their lives since Jay got killed. And it felt good to all three men. Nonetheless, when the last sip was gone it was right back to the business at hand.

The three young thugs jumped into Maine's Range Rover and hit the street. Their first stop was Chico's crib. Once Chico saw the untouched *fishscale* and heard the $18,500 tag he jumped all over the five brick purchase with no pressure at all. The only question was *when could he get some more*.

From there they hit Silver Blue. Jit and Blue were posted up in the hallway as always. Jit was happy to see Disco because he'd been out of powder for a while. He gave Disco the $3,750 that he owed him and Disco gave him a half-kilo, soft. He then turned to Blue and offered him the very same deal that he'd offered Jit, only Blue would be moving the hard. And just like any good hustler, Blue agreed. Disco gave him a half-brick hard and dropped $96,250 off to Londa's apartment before getting back in the wind.

$ $ $

The Range Rover exited Sunrise East and bussed a right on 16th Terrace just like before. Disco slow-rolled the expensive SUV, watching from behind tinted windows, as the young thugs mean-mugged the Dade County plates. 16th Terrace was mobbed *all-the-way* up. When they got to the end of the block where the store sat, the line of customers waiting to be served was unreal. Three dudes stood exchanging *product* for money, while two others sat at opposite ends with guns. *These young niggas makin' a muthafuckin' killin' out here!* Disco thought to himself as he bent the corner onto 16th Street and pulled in behind Boe's gray Charger. Before Disco, Lil Will, or Maine could exit the Range, both Boe and Cuz appeared from the side of the house. And just like before, Cuz had his AK-47. With a simple, *what they do, boy?!* The men all retraced Boe and Cuz's tracks around the side of the house. Disco introduced everybody and then got right down to business.

He handed Boe the 36 ounces of hard white and also half-a-key of soft. He explained to Boe that there was *plenty of cocaine in place*, so he was to serve *servers* and leave the fiends alone. He needed Boe and Cuz to supply the niggas that were supplying that line of customers on 16th Terrace. His closing words were, *if y'all two can do that we'll all be rich in eighteen months*. Boe shook his head because he understood. However, Cuz hated the niggas on 16th Terrace and did not want to be fucked up with them in any way. But he did not express his thoughts. He simply remained silent.

With that out of the way, Boe handed Disco the $10,000 that he had for him and the meeting was adjourned.

On the way back to the Range Rover, Disco locked eyes with a young thugged out nigga sitting on a crate just across from Boe's house. The dude had some big-ass dookie dread-locks and tattoos everywhere. His shirt was off and sitting across his lap. Disco knew that it was a gun beneath the shirt, so he continued to watch the sneaky looking red nigga with all of the tattoos and dread-locks as he slid into the Rover. *A nigga gon' end up paintin' that young nigga there*, Disco thought as the trio got back in traffic – *city bound*.

Again the Range Rover exited I-95, only this time it was on North West 79th Street. Disco bussed a left and rode down until he was due to make another left. It had been a little minute since he'd last stepped foot in Largemont Projects. It was basically Jay's spot, though the run-down projects and the go-hard people that resided there had made both into the hustlers that they were. Riding through Largemont brought back a lot of memories: Horace Mann Junior High, the first time a crackhead sucked his dick, days of being broke and fucked up, the first time Cannon Ball's sister gave him some pussy... *Damn, Jay, my nigga!* he thought, holding back a tear. Disco was sad that his man was gone, but even sadder to have learned that Jay'd been playing the fifty on the brick prices. Yet it was what it was, *dirty water under a condemned* bridge, because Jay was his *dog-at-heart* and life always went on.

  He spotted Charles Mills leaning against a mint-green Donk on eight's, talking to fine-ass Toosie. Disco had always wanted to fuck Toosie. Pulling the Rover over beside Charles' '75 Chevy, Disco rolled the window down and called Charles over.

  Charles had been Jay's lieutenant in Largemont, and since Disco planned to *put back down* in the projects he figured it best to give Charles the first shot at *running the rock*. Only difference was, Jay'd had Charles *working for him* — Lt'ing at a set salary. Disco planned to *give Charles the rock and let him run* — front him the work at $800 a zone just like he'd done with Boe, Blue and Jit.

  After hearing everything that Disco had to *say and offer*, Charles jumped on the opportunity — *just like Disco knew he would*. The two dapped it up and made plans for Charles to pick up a brick of hard in one hour. Disco smiled as he jumped back into the Rover. *Look at this bitch*, he said to himself. He'd noticed that Toosie had been seriously *jocking-his-fresh* the whole while he'd been rapping with Charles. Shit was coming together in every way and he loved it.

The last stop that Disco had to make was one that he truly did not want to make, because there'd been bad-blood and fucked up feelings surrounding a deal that his brother had made with the people along time ago. For real, it had all been a big misunderstanding.

Disco whipped the Range Rover up into Aswan Apartment Complex and shot straight to the back. The sun was just starting to set, which meant that he had to hurry up with his business and get the fuck out of there, because Aswan got real crazy after dark.

He stopped at the last building. There were about sixty-something people – male, female, old and young – all hanging out. Some of them stopped what they were doing to check out the fancy SUV. Others continued macking, selling dope, gambling, fighting or whatever else they might've been doing. The whole scene looked like a bad take from a hood movie.

Disco scanned the crowd in hopes of spotting his *used-to-be* man or his little brother. He saw neither. *Damn! This shit crazy,* he thought, not wanting to get out of the truck. After saying a fast prayer he told Maine and Lil Will to hold fast, but if he wasn't back in fifteen minutes to *tear the whole building down*. They nodded and he jumped out...

Chapter 34

Man: So whatchu doin' right now?

Joy: I betchu wanna know ☺

Man: u b'n thankin bouta nigga?

Joy: all day!

Man: whatchu b'n thankin?

Joy: come 2 the room and c!

Man: want 2 but handlin' somethin'.

Joy: I bet!

Man: don't play! Is u still naked?

Joy: Yep! N I'm bored. Bout 2 call a friend ☺

Man: U got jokes.

Joy: N u just don left me ☹

Man: I'm tryna get there now!

Joy: u no I gotta go 2 work 2night

Man: not if u don't wanna.

Joy: whatever!?!

Man: 4 real. I gotchu ma!

Joy: Heard it all b4!

Man: Not from me. N ain't nann nigga like me.

Joy: mayb not. But I gotta look out 4 me. So I gotta go to work

Man: ok. I'ma come getchu from work N we gon stay at the same   tel.   ·

Joy: 4 real!?!?

Man: 4 real ☺ ... it's all on u!

Joy: I'ma b @ KOD.

Man: OK

Joy and Maine texted one another as he sat in the Rover. They'd been at it all day. He could not wait to see her again. She was so damn pretty and fine! Her personality was also great. Maine wondered how she ended up in a strip club and not in some *big-boy's* mansion, because shorty had the complete package. *It's fucked up I gotta kill her fuck-ass brutha*, he thought.

Lil Will sat in the backseat talking to Trisha. He always called her *roxy* and *nosey as fuck*, but he never missed an opportunity to listen in on her latest gossip reports.

$$$

Disco had barely taken two steps and he was being called.

"Aye, fool! Aye! Fool, check this out!" he heard someone yelling. But he did not stop, he simply continued on towards the hallway's entrance. *Mmaann, I hope one of these niggas is in this fuckin' hallway!* he said to himself.

Entering the hallway, everything got dark as hell. The stale scent of piss attacked his nose. *Gotdamn! These niggas livin' low as fuck 'round this bitch!* he thought, covering his nose with the neck of his shirt.

As soon as he turned to mount the stairs a heavy hand came down on his shoulder.

"Aye, my nigga!" he said and went for his gun, but the hand on his shoulder pushed him hard into the stair-rails. The gun fell into the dark. "Man, get the fuck offa me, yo!"

Four more dudes walked up. One of which was the dude that had been calling him.

"You ain't heard a nigga callin' you, fool?" the dude asked, picking up Disco's gun.

"Nah," Disco retorted with much sarcasm.

"Whatchu want 'round here?"

"I'm lookin' for Ace, fool," Disco shot back.

"Ace? Who is you? Whatchu want wit' Ace?"

"Look, man, Ace my dog. I used to live next do-"

162

A voice from the top of the stairs cut him off. "Disco! That's yo' scary ass?"

"What?!" Disco exclaimed, looking for the person.

"Mmaaannn, y'all give fool his fi' back...he straight," the dude said, walking down the stairs.

Disco looked and saw Lil Danky. With an *East-Unit* firmly in place, Disco snatched his gun back and growled, "my nigga, you better holla atcha homeboys. 'Cause it almost happen to 'em."

Lil Danky laughed. "You just like yo' fuckin' brutha, fulla shit, my nigga," Danky fired back as him and Disco walked up to the apartment.

As soon as Lil Danky and Disco walked through the door, Ma Barker passed Ace the lace-blunt and rolled her evil-eyes at Disco. Ace's girl, Rena, sat there beside him watching QUEEN PEN on DVD.

"What it do, everybody?" Disco greeted and took the lace-blunt from Ace.

"Ain't shit," Ace said cooly.

"Hey, Disco," Rena said with a smile. She was such a pretty chick.

Ma Barker sucked her teeth and rolled her eyes again. She'd always been a mean, good hustling, ultra-ugly lady; but she seemed to be even meaner and uglier ever since that fucked up deal had gone down between them and Pretty Pulla. And even though Pulla had eventually paid them their money back, Ma Barker continued to grind the ax.

"Ace, umm, lemme holla atcha, pimp." Disco passed the blunt to Ma Barker, because Rena and Lil Danky didn't smoke lace, and mobbed off to the back room with Ace.

Ace really and truly had his shit laid out. His bedroom looked like a suite at the Executive Inn.

Disco took a seat in the fresh leather recliner and shot his stick. "Say, Ace, what they hittin' for, bruh?"

Ace eased down onto his big king-size water bed. "Depends on who you is and who you know, bruh. Why, what's up?"

163

Disco rubbed the small patch of hair on his chin. "I got 'em for twenty-two."

"Twenty-two?" Ace questioned, knowing that bricks were as high as $30,000 on the street, though most dudes that knew somebody only paid between $19,000 and $26,000.

"Yeah, my nigga. I got 'em cheap."

Ace remembered the last deal that he'd made with Disco's brother. The work had been pure *flam*. And even though he'd gotten his money back, the shit had been a real headache. "Sco, fool, I ain't wit' that fuck-shit, boy."

"Mmmaaannn, Ace, my nigga, slow down... you know a nigga fucks witchu! So why you on that old shit? Didn't a nigga straighten that lil' shit?"

Ace nodded his head. "How its swimmin'?"

"Shiid, it done swum already. Straight butter!"

Ace shook her head. "Hell nah, fool. I gotta have my shit in the jacket."

Wasn't that fuck-shit my brutha sold yo' ass in the wrapper? Disco wanted to ask his ass, but decided not to. "Look, Ace, it's butter, bruh. The only reason a nigga dropped it all is 'cause the container that the work came 'cross in flooded or some shit... all the work got wet, a *hunnid* units. So I been up two days scrappin' and bussin' wrappers to drop that shit, 'cause a nigga couldn't move the shit wet. You feel me?" Disco lied like a muthafucka.

Considering what Disco had just said, Ace stood up. "Lemme holla at my peoples right quick."

When Ace left the room Disco looked around at all of the sexy photos of Rena. *Damn! Rena a bad-ass-bitch! I'on know how my brutha let her get away?!* he thought before checking his watch. Fifteen minutes had passed since he'd exited the Rover. *I hope this nigga hurry up.*

"Yo," Ace said, re-entering the room. "I need one, Danky and my ole-girl need a half, and my lil' fool need a half. But, fool, we ain't payin' no twenty-two for no work that already been in the water, my nigga."

Disco thought for a minute. *Shiid, that's two and a half. I already done beat a quarter off each brick, so I done got $7,200 off 'em anyway. Fuck it!* he mused. "Twenty, my nigga."

"Nah, eighteen."

"Eighteen-five, fool, and you killin' a nigga."

"Eighteen, Sco. You know you done already done ya thang."

Disco shook his head. "Fool, I'm losin' on this shit already, Ace. I gotta get eighteen-five, my nigga."

Ace seen that Disco wasn't moving off of his price. "Aiight, look, just bring a nigga one. If it's whatchu say it is, we gon' snatch three tomorrow."

"You got that," Disco said as he stood up. "If I still have three. 'Cause these bitches jumpin' like fuck. Feel me?"

"I feel you. I'ma have the money for the one ready when you get back."

"Get back from where?" Disco asked. "Boy, I ain't comin' back over here!"

Ace laughed. "So I gotta come to you?"

"Hell yeah!" Disco shot back. "You already done robbed a nigga."

The two agreed to meet up in Silver Blue in one hour, both satisfied with their bargaining skills.

Chapter 35

The two had just left KOD's and could not wait to be alone. Upon entering the large ritzy hotel room, a sort of magnetic lust pulled their bodies together. Their lips met, tongues frolicked. Complete rapture became the focal point as Joy stepped out of Maine's tender embrace and began stripping naked. *Her body!* Though he'd seen her naked on occasions in times past, his nature stirred everytime like it was the first time. Tearing his eyes away from her bewitchingly perfect body, Maine came up out of his clothes. And like magic, they were once again pressed *body to body*, her wonderful tongue probing the whole of his hot mouth. He'd never been much of a kisser, but something about Joy made him appreciate the art of osculation. The skill of her fervent tongue and soft lips caused fantastic feelings of sexual want to multiply within him, making his entire body tingle as if someone was provoking his desires with sexually enhance electrodes.

"Damn, baby," Maine moaned softly in Joy's ear as his hands squeezed her soft ass for a spell, only to probe further and find her slit slippery and oozing her desires.

Maine quickly left her lips for her neck, then her hard *Chap Stick* cap size nipples, and down to her quivering stomach. He tickled her belly button for a while before lifting her leg over his shoulder and burying his tongue in her hot sex-hole.

Joy jumped and tried to remove her leg from his shoulder. She'd never had her pussy eaten – not by a man at least. She'd had a drunken fling with her homegirl Precious before, but it didn't last because *she was not gay* and soon found out that relations with a *confused female* were just as problematic as relations with a *dog-ass-nigga*.

Joy felt guilty, because she knew emphatically what she was – *a shone*. So she knew better than to let a real nigga eat her pussy. "Ut'un, Maine. You don't have to-"

Maine silenced her by forcefully pulling her down to the plush hotel carpet. On his back, Maine positioned Joy on his face and lightly began tapping her budding clitoris with his tongue.

Sssslll, ooooooh! Daaammmnnn! Joy sounded off inwardly. This was so much better with *a real man*. Maine wanted to taste her, so Joy now wanted to be tasted. She eased up, the slick slit of her pussy on Maine's mouth and her enlarged clitoris on the tip of his nose. Joy began rocking her hips at a fast pace. Maine's tongue jabbed in and out of her. She wanted to bathe his face in her lady-milk and then kiss his face free of her own juices. The thought of it, knowing that she'd soon be squirting in his mouth, drove her into an erotic frenzy.

"Baby, I'm cummin'!" she howled.

Maine pulled her down flush on his face and sucked hard on her clit until it began gushing that sweet love-honey that he loved. Joy's was thick and creamy. He'd just about consumed it all when Joy got off of his face and stuck her tongue in his mouth. She sucked his tongue, lips, and licked his face. Maine had never experienced such animal passion.

Joy reached beneath her and gasped as she felt Maine's big hard dick. She squeezed it firmly in her small hand, her pussy thumping as if it had a heart of its own.

Joy sat up, the head of Maine's thick love-organ at the soft slippery opening of her pussy, slowly and with some discomfort, Joy eased down on his dick. Gasping, she slowly began to ride him. With each deep plunge Maine stretched her fully and filled her pussy to capacity.

Maine grabbed her plump ass and squeezed it roughly as she found a new rhythm and began bucking faster. Her small titties bouncing as she went up and down his long cum coated pole.

"Ooooh, Maine, baby I'm cummin' again!" Joy yelled.

"Come on, baby!" Maine yelled back and instantly felt the warm sprays from her long clitoris pelting his lower abdomen with thick gobbets of cum.

He couldn't believe how tight her pussy was. *Damn, I thank I love this bitch!* he thought as she continued to ride him faster. She'd rise all the way up to the very tip of his dick, almost causing it to come out, but Joy's tight pussy walls never failed to suck him back in as she descended back down on it. The ride was driving Maine crazy!

"Joy, I'm finna nut, bay!" he moaned.

Joy slipped off the dick and took it into her small mouth. Working her lips around its large head, Joy sucked with all she had and was rewarded with a monstrous load of hot creamy nut. *Mmmmmm!* she moaned as she swallowed the most of it.

"Shawty, you a beast!" Maine groaned.

Joy smiled and laid beside him on the thick carpet, finding her way into his arms. "You ain't no pushover yo'self," she responded, her eyes dancing as she looked into his.

Maine sensed her happiness. She looked nothing like she looked the night he'd met her. Her eyes now expressed the truth of her happiness. Maine hugged her closer to him. "Shawty, it feels good to be beatIn' a real goon, don't it?"

Joy smiled brightly and nodded before closing her eyes, because it really did feel good...

BOOK 4OUR
LOOK AT ME! LOOK AT ME!

I fucked my money up/ now I can't re-up!/ I ran up in his spot/ just to get my stacks up... Now I'm back on deck/ so shordy what the fuck you want?/ Niggas talkin' shit/ but that ain't what the fuck they want!

-Wacka Flocka Flame [Oh Let's Do It]

Chapter 36

SIX MONTHS LATER

Disco woke up groggy. His head was killing him from all of the *Ace of Spade*, pills, weed and cocaine. Shaking his aching head, he tried to focus on his surrounding. It wasn't until the tall red-head with the gracile figure exited the lavish hotel room's bathroom that he somewhat remembered where he was and how he'd gotten there. He'd been partying with his new partner G. They'd gone to Club Levels and partied all the way to the top level before he blacked out.

The red-head walked over to the hotel dresser and bent over, inhaling a long line of cocaine before smiling back at Disco. She was completely naked and the meaty ripples of her labia gapped open to smile at him as well. He smiled back, but quickly realized that something was missing. Then the thick dark-skin Cuban chick sashayed out of the bathroom, naked as the day she was born. Her huge titties and ass bounced as she walked over and slipped back in bed with him, causing the other chick that had been asleep under the covers to wake up and look around. Her water-blue eyes scanned the room, sleepily. The red-head said something in Spanish and gestured with the half straw she was holding. Both girls giggled and shook their heads no. She then spoke to Disco in her native tongue, offering him the cocaine.

"Hell nah, bitch! I done told y'all hoes to speak English. We ain't in Havana and I don't speak that gwalla-gwalla shit!" he snapped.

They all giggled, because he was so cute to them. And just as he couldn't understand them, they didn't understand shit he'd said.

"Stupid-ass hoes," Disco mumbled as he fired up a lace-blunt.

A frown creased his face. He couldn't remember if he'd used rubbers on the loose Spanish chicks. *Oh well*, he thought. His cell phone began ringing. The ID showed that it was Maine. *I don't feel like fuckin' with Maine's pussy-whipped ass*, he said to himself and hit the ignore button. Further observation showed that he had 40 missed calls: two from Ace, three from Chico, one from Lil Danky, Charles Mills out of Largemont had called three times, Boe had called four times, five calls from Blue, two from Jit; Londa had called ten times, Lil Will had called four times and the last six were from Shoniece.

Fuck all them callin' me for? he wondered, because he was chilling. *Fuck Lil Will and Maine gettin' money for if everybody gon' bother me?*

Disco looked at the time on his *big face* Rollie. It was exactly 1:30 p.m.

The red-head with the small titties and long pussy slid in the bed, finding her way between his legs, she sucked his dick into her mouth and began bobbing smoothly. The other two girls giggled and moved in to help her; one easing behind the red-head to lick her pussy while the other slipped beneath the covers and started sucking Disco's balls. *Damn, look at me! Look at me! I'ma muthafuckin' boss!* he thought, smoking his lace-blunt as the three chicks entertained him like the true young boss he'd become.

$$$

The past six months had been nothing but stunting for Disco. After paying Bertto for the first work he'd given him, Disco used the extra money – the profit that he was supposed to give Lil Will and Maine as half of their money back – to cop three bricks, so instead of another fifteen kilos they'd received eighteen, twelve of which were already sold – seven to Chico for $129,500 and five to Ace for $100,000. He left one brick raw [soft] for Jit in Silver Blue, which brought him $28,800. The remaining five were whipped up into six and a quarter – two to Blue, two to Boe and Cuz, two to Charles and the quarter was strip club money. All together they'd made $176,100 – after the $255,000 that they owed Bertto – in a week's time. Yet again, instead of paying Lil Will and Maine their $127,500, Disco put $70,000 in his closet and copped five birds for $85,000, which left only $75,000 apiece for Lil Will and Maine. But they didn't trip because they saw the bigger picture. With every flip their money grew and so did their clientele. In three months they were copping fifteen and G – Bertto's right hand – was fronting them twenty-five, which only took them a week to move, because their traps were on fire and they had it for cheap.

And even though Disco had eventually given Maine and Lil Will $100,000 of the $127,500 that he owed them, things had changed between them. Disco begun spending less and less time with them and more time with G – who'd taken a liking to the hustling young thug. And because Disco was always out hanging loose or partying with G, all of the work fell on Maine and Lil Will's shoulders. They'd basically been regulated to workers in what was supposed to have been a partnership.

Of course, Lil Will and Maine weren't the only ones fallen to the wayside with *the boss*. Londa and Shoniece barely saw him, and when they did it was almost in passing – he'd give them a quick quicky, a few stacks to appease them and be gone before they could protest his leaving.

$$$

Disco's phone rang. He looked at the ID and saw that it was G. He pushed the red-head's bobbing head off of his dick and answered.

G was one room over with three or four animals of his own. This had become the normal for them. Every night was a party.

"You ready, man? We gotta go, bro," G said into the phone.

"Shiid, fool, it's all on you."

"Okay. I'll meet you at you car," G said and hung up.

Disco hopped up, showered and dressed quickly. He dropped three stacks on the counter for the Spanish bitches and cleared it.

Coming through the hotel lobby, chunks and Rollie blinging, every hoe in the building had their eyes locked on him as if they knew for certain that that Porsche Carrera GT convertible parked out front was his. It was a silver blue-pearl and topped out at 212 mph. G stood beside the car – on the passenger side. Disco dapped his new homeboy and hopped in – jumping over and into the car's cockpit without opening the door. G laughed and followed suit. With the top still down, Disco smoked tires out of the hotel's parking lot.

"You crazy, man. That's what I like about you," G said.

Disco didn't respond, he just continued pushing the high-end sports car, weaving in and out of traffic. Meek Mills' I'MA BOSS played loudly as they rode. Heads turned wherever they flew by. G tapped Disco on the arm and told him to hit Miami Lakes. Steadily whizzing through traffic, Disco came to the exit in no time.

"Where we goin'?" he asked G.

"Just turn up here and pull into that ice cream shop."

Disco shook his head and sucked his teeth. *This nigga always gotta nigga in these fuckin' ice cream shops,* he thought, parking his $480,000 whip.

Everybody – male and female – stared and pointed as they exited the car.

Sombra and Pito came out and escorted them inside. The cute little Spanish girl passed G and Disco a chocolate banana split with syrup and sprinkles. G immediately dug in.

"Love this stuff!" G exclaimed. "I want to show-a-you something."

They walked beyond the counter to an office at the rear of the ice cream shop. Pito closed the door and locked it. G opened a storage closet and placed a big gym bag on the desk.

"I gonna show you how to really make some money," G said to Disco. "Grab that bag and come with me."

Disco followed him through a back door which came out to a back alley. A gray Nissan Z was parked. G jumped in and Disco took the passenger side. They drove along for about twenty minutes before pulling up to a two-story brick house that sat midway the street.

"Come on, I show you," G said and hopped out.

Disco grabbed the gym bag and followed. The door opened before G could knock or produce a key. A big 5'11", 180 pound, naked black bitch answered the door. Her hair was fire red, she had a gap between her front four gold-teeth, and her large titties hung to her protruding belly.

"'Bout damn time! We been outta cut for the longest now. How the fuck we s'posed to finish shit if we ain't got shit?" the naked chick snapped.

"Take it easy, baby. Everything is absolutely handsome... I brought you-a-ice cream but this guy ate it," G said, pointing at Disco.

The lady gave Disco the evil-eye and snatched the gym bag from him. "Make me so sick," she mumbled and strutted off, her wide fat-ass juddering as she walked.

Disco looked to G for an explanation. G shrugged and waved him to follow.

They came to a large den. There were about six naked chicks bussing down bricks, mixing them, recompressing them and then re-taping them. G picked up a mask and handed it to Disco. They walked along, watching the women work. Stopping at the mix station, G picked up some of the cut.

"See this? It's thee absolute best in the galaxy. With the premier yayo that I give you, you mix e-leven ounces of these with each kilo, you still bring-a-back twenty-a-five e-asy!" G explained.

Disco looked at the cut. "What is it, my nigga?"

"Cut. Ben-en-a-chloride. $1,500 a kilo."

"Where you get it from?"

"Slow down now. You-a-speeding," G said. "Take this."

G gave him some cocaine that had already been mixed.

"What I s'posed to do wit' this?"

"Snort it. Cook it." G shrugged his solid shoulders. "I don't care. But when you finish it, come see me. I put all you coca here too. These house go six days a week, at least 30 kilos a day. It cost me $3,000 a day to run. You pay Tuesday, you do you yayo."

"For real?"

"No," G said. "For play."

Disco smiled and dapped G up.

"I like you... you-a-boss, like that nigga, ummm, Rozay... I boss like Sosa. You, me, we rule the city. Then the state... then the world."

"I'm feelin' that, my nigga," Disco replied, loving what he heard.

"But don't... I mean ever... cross me. Because there is no second chances," G warned. His face betrayed no emotion.

Disco nodded and they headed back to the ice cream shop.

175

"Sco, let's do it again, pleeease," Londa whined from the Executive Suite's heart shaped bed. Her and Disco – finally after two weeks of not seeing each other – had hung out all day and spent the night making sex faces. Londa had truly enjoyed, and understood fully that another two weeks would probably pass before she experienced another occasion such as this. True, even when she didn't get the *quality time* that she lived for, he always made sure that Blue or Jit dropped her a few stacks every four or five days. But something had changed in Londa. The money was no longer exciting. She wanted the man behind the money – Disco. The man she'd fallen so in love with.

"Londa, didn't we do it all night? I nigga got shit to do!" Disco shot back.

She sucked her teeth just as his phone rung. It was Lil Will.

"What's good, fool?"

"Ain't shit, what they doin'?" Lil Will shot back.

"Whatever I tell 'em, my nigga. 'Cause I'm the boss!" Disco capped, latching the fixture on his new Audemars Piquet watch. It was exactly like the one that his brother had given him before going to prison – the one that was stolen when Maine got home invaded.

Lil Will laughed at Disco's cap. He'd been knowing his fool for years and understood his natural need to be out front. Him, Maine, and Disco kind of shared that – they were born *stunt men*.

"I feel you, fool. Whatchu need me to do? I'm downstairs now."

"Aiight, hold up. We comin' down now!" Disco said and hung up.

$$$

When they made it downstairs they found Lil Will sitting in his new Corvette ZR1. It was beige with the gold-pearl in color, limo tinted windows and sat on 23" customized chrome rims. Disco smiled, the car was cute to him, especially since it was parked next to his $480,000 Porsche Carrera.

Lil Will jumped out and greeted Londa and his man. The $680,000 *buy money* was in Lil Will's trunk, so Disco took his partner's keys and gave them to Londa with instructions on how to get to the ice cream parlor and what to do when she got there. She nodded, kissed him, and sped off in Lil Will's fast car. Lil Will and Disco jumped in his faster car and sped off in the opposite direction. They bent corners until they caught I-95, flushing it to the 103rd Street exit. It had been almost three months since Disco had cruised his old hood. Everything still seemed to be the same as he entered the Silver Blue Lakes Apartment Complex. He parked the Porsche Vert in the middle of the lot and hopped out, Young Jezzy's TRAP STAR sounded off loudly from the car's sound system.

It seemed that everybody was out – hoes and niggas alike – and they all stepped over to where Disco and Lil Will stood, to greet them. *Look at me! Look at me!* Disco thought as the *low-lives* paid homage to *the boss*.

"What they do, boy?!" Blue greeted his partner excitedly.

"My nigga, you already know... they do what the fuck the boss tell 'em. You feel me?!" Disco capped back and dapped Blue.

"Must be nice, my nigga," Blue returned.

"You thank it ain't," Disco told him. "I see you lightweight steppin' it up too."

Blue looked over at his Ford F-150, twin cab, with 24" chrome ENKEI rims. Beside it sat Jit's four door '71 Chevy Donk. It was painted [wet] with 23" rims and beat. They were both painted the same wet royal-blue – representing their projects.

"Lil' somethin', my nigga. But you shittin' on 'em wit' this Porsche thang, boy... I swear to God, if I had yo' hand I'd cut my shit off."

"I feel that. 'Cause if I was you, I'd feel the same way... where Jit?"

"In the abandon 'partment wit' Fannie Mae."

Disco laughed. "They might as well get they own 'partment and just do the muthafucka, my nigga, much as he trick wit' her."

"Huh, man?!"

They both laughed some more.

"Aye, Sco!" he heard somebody yell. It was a female voice. He looked over towards the building and saw thick-ass Kawannah standing on the second floor. "Check this out, Sco. Lemme holla atchu!"

Fuck this bitch want? he asked himself and walked over. "What's good, thickness?"

"You," she shot back, licking those fat-ass lips of hers and batting her big eyes. "Come in for a minute. I need to show you something and put a bug in ya ear."

Yeah, and I wouldn't mind puttin' a dick in yo' mouth, he mused, following her inside of her apartment. Kwannah had a big-stupid ass! And her little booty-shorts had its entirety on display, enticing him to squeeze. *I know bruh done dug deep off in that ass!*

Kwannah turned around and caught him staring at her big juicy ass. She smiled. "Boy, what is you lookin' at?"

Disco frowned at her. "Kwannah, whatchu want?"

She sucked her teeth and rolled her big eyes. "Where you been? And who Porsche thang you whippin'?"

"Mine and mine and mine," he answered.

"What?"

"I been *mindin' mine* and whippin' *what's mine*, feel me. Now I know you ain't call me up here for that shit."

Kwannah sucked her teeth again. "You ain't gotta be gettin' smart. I guess you think you the shit now witcha lil' Audemars and Porsche, but I was ya girl befo' yo' ass blew up. Now you actin' all stank."

Stupid ass bitch! You my brutha hoe and I don't owe you shit, he wanted to say, but out of respect for Pulla he chilled. "It ain't like that, shawty. A nigga just been dumb busy. Now what's up?"

"Yeah," Kwannah said, slightly rolling her eyes. "You ain't never holla back 'bout them flicks for Pulla, so I went 'head and had my friend take these. You think he gon' like 'em?"

Kwannah passed Disco an envelope full of pictures. He opened it and got an eyeful! His dick rocked straight up! Kwannah was pictured in a G-string with no bra holding those big ass D-cups – only whip cream covered her nipples... one with her bent over – pussy lips hanging... one with her legs bussed wide open and her tongue out... another with her tongue licking two cherries... *damn!* he almost let slip when he saw the one with a big banana halfway down her throat. He could feel his dick pulsating.

"Whatchu thank?" she asked, smiling at his erection.

"Ye-yeah," he stuttered, still staring at the pictures. "He, gon' love these."

"How 'bout you?" she asked. "Do you love 'em?"

"What?!"

"Boy, don't play!" she said, grabbing his dick. "This thang ain't hard for nothin'!"

Kwannah pushed him down on the love seat and pulled his dick out. She didn't waste anytime playing with it, she went straight deep throat!

"Goddamn, girl!" he moaned.

She held the head of his dick in her throat and began swallowing – making her throat muscles massage it. Disco had never felt no shit like that. He started squirming in his seat. Kwannah spit the dick up, only holding the head between her thick lips. She applied maximum pressure and began working her lips up and down his shaft. Disco pumped his hips, loving the feeling of her wet, strong dick-suckers.

"Mmmm, hmmm! Come on, baby!" she moaned, licking his balls and the underside of his shaft before sucking it whole again.

And in 60 seconds flat, Disco was feeding her his children. *Mmmm!* she moaned, taking all of his thick slimy semen into her mouth. When she'd caught the last of it, she stood and walked to the bathroom. Disco heard the toilet flush and then heard her running water. She returned a minute later with a wash cloth and a smile.

While wiping his dick off she asked, "you straight?"

He nodded, eyeing her strangely.

"What?!" she asked, laughing.

"Whatchu just did in the bathroom?"

"Shiid, I spit yo' nut out and brushed my teeth. Why?"

"Why you ain't swallow it?"

"Boy, please!" Kwannah said, rucking her brow. "I'll get it up outcha, but I am not swallowin' that shit!"

Disco frowned at her. "You a trip... is you finish?"

"Nah," she said. "Take them flicks witchu... and make sho' yo' brutha get some of 'em." A nasty smile was covering her face.

"Aiight," Disco replied, standing to leave.

"Hold up, boy. It's one more thang."

"What?"

"Look, don't put my name in this shit, okay... but, the other day, probably 'bout three weeks ago, Blue and 'em was outside my door talkin'. It was him, Jit, them animal-ass hoes off the end, Lil Henry, Ziggy, and Shelton's soft-ass. The –"

Disco cut her off. "Ziggy and Shelton was 'round here?" he asked, knowing damn well he'd told both of them to *stay the fuck outta the Blue!* Besides, he knew that they were the suckas that broke into his rental and stole his gun.

"Yeah. They been comin' through a lot lately."

"And they was kickin' it wit' Blue and Jit?"

"Yeah, bay. Smokin' and drinkin'. They be 'round here hangin' out."

Disco gritted his teeth. *I'ma kill them fuck-niggas!* he thought before Kwannah continued.

"Anyway," she said, popping those big lips of hers. "They must be ain't know I was home, 'cause I usually be at work, but I had done been out all night and was tired, so I called in... so look, they was by my door talkin' all loud and shit. So I got up and was 'bout to cuss they asses out, 'cause I don't really do Shelton and them *shone-ass-hoes* off the end know I don't like they nasty asses. Bitches 'round her fucking bruthas and fuckin' hoes' mans for a lil' change... ooww, I can't stand them nasty bitches!"

Disco looked at her like she was crazy! *Didn't this hoe just suck my dick, knowin' damn well that I fuck wit' Londa and she's s'posed to be my brutha peoples?!* Disco shook his head sadly. *Shit crazy!?*

"Yeah, Sco, but look," Kwannah continued. "They talkin' all loud. So when I got to the door, 'bout to open it and *read* they asses, I heard the hoes like ...'nigga you sleep, Sco run this shit! He gotta $400,000 whip and he boss this shit. The nigga bought the bar at Club Space for a month! So you better wake up. That nigga a boss!'... Yeah, the hoes was all on yo' nut sack. Blue and Jit was just laughin'. But Ziggy and Shelton went off... 'fuck that pussy-nigga! We gon' rob his soft-ass! That nigga pussy. He only shinin' 'cause he got his brutha plug! He ain't no go-getta! That's why we broke in that nigga car and gon' rob his ass wit' his own gun! Fuck Disco!'... They was lettin' you have it, honey."

"What?!" Disco shouted. "Them pussy-niggas said that? In my 'partments?"

"Yep."

"And Blue and Jit ain't say shit?" Disco was .38 hot!

"They was only laughin' at first. But then Blue was like, 'slowdown, fool. It ain't that serious.' And Jit was like, 'for real, fool be lookin' out.' But Shelton 'em wasn't hearin' that shit."

Disco nodded his head. "Bet that up, K-Girl." He reached in his pocket and extracted a big $20,000 knot. "This for my brutha flicks." He handed her $150. "This for the info." He gave her $250. "And this for suckin' my dick." He passed her $25.

"Ppsstt!" Kwannah sounded, rolling her neck and eyes. "You mighta tried me!"

"Nah, any hoe can *get it up out me*. That's the easy part, ma. The hard part is swallowin' what you produced... hit a nigga when you learn how to swallow," Disco said and walked out with the flicks for his brother and a new problem to solve.

When Disco made it back downstairs, Blue, Lil Will, Jit and the *animal-ass-hoes* from the end were surrounding his car, smoking weed and bullshitting.

"Heeeyyy, Sco!" the hoes sang in unison.

"What's up, hoes," he shot back and hopped in his car. "Let's hit it, fool."

"Maine on his way, bruh," Lil Will replied.

"Well you wait on him, I'm out! I'll holla when I get that," Disco told his man and fired off.

Chapter 38

After getting a call from G, Disco changed cars – out of the Porsche and into his reliable rental. When he pulled up to the parlor Lil Will's Vette was parked out front and Londa was busying herself with a chocolate banana split – syrup and sprinkles included. G sat in front of her eating one of the same.

"Looky what-a-the house-dog pulled in," G said, standing and giving Disco a half-hug.

"It's *what the cat drug in*, G," Londa corrected as she also stood and hugged her man.

"Thee *house-cat!* I forget... dog, cat, it's thee same. As long as it's not thee rat. I hate rats!" G stated, his demeanor had gone from comical to deadly serious just that fast.

Disco went into his pocket and peeled $2,500 off of his knot. He handed it to Londa.

"Go play in the mall for a lil' while, take my rental. I'ma holla atcha if I need you."

Londa took the money and kissed Disco on the lips. "I'ma see you tonight?"

"I said I'll holla if I need you."

Disappointed with his rash reply, Londa waved by to G and the cute little Spanish girl that had fixed her ice cream and then sauntered off.

G watched her *nice ass* judder as she walked. "That's a very handsome woman you have."

"Yeah," Disco said, catching his vibe as well as peeping his stare. Disco laughed within. "She aiight, my nigga."

The two jumped in the Vette and sped off to the two-story brick house. Grabbing the two duffle bags that contained Disco's 40 kilos from the Corvette's trunk, they made their way inside. Everything was already set up. The big black naked lady with the huge ass and large sagging titties took the bags and began yelling orders. The other naked women immediately went into action – breaking down the bricks and rebuilding them. The process was simple and did not take very long. Disco watched with sheer amazement. A slight erection ensued. But not from the naked women – they were nonessential at present and *so not on his calculating mind* at the moment. His erection stemmed from b*oss visions of bigger profits and further expanding the fundamentals of stunting.*

Disco smiled a broad smile as the last three kilos were wrapped up, 52 units and eight ounces in total. *That's twelve bricks and eight ounces for three stacks!* he thought, quickly pulling out his money roll and giving G five stacks.

"What's this? It's only three."

"Man, give it to them naked hoes, keep it, I don't give a fuck! Just lemme get that work and get the fuck outta here, my nigga. I gotta million to make! You feel me?!"

G laughed and patted his little eager partner on the back.

"You didn't get here, at these point, in one day... Patient! You have every-a-thing. Me," G said, tapping himself on his muscular chest. "I *looove* Ice cream! The pro-cess. It takes patient. But the results are always very handsome. Me parlor, only thee best ice cream. One week to *makey* ten gallons of ice cream be-a-cause I only use the premier in-gredients. *You* will be a bigger boss than me, Rozan or Sosa."

Disco laughed, not knowing who the fuck Rozan was, and dapped G up. He also hadn't understood none of that *ice cream and patience shit.* All he'd heard was b*oss* and all he saw was *his first million.*

Hell yeah! When my brutha come home in nine months, we gon' rule the world! Bosses! he thought.

G seemed to be reading his mind. "Don't count you eggs before thee cock crow," he said, eyeing Disco.

"It's *count your eggs befo' they hatch*, my nigga." Disco laughed at his man, always fucking up meaningless quotes.

"Chicken, cock, hatch, crow, same difference. They all birds. But the meaning is, how *mush* money you have-a-saved?"

Disco eyed G, not sure where this was headed. "I got $250,000 put up," he lied, knowing damn well he only had $76,000 in his safe.

G shook his head sadly. "How you have car, even watch, more than you have-a-saved?" G asked, then put his index-finger to his temple. "Think. You didn't get it in-a-one day. So don't spend it in-a-one day. Patient!" he said and left Disco to his thoughts.

Chapter 39

Mac-90 sat on the screened porch of the newly leased house that him and Varray shared in Miami Lakes. Already on three good-pills and a can of 211 Stainless Steel, Mac-90 fired up a choppa-square and pulled hard on it. He got an instant head rush as he gazed out at his new neighborhood.

It's too quiet out this muthafucka! he thought to himself. *Damn I miss Town!*

The only thing good about his new hood was the fact that he didn't have to worry about running into the *fuck-niggas* that he and Varray robbed for a living and the two animal-ass white hoes that lived next door. They were both nurses and both loved pills – any kind of pills – and black dick. He and Varray had met the two skinny, big breasted bitches the first day that they moved in and had been fucking them ever since.

I wonder where them nut-drinkin' ass hoes at now? Mac-90 wondered to himself. He looked next door, their white VW Limited Edition Jetta was gone. He then looked across the street from his house – where all of the fine-ass Spanish hoes hung out with the big, thick black chick. He'd been meaning to pull up on *thick-black* for a minute, but couldn't quite figure an angle to approach her from. *Damn, I'll do somethin' big wit' that big bitch! Believe that!* he assured himself, fondling his crotch as he smoked the last of his choppa.

Just then the door opened across the street. A black dude and a freaky walking Spanish dude walked out carrying duffle bags. He'd seen the Spanish dude plenty of times at the hoes' house, simply figuring him to be their gay partner, because faggots always hung out with bad hoes. The black dude looked familiar too.

Ain't that that fuck-nigga from, nnnaaahhh, can't be, Mac-90 told himself. *I'm trippin'*, he figured and fired up another choppa.

The two men placed the two duffle bags in the Corvette's trunk and whipped off.

I gotta keep a eye on them, Mac-90 thought. *They might be on somethin'.*

Before the thought could clear his mind the white Jetta whipped up next door and Lynn and Halle jumped out wearing next to nothing.

Shiid, Varray gone, I got both of these hoes to myelf! I'm 'bout to get off-the-muthafuckin-chain! Mac-90 thought and stepped outside of the porch's screened enclosure. He wore only his jeans and boxers beneath, having left his shirt, socks and shoes next to the living room couch. The noon sun reflected off of his baldhead and his loud high-pitched voice shattered the quiet, still air.

"Aye! Aye! Y'all hoes check this out! Fuck y'all finna get into?" he yelled, walking towards them.

The two airheads – a short haired natural brunette with light-brown eyes [Halle] and the long haired fake blond with the dark-brown eyes [Lynn] – giggled aloud and met Mac-90 at the edge of his property.

"We were totally just talking about you," Halle said, holding Lynn close to her.

"We sure were!" Lynn said. "This guy, Brad, just gave us a *fifty-pack* of *Bars*!"

"What he want for 'em?"

"Umm, two-hundred," Halle said.

Lyin' ass bitch! Mac-90 thought. "I'll give y'all hoes one-fifty for 'em and pop-off wit' y'all. What's up?"

"Deal!" Lynn said, giggling gleefully, because they'd fucked Brad and gotten the pills for only $50.

"Y'all hoes come on," Mac-90 commanded and walked back to his house. He had some big plans for the two sneaky-ass, good pussy white hoes...

Chapter 40

FOUR DAYS LATER

Shoniece shook Disco awake. He was tired as hell. The two of them had just returned from *Fantasy Island* [The Hedonism Resort in Negril, Jamaica]. It was a complete blast! – and the best $50,000 he'd ever blown in three days. Naked bitches of all ages, colors, and descriptions walked the resort with S-E-X in their every movement. Before then he'd never taken ecstasy, but the way Shoniece and every bitch on the island had been throwing the pussy at him he had to pop something to keep up. He'd never in life fucked so much!

"Disco, bay... the phone, bay. It's yo' brutha," Shoniece said sleepily.

"Goddamn, man," Disco complained, taking the phone. Shoniece got up and left the room. "Yeah, what's up?"

"Damn, boy, it's like that? A nigga can't never catch you. What, you a star now, my nigga?" Pretty Pulla capped at his little brother.

"Nah, dog, somebody lied, 'cause I gotta choppa in the ride. You feel me?!" Disco capped back, loving the fact that his big brother was open.

"I heard that, my nigga. I got that cake, too. It must be yo' birthday."

Disco had sent him $5,000 before leaving for Fantasy Island. "Nah, not yet, but I got my name on the cake. You feel me?!"

"Believe me, nigga, I feel you! I got like seven left, slim."

"Yeah, and I can't wait, bruh. The world is ours, my nigga."

"Yeah, yeah... but, umm, man, where my car at?"

"Nigga, that old-ass shit in the garage... I'm snatchin' out here, bruh, I promise! When you hit, we goin' to get that Boo Thang, my nigga."

"Boo Thang?!" Pulla questioned.

"Yeah, nigga, that Bugatti Veyron 16.4! I been checkin' that shit out, $1,700,000."

"Nigga, you trippin'!"

"Nah, nigga, you trippin'! I already got that Porsche Carrera GT Vert, nigga! $484,000," Disco corrected his big brother.

"For real, boy?!"

"I told you I'm snatchin' out here, I tell ya, I promise!" Disco was feeling hella good. "I got my name on the cake, bruh-bruh."

"Damn, boy! That's real. I can't wait to get there!"

"Yeah, but bruh... umm, lemme ask you somethin'."

"What's good?"

"Why you fucked Shoniece, bruh?" Disco asked sadly.

"Boy! I ain't never had none of Shoniece's pussy!"

Lyin' ass nigga! 'Cause that's the same shit she said, Disco thought. *They done rehearsed that shit!* "My nigga, you ain't gotta lie to a nigga, my nigga. A hoe ain't gon' never come between us. I just wanna know so I'll know how to carry this hoe, bruh."

"Bruh, you trippin'!"

"Bruh, I know 'bout the trip to ATL. The hoe done told me everythang," Disco lied.

"Well, the bitch lyin', my nigga. On Lil Arthur and B head, my nigga, I ain't never fucked Shoniece... in the pussy," Pretty Pulla swore.

"Maann, I woulda never done it to you, bruh. You know that, right?" Disco said, knowing he'd gotten head from Kwannah, which Pulla didn't know about.

"Nigga, you fuck my hoe, Pie!"

"Maann, everybody was fucking Pie!"

And fool, everybody fuckin' Shoniece! Pulla wanted to tell his little brother, but instead said, "Well, my nigga, I still ain't never had none of Shoniece's pussy."

Disco wanted to believe him, so he did. Feeling better about his hoe now, he got back in the groove. "So what's up?"

"Shiid, Lil Disco left last week. He ready to go."

"Maann, I'm not fuckin' wit' 30 Row crazy ass," Disco shot back.

"Bruh, give the nigga somethin' for me. On stacks it's gon' be straight."

"Aiight, give him my number."

"Bet that up, bruh... Love ya, my nigga... and I'm proud of you."

That made Disco feel hella good. "No pressure, bruh-bruh. And a nigga love you too."

Disco hung up just as Shoniece walked in.

"You ready for momma to milk that dick?" she asked, slithering onto the bed.

"Nah, ma, chill," Disco said, halting her. Sex was the last thing on his mind. "Is you ready to go home?"

"No! Boy, I'm straight! Whatcho lyin' ass brutha done told you? 'Cause you trippin', Sco. I—"

"Londa! Shut the fuck up! You always—"

"Ut'un! No!" Shoniece cut him off. "Nigga, what did you just call me?"

"Umm, shit, I called you a *bitch*!" Disco bassed on her, not really knowing what the fuck he'd just called her. He felt it had to have been derogatory because she acted like she was offended. Why? He couldn't understand because he always called his hoes *bitches*.

"Nah, nigga! You called me *Londa*."

"What?!"

"You called me Londa, Sco. Why that bitch on yo' mind?"

"That bitch ain't on my mind... you trippin'!"

191

Disco got out of the bed and headed to the bathroom. He showered, cleaned up and came back out to get dressed. Shoniece was still sitting in the same spot, crying.

"What's wrong witchu?"

"You wanna send me home so you can fuck that bitch," she said sadly.

"Shoniece, you trippin' for nothin'. You know a nigga love you, girl," Disco capped, taking her into his arms. "You my boo thang, lil' momma."

"Then why you wanna send me back?"

"'Cause Lil Disco out and we 'bout to crank 30 Row back up, feel me?! I need you to *get it in on that road*, feel me?! I know you know how to move and I don't trust nobody but you wit' that bread, *feel me?!*" Disco capped soothingly to his baby, but made a quick mental note to be sure to tell Lil Disco, *don't give Shoniece's ass one dime of my muthafuckin' money! Either brang my shit yo'self or send it UPS.*

Shoniece nodded slowly, indicating yes, *she felt him.*

"Good, now gimme some of that fi' pussy befo' Lil Disco call back. 'Cause when he hit we gotta get you outta here."

Shoniece smiled and came at him headfirst like a soccer player, taking his semi-erection into her mouth and sucking it with unadulterated passion.

Chapter 41

Having fucked the air out of Shoniece and received the call from his brother's man, Lil Disco in Anniston, Alabama's notorious *30 Row*, Disco had promptly grabbed the two kilos and eight ounces from his stash, got Shoniece a fresh rental and got her ass on the road. He'd negotiated a sweet deal with Lil Disco – whose real name was J-Roc. His brother Pulla had named J-Roc *Lil Disco* because the big youngster reminded him of Disco, his little brother, who was older than J-Roc, and began treating him like family while they were all hustling big in Anniston. They'd made a lot of money together and Disco had gained a lot of respect for Lil Disco when he'd taken a federal gun charge for his brother Pretty Pulla. So to help him get right, Disco told him to pay Shoniece $5,000 for *hitting the road* and to just give him $35,000 for the 44 ounces of clean soft. He knew that Lil Disco was going to make a killing off of the work, *so his ass gon' be payin' the full $20,000 plus payin' Shoniece her shit the next time*, he thought as he followed Londa to the ice cream parlor.

Damn I'm 'bout to kill 'em! he kept telling himself. He and Londa had counted out $1,100,000. It was the most he'd ever touched – and it was all off of the 50 kilos that he'd given to Lil Will and Maine. Some went wholesale, others went retail. Several were served in the wrapper, yet even more had been *whipped up* and sold hard. They were gaining new weight customers and opening new traps weekly. Everything was coming together like two fat lesbians in a phone booth.

Of the $1,100,000, they owed G $425,000, which was for twenty-five kilos. However, Disco had Lil Wil and Maine believing that the extra ten bricks he'd given them – 50 in total – were also from G, so instead of splitting $420,000 three ways, they were splitting $250,000 three ways and Disco was sitting on $250,000 with another $35,000 to come.

When they got to the ice cream shop, Pito and Sombra quickly jumped in Londa's Volvo after she'd gotten out and whizzed off with the $500,000 that he was spending and the $425,000 that he owed G. Disco was upping the ante and G respected it, so he was giving him thirty bricks for $500,000 instead of the normal $510,000 – a $10,000 break.

"Me want to see-a-you do good, Disco," G said over ice cream. "I like you."

"I 'preciate that shit too, my nigga," Disco said. "You still gon' front a nigga the twenty-five though, right?"

"Of course. I got you, man... but just-a-like I got you, you got-a-to play fair with you men. Everybody got-a-to have some food."

Disco nodded his head. He felt that he was playing fair with Lil Will and Maine. He was thugging and everybody was *whipped up and stunting*. So nothing else really mattered. But hadn't he been upset with Jay for similar infractions? *But that was different*, he concluded.

When Londa's Volvo pulled back up, Disco gave her $2,500 and a tongue kiss. She took his rental and left.

As he and G hopped in the Volvo his stomach began to bubble. There were millions in *product* in his trunk. *We 'bout to turn this 55 into 71 bricks and twenty-nine ounces! And I'm 'bout to lose my mind!* he thought as they exited the parking lot and whipped off towards the two-story brick house. *Boy! Look at me, look at me!*

Chapter 42

The clean Chrysler 300 bent the corner en route to its home base. Tupac's CHANGE loomed softly as it cruised. Mac-90 shook his head sadly and looked at Varray, whom drove the Chrysler. They'd just left the motel after having hung out at *The After Hour* – a sleazy hole in the wall club in Overtown – for most of the night. They'd both picked up some *action* in the club and took them to the motel. Mac-90 had snatched Toya – a freaky ass *shone* hoe out of 20th Street apartments – and was very pleased with her performance. However, he was shocked and totally dumbfounded at who Varray had snatched. He just couldn't believe it!

"Varray, my nigga, how long you been smashin' Vanessa, dog?"

"Man, I'on 'member. Why?"

"Why? My nigga, Jack dead and you fuckin' the man's baby-momma! My nigga, that's some *slimy-ass-shit*, dog."

"Shiid, somebody gotta fuck the dick-eatin' bitch! Why not me? I'ma real nigga and I look out for the bitch and Lil Jack... shiid, I jut gave the hoe $200."

"$200? $200? A nigga spend $200 on pills and coc', bruh," Mac-90 shot back. He really didn't like the idea of Varray fucking Jack's girl, especially since Jack was dead, because he truly believed that disrespecting the dead brought niggas *bad luck*. Because whether Varray wanted to believe it or not, the dead were actually living – in the spirit – and could see everything that niggas were doing and could either help niggas or *fuck niggas up*.

"Mac, my nigga, the hoe came at me, dog. But if you gon' have a sucka stroke over the shit, I'll-" Varray stopped mid-sentence upon seeing the silver Volvo Vert on his block. "What the fuck?! Mac, look!"

Mac-90 looked at the car that Varray had pointed out. "You like that shit?"

"Nah, fool! Ain't that that hoe Londa's car?"

"The fine-ass red hoe that you used to smash?"

"Yeah!"

Staring hard at the car, Mac-90 said, "Damn sho' is, bruh! And that's where I know that fuck-ass nigga from!"

"What fuck-ass nigga?"

"Last Tuesday... I was on the porch smokin' a choppa. You was probably fornicatin' wit' Jack hoe... but, my nigga, I seen one of them niggas come outta that house wit' a gay lookin' cracka."

"One of what niggas?"

"One of them suckas from the Rollexxx... the fuck-niggas we licked. The fuck-"

"Niggas that killed Jack," Varray cut in, finishing Mac-90's sentence.

"That!" Mac-90 stated. "That fuck-nigga was in another car last week, a Vette. That's why I ain't peep it. They came out wit' duffle bags, boy...they got it in that house and them hoes sittin' on it for 'em."

"Yeah," Varray said, driving past their house. He parked on the next block, not wanting to chance them spotting his black 300. They walked back and sat on the screened in porch, where they could watch and not be seen. Mac-90 fired up and smoked damn near half a pack of choppa-squares before the front door of the house finally opened. It was G stepping out to use the phone.

"Mac, that's that Spanish nigga that be wit' Bertto, my nigga!"

Mac-90 snapped his finger. "Damn sho' is! I knew I knew that loose walkin' ass cracka! He muscle. That nigga will kill somethin'!"

196

"Boooyyy, if that's Bertto's man, then that's Bertto's house."

"And I done took from that gay-ass cracka one time and I'll take his shit again! I'm tellin' you, Var, my nigga, it's in there."

"We gon' see," Varray said as they watched G re-enter the house.

"Aye, Var."

"Yeah?"

"Lemme ask you somethin', my nigga."

"Go 'head."

Mac-90 looked at his partner. *Jack, forgive me*, he prayed quickly and asked, "Is that pussy good?"

"Who? The hoe Londa?"

"Hell nawl, nigga! Vanessa, Jack hoe."

"Man, you trippin'."

"Nah, Var, my nigga. I'm just askin', 'cause she walk like that pussy good. Plus that hoe –"

"Hold up," Varray cut him off. "That's the nigga Disco!"

Mac-90 looked. Disco and G were both putting duffle bags in the Volvo's trunk.

"I told you, boy! It's in there, boy! Them hoes sittin' on it," Mac-90 almost yelled.

Varray nodded his head. A smile spread his face. "And we gon' get it," he said as both men hopped in the Volvo and sped off.

Chapter 43

"Ooooh, baby, yeeesss, lick it right there, Daddy Maine," Joy moaned. Her and Maine were at Maine's house enjoying the pleasures of each others lustful joy.

Maine licked and savored the perfumed warmth of her musky opening. He loved the scent of her sex just as much as she loved his oral stimulation. She had already came twice and was on the verge of spurting her love again, but Maine's HUSTLING special ring-tone sounded.

"Damn!" he said, removing his mouth from Joy's tumid vulva.

"Noooo! Ba-be, let it ring!" she whined. Her orgasm was *right there.*

Maine wanted to please his b*oo thang*, but the HUSTLING ring-tone was for one of two people – neither could he see himself ignoring or letting down.

He rolled over and answered the phone. "Yeah?"

"My nigga, where Lil Will?" Disco asked, apparent agitation in his voice. "I been callin' this nigga for the last hour!"

"Oh, fool cleared it. Him and Trisha went to Universal Studios with they daughter."

"What?! Who the fuck told that nigga he could leave? My nigga, we got work!" Disco screamed into the phone.

Maine took the phone from his ear and looked at it crazy. *Who told him he could leave? This nigga trippin'!* Maine thought, but simply said, "what?"

Disco sucked his teeth. "Maann, fuck it! It's on you then. Come get this shit, fool. Washhouse on 22nd in forty-five minutes," Disco said and hung up before Maine could reply.

Pulling into Chico's yard, Disco hopped out with a duffle bag – twenty bricks inside. Chico had some Four-Corner-Hustler niggas out of Arkansas that needed five units and he needed fifteen himself. Disco was in and out with $370,000 – which he didn't bother to count because Chico was always on point.

From there he hit Aswan to serve Ace, Lil Danky and their mean ass momma – Ma Barker. They needed five – together. Again, he was in and out, this time with $100,000.

That left him six kilos and twenty-nine ounces from his personal shit.

Pushing it down 27th, Disco broke right on 95th and rode to 22nd Avenue. He then bent a right and whipped up into the wash house. Maine's BMW was parked there. He could see that a female was riding with him.

Maine slid into the clean Volvo Vert.

"What's hood, fool?" Maine capped.

"Ain't shit, my nigga. That forty bricks in that bag... y'all tighten up, my nigga."

This nigga really gone on this boss shit, Maine thought to himself. But Disco was just like that. He meant no harm, and besides, everybody was eating. "I'ma hit you later on," Maine said.

"Yeah," Disco replied dryly, speed dialing a phone number.

Maine hopped out with the forty kilos and cleared it.

$$$

With that taken care of Disco shot to his house and put the $470,000 into his safe, along with five kilos for Lil Disco. The odd brick and twenty-nine ounces he quickly whipped up into seventy-two ounces of *straight butter*. He'd already called Boe and Cuz, letting them know that he was en route. This would be another $57,000 to grow on. *Don't count yo' chicken befo' they hatch,* he remembered G trying to tell him. He laughed, *look at me, look at me!*

Chapter 44

The loud sharp horns blared, the bassline and the 808 thundered as Young Jeezy delivered his classic verse on Shawdy Lo's DEY KNOW... *I'm in my cool whip/ outside jello/ hopped up out that pretty muthafucka like hello... Hello/ ladies how you doin'/ that nigga crazy girl / don't say nothin' to him... Got snow /got white/ jack who/ take what/ Click Clack/ hello...*

The song filled the air with a jovial – triumphant vibe. The speeding Porsche Vert from which the sounds emitted was en rout to Club Wet-Wetz – Nephew Mal at the wheel, his long thick dreadlocks blowing in the breeze. Disco leaned on the passenger side, the top was down and there were so many lights. *The lights.* So many lights. *The money.* So much money. *The suckers.* There were so many haters. *Jack who? Take what?* Disco thought to himself as he stared at the lights. *So many lights.*

He and Nephew Mal had been out shopping and *popping off* all day. Beside that weekend on *Fantasy Island* with Shoniece, Disco'd never fucked with pills, but fucking with Nephew Mal the past two days had changed that. Mal was a *live wire.* He was the embodiment of thugging: *Young, On Pills, and Down for Whatever!*

With the modified Bin Laden style *Scorpion* on his lap, Mal pushed the *fast car* and rapped with the song, modifying the lyrics to reflect his vibe – his come up. *The triumph!*

"...I went from a half-ounce to a Mazzarotti / first real nigga to put on for Broward County..." Mal turned up into Wet-

Wetz and parked near the front. The assault rifle he slid beneath the seat.

"Here," Disco said, passing him a .40. "We can get this in. The owner's my man."

They hopped out, fresh to death. Mal rocked the all black Polo silk set, black J's, stupid Cuban link with the frosted Jesus piece, stainless steel Rolex, and dark Ray Ban shades. Disco was hurting them with the light-gray, yellow and pink Polo linen set, three-color matching gators, his Audemars and gold *Carties* – pockets threatening to burst at the seams.

"Got-damn, you might as well *pop-off*, got-damn," Mal said, passing Disco a pill before chewing two himself.

Disco chewed his and the two walked in.

The club was full as fuck! Everybody trying to *out stunt* the other. It was something like a ballers' fest. Disco spotted Lil Will, Trisha, Maine, and Londa up in VIP. Yet he chose to take a table on the far wall of the large club – near the bar. The chubby waitress quickly recognized money and made her way over. Disco ordered six bottles of bubbles, handing the waitress ten stacks.

"Brang a nigga nine stacks in ones, the four-hunnid odd is yo' tip," he told the smiling young lady.

She thanked him and hurried off to fill his order.

Mal tapped Disco on the arm and pointed at the two scanty dressed white chicks seated next to them. Fake blonde and a brunette. Cut off *Daisy Dukes* and halter tops. Long heels, red bottoms. Fat pussies, big titties. Airheads, nothing to think with. All of this was apparent as Mal peeped them *popping off*, back-to-back. They had a tall, full-figured black chick bent over in front of them, legs spread, pussy open. The two white hoes giggled and whispered to each other as they stared into the naked dancer's *worn-hole*.

Mal had never fucked a white bitch before and wanted to bad as fuck. He caught the blonde's eye and put up the X sign – crossing his forearms in front of him. The blonde giggled some more and showed the brunette, who in turn giggled also. They both threw the X sign back at Mal. He nodded, *I'ma get them hoes!* he thought, already picturing the penetration.

The waitress returned with two bouncers and Disco's order. The bouncers sat the six silver buckets around their table – all filled with ice and a champagne bottle. The chubby waitress sat the 90 crispy $100 stacks on the table – in a neat pile.

"If you need *anything*, baby, just wave for me, okay?" she flirted, batting her pretty eyes.

Disco chuckled. *Picture me dead broke, look at me rich now!* he thought of Meek Mills' lyrics, they were so true. "I gotchu, lil' momma," he said, smiling a solid gold smile back at her.

She sauntered away and the bottle popping began.

$$$

Lil Wayne's HOW TO LOVE loomed loudly from the club's sound system. Londa, a bit tipsy, sat in the VIP between Maine and Trisha, swaying to the music. The words from the song seem to strum her heart, mesmerizing her with their truth. Her mind was fixed on Disco. Thoughts of the last time they'd wedged their hot body parts together in what she perceived as love. But was it love? And if by chance it were, Londa knew that she needed more. She'd given him all of her – physically, mentally and financially. Nevertheless, now that he was on top she'd seemingly been relegated to the bottom and stripped of her rightful position at his side.

Trisha looked at her *partner-best friend-sister* and felt bad for her. She nudged her and made a silly face. Londa looked at her and smiled. It was a half-smile, yet beautiful nonetheless, because Londa was truly one of the prettiest women that God had ever created.

"Hoe! Is you aiight?" Trisha asked jokingly.

"Yeah, girl, you know I'm straight. My account good, I'm lookin' good, what else a real bitch need?" she said half-heartedly and poured herself another glass of Moet. Downing the glass she smiled. However, inside she frowned. Disco, that's what else the *real bitch* needed.

"Aye!" Lil Will said all of a sudden. "Ain't that Sco right there."

"Where?!" Londa jumped, scanning the club.

"Over there!" Lil Will pointed and everybody looked. "Wit' the gray shit on...sittin' wit' the red nigga wit' the wicks and the two white hoes."

"Yeah," Maine said, recognizing his partner. "That is fool."

"I wonder why he sittin' way over by the bar. Y'all told him we was comin'?" Trisha asked.

"I told him...well, I left that nigga a message, 'cause he ain't answer his phone."

"He probably ain't get it, boy!" Londa said and began leaving. "I'ma go get him. I'll be right back."

They all watched her exit, damn near running in her expensive high heels.

Trisha shook her head sadly. "Sco must be got platinum on that dick, bay! Because he got my chick fucked up!"

"She'll be aiight," Maine said.

"Yeah, Londa a *go-getta*," Lil Will chimed in.

"Well, yo' ass bet' not never try me like that! Or I'ma kill yo' ass!" Trisha told her *lover-baby daddy-partner*, and she meant every word of it.

$$$

Disco, Nephew Mal, and their two new white female friends were on their third round of bottles – twelve bottles deep – and halfway through Mal's *happy-sack* of pills. The vibe was live and the *horny-white-sluts* were *wide-ass-open*. Mal had the brunette and the fake blonde was all over Disco as Amazon, White Chocolate, Bubbles, and Purple Thunder worked up a sweat trying to impress the two big money ballers.

Disco had his middle and pointer finger deep off in the blonde's pussy – her shorts pulled to the side – as she threw his money to the dancers. Her pussy was super-wet and they were *rrrroooollllllliiiinnnnggggg!*

Mal had his brunette finger-fucking Bubbles as he poured champagne down her back and into her big round ass. A badass bitch in ripped up blue jeans, Red Bottom heels and a Nadia Terrel studded half-T caught Mal's eyes. She stood staring at Disco with evil-eyes. Mal nudged his partner.

"Aye, bruh, I thank that lil' momma right there want you," Mal said, staring at the *boss-ass* red-bone.

Disco looked up, drunk and high as fuck. The pills had him tripping. He pulled his two fingers out of the white hoe's big wet pussy and smelt it. Frowning, he addressed Londa.

"What's up, Londa? Fuck you doin' in Wet-Wetz? You dykin' now?" he slurred, smiling at her mischievously.

"Disco, do – not – play – wit' me, boy...why you down here wit' this," she said, eyeing the two white girls. She could see that they were high. "Wit' this trash! Why you ain't in the VIP wit' us? Come on."

"Nah," Disco slurred.

"Why?!" Londa shrieked, surprise registering on her face.

"Mal!" Disco called.

"Yeah, what's up, bruh?"

"Why we ain't in the VIP?" Disco asked.

"Shiid, 'cause we thuggin'! The VIP for suckas," Mal answered, causing the white chicks to laugh.

"Well, you might as well tell her to move, 'cause I'ma just chill wit' you," Londa said, moving towards Disco's side.

"Nah," he stopped her. "Londa, you might as well start dykin', 'cause yo' pussy all big and loose and yo' head ain't on nothin'. For real, hoes like you need to dyke."

"What?!" Londa shrieked. Tears began to fall. She couldn't believe he'd said that. "Don't say that, Disco! Don't do this!"

"Do what? Ma, I'm serious. Me, you and this white bitch right here can dip right now. 'Cause for real-"

"Fuck you, Disco! Fuck you!" Londa yelled and stormed off.

Disco looked at Nephew Mal and the white hoes. "Fuck wrong wit' her?"

They all bussed up laughing. Shit was funny to them, because they were all drunk and *rrrrooooollllllliiiinnnngggggg!*

Mal felt the phone vibrating at his side. He answered, "Young and thuggin'! Whatchu need?"

"Where Sco?" the female voice asked.

"Who the fuck this is?"

"His wife, nigga!" Shoniece yelled.

"Well what the fuck his wife name?" Mal shouted back.

"Shoniece!"

"Hold on," Mal said and muted the phone. "Bruh, some hoe name Shoniece on the phone," he told Disco.

"Lemme get that lil', fool," Disco popped, taking the phone from Mal. "What's up, baby boo?"

"And who the fuck was that?" Shoniece yelled.

"Death. What difference it make?"

"See, Sco, that's the shit I be-"

"Shoniece, where the fuck you at?" Disco asked, cutting her off.

She sighed heavily into the phone. "We crossin' County Line Road."

"Who is we?"

"Me, Lil Disco and one of his partners."

"Y'all got my money?"

Shoniece sighed again. "Yeah, boy!"

"Aiight, y'all come to Wet-Wetz. Bottles on me!"

"But I'm not dressed-"

"Bottle on the boss-man," Disco stated and hung up on her.

$$$

Twenty-nine minutes later, Lil Disco, Shoniece and Lil Disco's partner approached the table. Amazon, Bubbles, Purple Thunder and White Chocolate were still sweating their asses off. The white hoes were still in place. All six champagne buckets were full.

"Ut'un. No! Sco, who is these people?" Shoniece asked without even saying hello.

Disco laughed. "These fine hoes that's dancin' is, umm, Amazon, Bubbles, Purple Thunder and White Chocolate... but, umm," he announced and turned to the white chicks. "What's y'all hoes name?"

They giggled and answered, "Lynn," and the other said, "Halle."

Shoniece rucked her brow, staring at Disco with absolute contempt.

"Them hoes wit' my dog, Mal. Nephew Mal, this Shoniece and my brutha Lil Disco." He stared at Lil Disco's outfit. *This nigga dougie-as-fuck!* he thought, loving the colorful Polo shirt.

Mal and Lil Disco exchanged greetings. Shoniece sat down between Disco and Lynn. Lil Disco introduced his man, who looked like a young Bobby Brown. He had one gold trimmer on his front tooth and rocked a low one with the grain — nice waves. His attire was urban, whereas Lil Disco rocked classic Ralph Lauren with all types of sour-apple colors and plaid.

"Disco, this my man, Turk," Lil Disco said.

Turk dapped Disco up. "Turky D, and the D is for Dollars, pimp...I'm tryna buy two, so I hope that shit right."

Disco looked at the little funny looking nigga and laughed. "I gotchu, fool." He liked the little dude off rip.

"Aiight, now, I know yo' brutha! So bottles on me," Turky D said and sat down next to Lil Disco, who was already blowing in Amazon's pussy.

Disco whispered to Shoniece to go and put all of the money in the trunk of his car. While she was gone they all *popped off* again and talked business. Lynn eyed Disco hungrily as Turk tried to rap to her. Disco looked at Mal, pouring champagne down Halle's throat, and thought about his situation. He played back how he and Nephew Mal had arrived to this point...

$$$

TWO DAYS AGO IN BROWARD COUNTY
Disco had exited Sunrise East and found his way to 16th Terrace as he'd always done. Cruising the block, he came to the corner store. A brown box Chevy sat there, about three dudes stood beside it, nothing like it'd normally been. Usually the block was full – niggas and bitches everywhere doing everything.

The three dudes stared at Disco as he floated by, looking as if they'd wanted to stop him. Nevertheless, he'd kept pushing it to Boe and Cuz's spot. The Dodge was parked out front. The block was semi-crowded, not like it normally was, but doing a lot more than 16th Terrace was. Cuz and Boe was in the yard, Cuz holding a choppa and Boe's face all balled up like he wanted war.

Disco hopped out, two kilos of crack in a bag, and immediately peeped the slim red dude with the dreads and tattoos. *Everytime I come 'round here this nigga posted up,* he thought, mugging the dude. The dude sort of mugged back but remained on his crate, which was closer to the house than it usually was. *I'ma end up puttin' it in fool life,* Disco had thought, stopping next to Boe and Cuz.

The two were arguing about the dudes around the corner.

"Fuck-niggas talkin' 'bout they gon' rob us!" Boe'd said.

"Y'all holla'd at 'em?" Disco asked.

"Bruh, fuck holla'n at them *duck-ass* niggas. I'm finna go let this *stick* holla!" Cuz shot back.

"Nah fool, hold up. That's gon' brang shit right back to the spot. We gettin' *boss-money* 'round this bitch. A nigga don't need to fuck that up... gimme the stick, I'll fi' they ass up 'cause I ain't from 'round here," Disco had stated.

"Hell nah, boy! You the boss, we lose you we lose everythang!" Boe had smartly replied.

"So what we gon' do? 'Cause fool 'em thank we pussy."

"Them pussy niggas know. That's why they just talkin'! Niggas that talk ain't gon' do shit!" Boe'd stated.

Boe was partly right. Disco spoke up. "Yeah, niggas rap but don't really be 'bout they lyrics, but when other niggas hear these fuck-niggas songs and they know that we done heard the *fuck-shit* too, and ain't nothin' done happened to the niggas-" Disco paused and shook his head. "-niggas thank we as pussy as the niggas rappin' and feel they wanna test the water. So we gotta do somethin', our hands been forced."

Disco had seen his big brother in a familiar situation. And though he was *'bout his money* and *Ray Charles to the bullshit*, the moment had its own demands.

"So who gon' go?" Cuz asked.

"Shiid, I'll go!"

All three men looked in the direction of the voice. It was the slim red dude on the crate. He was now standing.

"Fuck is this nigga?" Disco asked Boe.

"That's Nephew, he a lil' pill head. But he keep that iron on him."

"Shawty, you 'bout that life?" Disco asked, sizing the young dude.

"Hell yeah, got-damn, I'm 'bout that."

"Whatchu want?"

"Shiid, got-damn, put me on. I'm tryna get me some more tats, some fits and a Donk! I'm tryna stunt, got-damn."

This lil' nigga crazy! Disco had thought to himself. "You got fi'?"

"Hell yeah," Nephew Mal answered, pulling a chrome .357 from his waistband.

Disco chuckled. "Nah fool, you gon' need more than that. It's three niggas out there and ain't no tellin' if some more in the store... Cuz, give him that *stick*." He then turned back to Mal and said, "my nigga, go 'round there and kill 'em fuck-niggas. Don't play wit' 'em! Fuck 'em over and break. I'ma snatch you up... and on my brutha head, shawty, you do this shit right I'ma change yo' life, and that's on stacks."

Mal nodded, chambered the assault rifle and broke out through the houses, running low.

Cuz and Boe jumped in the Dodge. They didn't want to be nowhere around when BSO came through.

Disco jumped in the Volvo and slowly rounded the block.

Yyyyyyaaaaaaaaaaaaaakkkkkkkkkk!!! Sounded loudly. *Yyyyyaaaaakkk!!!* Hit again.

Damn, that lil' nigga gettin' off, Disco thought to himself, smashing the gas. As he came up on the store he saw two bodies twisted next to the brown Chevy. *Where this lil' nigga at?* he wondered. Then he heard, *Yyyaaakkk! Yyyaaakkk! Yyyaaakkk!* Go off in the store. Mal came running out of the store with a duffle bag and the smoking assault rifle.

"Come on!" Disco yelled, scared to death!

The wild young thug had jumped in and off they were – together ever since that day. *Young and muthafuckin' thuggin...*

$$$

"Sco! My nigga! Aye, Sco!" Disco heard his name being yelled over the music. He looked around quicky, fresh out of his reflections, not quite remembering where he was.

"My nigga, you trippin' over there!" Mal said, laughing at his partner. The two white hoes, both all up under him, also started laughing.

"What's up?" Disco asked, realizing that he'd indeed been tripping. Shoniece was back at his side and Lil Disco and Turk were both doing their things with two of the strippers.

"Phone, my nigga. Some hoe name Kwannah. She say it's super-important," Mal told Disco, passing him the phone.

"What?!" Disco yelled, holding the phone to his ear. "What?!... You sho'?!... And they 'round there right now?!... Don't say shit! I'm on my way!... Yeah, I gotchu! Just chill , I'm comin'!"

"What's up, bruh?" Mal asked, seeing the fucked up expression on Disco's face.

"We gotta roll! Come on! Lil Disco, y'all follow us!" he said and exited the club.

"What about us? Like, we'd totally love to come. I totally mean cum," Halle said seductively, rubbing her big titties as she spoke.

"Shiid, got-damn, y'all hoes gotta car?" Mal asked.

"Yes!" Lynn answered.

"Then follow us," Mal said and followed Disco out.

$$$

Lil Will had been watching Disco and his little clique all night. He wanted to holla at his man and see what was good, but he saw that Disco was drunk and really feeling himself. Especially after seeing Londa come back to the VIP in tears, he knew that his friend was *on one*.

"Aye Maine, you see that?"

"What?"

"Sco just gotta call and everybody tore out... his face was balled up," Lil Will informed.

"You think it's fucked up?"

"I'on know. But he drunk and I'on know them niggas wit' 'im. We better ride."

"Let's go!"

Him and Maine ran out to follow them.

"Come on, Trish. Let's go!" Londa said and hopped up. She needed to see what was up, because even though Disco had dissed her and hurt her so bad, she still loved him.

Chapter 45

...I be ridin' through my old hood/ but I'm in my new whip/ same old attitude/ but I'm on some new shit... niggas say they gon' rob me/ see me never do shit/ 'cause they know that's the reason they gon' end up on the news quick... Audemars on my wrist/ buss down/ [bling] poppin' bottles like I scored the winnin' touchdown [score]... picture me dead broke/ looka me rich now/ I run my city from South Philly to Uptown... I thank God for all these bottles I done popped/ all this money that I'm gettin'/ All these models I done popped...

Meek Mills' energetic flow boomed from the Porche's speakers as Disco whipped it up into Silver Blue. A procession of vehicles flowed: Lil Disco, Turkey D and Shoniece in the rental van; Halle and Lynn in their Jetta; Maine and Lil Will in Lil Will's Corvette; and Londa and Trisha in Trisha's Infinity SUV. The line of vehicles sped through the parking lot and all came to a quick halt in the middle of the parking lot, down near the cut where everybody hung and slung drugs.

Nephew Mal raised up the modified Scorpion and aimed at the crowd of gamblers.

"Run! One of y'all fuck-niggas run and I'ma flip ya!" Mal yelled, hoping one of them bucked.

The crowd looked up, all of them scared to death until they saw Disco get out of the car. Blue was the first to speak.

"Damn, Sco, what's up?!" Blue asked.

"Yeah, dog." Jit was also out there. He looked from Disco to Mal – who still had the assault rifle trained on them – to Maine and Lil Will, who'd just gotten out of the Vette.

"My nigga, don't try me! Y'all niggas 'round here talkin' 'bout robbin' me? Y'all fuck-niggas thank a nigga sweet?" Disco said, walking over towards the group, Mal was out of the car trailing his road-dog – gun still aimed.

Blue, Jit, Maine, and Lil Will were all puzzled at Disco's statement. But Ziggy and Shelton new exactly what it was. Kwannah was standing on the second floor watching. The hoodrats from down by the end – who were standing with the crowd of dudes when the cars had pulled up – had moved over to where Londa, Trisha, and the two white chicks stood.

"Sco, what's up, bruh? Tell a nigga somethin'!" Lil Will said.

"Why don't you tell him, Ziggy," Disco said.

"Dog, I don't know-"

"Pussy-nigga! Lift yo' shirt up!" Disco demanded. "You too, Shelton!"

They both lifted up their shirts. Disco spotted his .40 caliber on Ziggy's waistband. Disco took the gun and gave it to Lil Disco, instructing Lil Disco to run both dudes pockets. Once they'd been searched and had their money and drugs took, Disco went into action, pistol whipping Ziggy badly. Blood flew with each swing of the pistol until Ziggy finally stopped screaming and moving altogether.

Breathing heavily, Disco turned to Shelton. "Y'all fuck-niggas thank I'm pussy?"

"Disco, man, come on, dog... I-"

Disco shot him in the stomach, *BOOM!* the gun exploded, sending Shelton to the pavement. Everybody ducked, surprised at the sudden explosion.

"Damn, Sco! Whatchu doin', bruh?!" Maine asked. "You wildin'!"

214

"Nah, nigga, I'm thuggin'! And y'all gon' respect my fuckin' mind... Blue, Jit, y'all some fuck-niggas! But outta love I ain't gon' fuck y'all over!"

"Damn, Disco, what a nigga done?" Jit asked.

"It's whatchu *ain't do!* I'm feedin' y'all niggas and y'all listening to niggas talkin' 'bout bringin' me harm or robbin' me?! Huh?!"

"Mmaann, Sco, you know them niggas –" Blue tried to explain.

"Shut the fuck up, Blue! Befo' a nigga beat yo' bitch-ass! I told you I ain't want them fuck-niggas 'round here. But you still 'round here wit' 'em! But guess what... y'all guess what." Disco walked over to his Porsche and popped the trunk. He removed two duffle bags full of money and dumped it all on the Porsche's seats, yelling, "I got bond money, niggas! I got bond money! And I'll kill you niggas and bond out! I got hit money! I gotta 'nough money to get every nigga in this parkin' lot hit!"

Maine tried to grab Disco and claim him, but Mal pushed him off and aimed the gun at him.

"Whatchu doin', dog? Don't touch my dog! He say what he wanna say and do what he wanna do! Now fall back!" Mal snapped.

Maine looked at Disco.

Disco said, "You heard him! I say what I wanna say and do what I wanna do! Believe that! Now all y'all fuck-niggas be careful when you speakin' 'bout a boss."

Boom! Boom! Boom! he let the .40 pop and jumped in the Porsche. Mal jumped in with him.

"Lil Disco, take Shoniece home!" Disco said and snatched off.

The white hoes in the Jetta followed...

Chapter 46

Disco's eyes flickered. The sun shone brightly through the bedroom window. The large bedroom smelt like ass. He was completely naked and so was the fake blonde with the big tits that lay on his chest. *Fuck I'm doin' here*, he wondered, a throbbing pain in both his head and his *dick* head. He was drained of energy, dehydrated, and totally lost.

Lifting himself, he caused the white chick to wake up also. She stared at him, genuine lust in her sexy eyes, and smiled at her latest conquest.

"Hey, tiger," she purred.

Disco frowned. "Who is you?" he asked, because he couldn't remember shit.

"I'm Lynn, baby... like, it's not even twenty-four hours and you've like, totally forgotten me already. Oh my God?!"

Disco looked at the dingy white bitch and thought, *Lord I hope I used a rubber*. Then he fanned the air in front of his face. "Shawdy, open a window! Why it smell like ass in here?"

"Oh-my-God? What do you expect? You've been fucking me in my butt all night!" she sort of snapped at him and got up to open the window.

Shaking his head, Disco threw his legs over the bed's edge and stood up, but quickly moved his foot – feeling it pressing on something large and hard.

"Ooouuuch!" the other white chick with the brunette hair yelled.

Disco looked down and seen that he'd stepped on the sleeping naked girl's head. A naked Mal lay beside her. He looked up, laughing.

"You gon' kill the lil' momma, huh, playa?!" Nephew Mal said, still laughing.

Lynn and Halle were both now laughing also.

Disco shook his head. *Lord, please, let me have used a rubber. I swear I won't take no more of them pills,* he thought introspectively.

Clothes were all over the floor. He searched until he found enough to make an outfit. He then began searching for his phone. By the time he found it Mal was up and dressed also. There were crazy missed calls on his phone.

"Damn, bruh, we gotta go!" His Audemars said it was already 1:35pm. *Damn! I ain't fuckin' wit' them pills no more!*

"Like, umm, when will we see you two again, because we like *totally* had a *fucking great* time with you guys. The money throwing, the guns and violence, and the sex... oh-my-God! You two guys are like the ultimate thugs," Halle rambled off.

"Yes-way! You guys are super-thuggs. Totally!" Lynn chimed in.

"Got-damn, I'on know 'bout my dog, but I'll be back tonight!" Mal said, gripping his dick. He'd never fucked with white hoes before last night and he'd also never fucked a hoe in the ass, Halle had introduced him to both worlds and *goddamit* he loved them both.

Guns and violence? Disco reflected on Halle's words as he and Mal exited the house. *What muthafuckin' gun and violence?* he asked himself.

He made his way to the passenger side of the Porsche – the top was down – and stood dumbfounded. "Man, where the fuck all this money come from?!"

Cash was strewed all over the car's seats and floorboard like liter on an expansive wasteland.

Mal nodded his head – long thick dreads shaking – a broad smile on his young face. "*Sssstttuuunnnntttiiiinnnn'*! You had yo' deuces in the air last night, 'cause you shitted on 'em, got-damn!" Mal capped and jumped in the car.

"This shit crazy," Disco mumbled and climbed in. "I ain't never fuckin' wit' them pills no more, my nigga. And that's on stacks, boy!"

"I told you!" Mal laughed as he whipped out and sped off.

"Fuck you mean? *I told you.* Nigga, you the one that got me on these shits!"

"Nah, I gave you X, got-damn. Them two cracka hoes had *bars*, got-damn. Them shits make a nigga black-out! That's why I'on fuck wit' 'em. And I told yo' ass, got-damn, don't take them shits."

"Whatever, nigga! Go to my crib," Disco said and laid back with his eyes closed.

$$\$\$\$$$

When they pulled up to Disco's house the white rental van was parked out front, next to Londa's Volvo. As soon as Disco and Mal walked through the door the little Bobby Brown look-a-like jumped up off of the couch.

"Goddamn, bitch! 'Bout time!" he shouted.

"What the fuck you just said?!" Disco asked.

Lil Disco had been on the couch also, talking on his cell phone. He quickly hung up.

Turky D repeated what he'd said. "I said, *bitch, 'bout time.*"

"You just called my dog a bitch?" Mal asked, walking towards Turk.

Turk looked at Mal, then at Lil Disco and Disco. "What?! Y'all don't say that 'round *hurr*?!" Without waiting for an answer to his question Turk copped out. "Well, look, my bad y'all, my bad. Is y'all GD's, 'cause you-" He pointed at Disco. "-you real crazy. I mean, you acted real bad last night, so I'm sorry. My name Turky

218

D, and the D's for Departure! So lemme get my two keys that I already done paid for and lemme go."

Lil Disco got up and gave Disco the .40 caliber and the $835 that he'd taken off of Ziggy and Shelton.

Disco looked at the stuff and then at Lil Disco. "What the fuck this for?"

"That's from the two dudes you pistol whipped and shot."

"Man, I ain't pistol whipped and shot no niggas last night!" Disco fired back, seriously unable to remember the events.

Turky D threw his hands up and sighed loudly. "Ooh, Lord! I told you, Lil Disco, this bit—. I mean, this dude real crazy!"

Ignoring Turk, Disco asked Lil Disco, "you serious?"

Turk spoke up before Lil Disco could. "Yeah he serious, crazy-ass-man! You acted real, real ugly last night in them 'partments. Them two boys probably dead. And the po'lice is probably comin', so please gimme mine and let me go, brutha."

Disco shook his head, trying to remember.

Nephew Mal laughed. "Them *bars*. My dog gone off them *bars*, got-damn!"

This shit crazy! That must be what them hoes was talkin' 'bout... Lord don't let them two niggas be dead! Shiid, who is the two niggas?! Disco thought and wondered as he walked off to his bedroom. Shoniece was in the bed, sound asleep. He crept in the walk-in closet and removed the far wall panel. Toyed with the safe's dial, removed the five kilos and placed the money – the money that was all over his car's seats and floor – inside. He hadn't counted it and wasn't sure if it was right or not. At that instance he didn't really care.

Placing the panel back in place he returned to the living room.

"Here, this five... but, umm, whatchu gave me?" he asked Lil Disco.

"That was $40,000 for Turk two, the $35,000 I owed and my money for one," Lil Disco answered.

"Aiight, you still owe me for two then."

"Good! That's out the way, man, wake that bitch up and let's go!" Turk said, anxious to get the fuck away from Miami.

Disco's phone rang. He answered it without thought. "Yeah?!"

"Brang me my car!"

"Who this?!"

"Sco, do – not – play – wit' – me, okay. Just brang me my car!" Londa snapped.

"Ain't you got the rental?"

"I don't want the rental! I want my muthafuckin' car!"

This who I shoulda pistol whipped and shot! he thought. "Did I do somethin' to you?" he asked her.

"Look, save that bullshit, please! Just brang my damn car!"

"Aiight, look, meet me at the Krispy Kream on 163rd Street in three hours."

"Why the fuck come I gotta drive way the fuck out there to get my car? Why you just can't brang me my shit?"

Disco looked at the phone and started to hang up. He'd never heard Londa talk crazy like that – not to him anyway. "Look, Londa, I'm tired and I'm busy. If you want the car, be in place," he said and simply hung up.

By now Shoniece was woke and standing before him.

"You ready to go?" he asked her.

"I ain't goin'."

"Yeah the fuck you is," he told her.

"No the fuck I ain't!"

Is all these hoes done went crazy in one night?! he wondered. "Shoniece, I ain't 'bout to go through this witchu. Go pack yo' shit and get the fuck on!"

"So you can fuck that bitch, Londa! Or them two nasty white bitches you fucked last night, huh? Why you ain't come home?!"

"Listen, fuck them white hoes and Londa. You gon' go back because that's what the fuck I said do. Now go pack... I'll be up there Thursday."

She looked at him. "For real, you comin' back to Anniston?"

"Yeah. I gotta handle a few thangs, re-up and I'm outta here... shit gettin' crazy."

Shoniece kissed him and done as he had told her.

Chapter 47

After getting Shoniece, Lil Disco and Turky D on the road, Disco rapped with Nephew Mal for a spell and fastly found his way to his large empty bed. Mal collected a big happy-sack of pills, snatched up the Scorpion and jumped in Londa's Volvo, destination the Krispy Krèam on 163rd Street.

He whipped up, chewed two pills and scanned the parking lot. He peeped Londa's *super-fine* ass exit a clean blue-gray Impala LS. NOBODY GREATER THAN JESUS played softly on the Volvo's radio. Londa promenaded towards the Volvo. She wore some little stank shorts – showcasing the plumpness of her vulva and dark palms – and a tight baby-T that announced in loud pink and green letters GEORGE WASHINGTON & ABRAHAM LINCOLN OWNED SLAVES.

I'll be her slave! That lil' mamma a bad muthafucka! Mal thought, eyeing the sultry red-bone. Her big full titties bounced and demanded everyone's full attention as she *walked like a hoe.* Her dark Nadia Terrell shades masked her expression – her mood.

Mal cut the Volvo's engine off and hopped out.

Upon seeing him – instead of Disco – Londa stopped short and removed her shades. A deep frown covered her pretty face. For she'd been expecting Disco. She wanted to see him – her love. She needed to see him – her everything. Instead she now stood before Nephew Mal – the fucking help. She didn't even know him.

"And where is Disco?" she asked with definite attitude.

Mal ignored the question and asked his own. "You that lil' momma from last night, huh? The one that was cryin'."

Londa sighed and switched her weight from one toned bowleg to the other.

"Where – is – Disco?" she asked slowly, as if he was *slow*.

Again Mal side-stepped her question. "You shouldn't never cry. 'Cause you the most prettiest girl in the world when you not cryin'."

Londa shook her head and covered her eyes with the dark $370 shades. "My keys, please." She really wanted to cry. But he – the help, this stranger – had said that she shouldn't cry. So she wouldn't allow him to see her cry.

"Here you go," Mal said, passing her the keys and taking the keys to Disco's Impala rental.

Londa walked beyond him without saying another word. The perfume she wore tickled his nose. He wanted to turn around and steal a view of that ass, he knew it was bouncing. But Disco was him man and she was his hoe.

He slid into the Impala and looked the car over. He peeped a big designer bag on the backseat. *She left her shit*, he thought, grabbing the bag and jumping out.

She was backing the Volvo out.

Mal stepped in her car's path and knocked on the trunk.

Londa quickly stopped and lowered her window.

"What?!" A tear was about to fall.

"Yo' bag, lil' momma."

"My bag?!" she questioned, then looked at the Familiar Line bag. It was Disco's bag. A bag of DVD's. "Oh, thank you."

Londa got out, her shorts had really dug up in her pussy lips, giving Mal a full view and a slight woody.

"No problem," he said, staring at her fat pussy.

She threw the bag inside her backseat, thinking that she'd simply keep the DVD's until Disco came and got them, and if he never came and got them she'd simply keep them and watch them. *They must be some good movies if his ass ridin' 'round wit' 'em*, she thought as she closed her door and zoomed off.

223

I wonder if them cracka hoes got some liquor, Mal wondered getting back in the Impala and heading off for a night of pill popping and wild sex with his two new white female friends. The car's system blaring... *I'ma boss like my nigga Rozay/ bitch asked me for a check/ I told that bitch like no way... 'cause I hustled from the bottom/ there was never no way/ see I never had a job/ so I had to serve yay...*

Chapter 48

Before returning to her apartment, Londa stopped by Winn Dixie and bought two gallons of Double Berry ice cream and a gallon of white wine. She'd decided to drink her wine and eat her ice cream while watching a few of Disco's DVD's.

She fixed herself a very tall glass of wine and drained it all in what seemed like one big gulp. *Mmm, better*, she said to herself and poured another glassful. The ice cream she'd decided to eat straight out of the container, so she got a big spoon and hit the couch in front of the TV.

Opening the bag of DVD's she frowned. *All of these damn bootleg shits*, she thought. *They coulda at least wrote the damn names of the fuckin' movie on the damn DVD,* she fussed inwardly.

Randomly picking one, Londa put a DVD in, hit play and fell back. Big spoon in hand, she dug in her Double Berry and waited for the movie to begin. And when it did Londa damn near dropped her ice cream.

"What the fuck?!" she yelled and leaned forward, a frown on her face. "I can't believe this fuck-ass shit!" Her mouth was wide-ass-open.

On her screen was Bertto, ass naked, getting fucked doggie-style. The dude fucking him was a black dude. And he was damn sure fucking the hell out of Bertto, who screamed like a real bitch, but never once asked the dude to stop. In fact, he begged the dude to *fuck him harder* and asked his homosexual lover to *please fuck him with his legs up.*

The dude complied, pulling about a yard of naked dick out of Bertto, who then laid on his back and cocked his legs up. Up until then the dude's identity had been a mystery. But as they changed positions – the dude now had Bertto's quivering legs on his shoulders pounding him – Londa got a clear view of buddy's face.

"Oh, hell nawl! No this bitch ain't gay?! Oh my God!" she sceamed, recognizing the dude. "That's Omar!"

Omar was from the Lil Haiti area in Miami and was known to be a gangster throughout the city. "That explains everythang!" Londa said out loud. She'd ran into the wannabe thug a few times at events and knew that he wasn't a *dope-boy* or *robber* or *paper hanger*, but he'd always had cake and always flossed at the happening spots. They'd talked a few times, but something about him had always made her keep her panties up and legs closed.

"Gay, fuck-ass, AIDS, dick-in-the-booty ass nigga! I'm sooo glad I ain't fuck that gay-ass nigga. 'Round here fakin' like a 'G'," Londa ranted and raved.

Sick at the sight of the nasty shit, she popped the DVD out and popped in another one. Same shit, different dude. She put in DVD after DVD, praying that she didn't see Disco fucking Bertto – him or no other nigga she'd fucked with. Then she wondered, *what the fuck is Sco doin' wit' these nasty, gay-ass DVD's?*

She dug in her ice cream and licked the rich strawberry ice cream off of the spoon. Then it hit her like a ton of bricks. *Ice cream!* she thought about when Disco was fucked up financially and the rumors about Bertto's safe house getting robbed. It was about the same time. *And they said the niggas had took some DVD's from Bertto and he wanted his shit back*, Londa mused. *And it's a reward too!* she remembered. And she could see why Bertto wanted the DVD's back so bad. They were *nasty as fuck!* Showing him getting *beat out* in positions that she'd never been fucked in. There were also scenes of Bertto sucking dick – sometimes two at a time – and black dudes nutting all in his mouth and face. It was totally disgusting!!!

Ice cream, Londa thought again and began putting all of the DVD's back into the expensive designer bag. *I know just what to do wit' these shits!*

Chapter 49

The Following Night
Disco and Nephew Mal were *blacked out* – hoodies, jeans, boots
and guns. They were situated in a hedge between the white hoe's
house and Varray and Mac-90's crib. The sun was just setting and
the two would-be killers were ready to get the bloody ordeal over
with. Espcially Disco, who'd been looking to *see* the two home
invaders/killers for a long while. His face and palms were wet as
rivers in murderous anticipation. They'd robbed him for his re-up
and his watch – via laying Maine down. They'd also killed his dog.
Both infractions were punishable by death and it was their time to
pay.

Mal sat in the bushes beside his man, his mind set on the
deadly mission at hand – a doppelganger of eternal rest. He was
ready and willing to issue death for his homeboy. Or even accept
it if that's what it came to. Why? Because in four days he'd lived a
lifetime. And he owed it all to his homeboy... Rolex watch. Chunky
jewelry. Access to $400,000 cars. Money to blow. Every shade and
shape of hoe on deck. Menage a trios. $1,000 fits. Big 'dro and pill
sacks. Misery was memorable, but minus any meaning in his
manner of existence. He'd reached a milestone in his young life. In
four days he'd done what a lot of his other homeboys – up in
Broward – would never do. So it was *whatever-whatever.*

Got-damn, I'm young and I'm thuggin... I might die young
because of my thuggin... but God, a nigga woulda been dead if it
wasn't for thuggin... probably starved to death or gun down by

228

another nigga thuggin... my old-boy was thuggin. My old-girl loved him. Gave birth to his thuggin... for real, God, all you ever gave a young fool like me in this life is this thug shit... so I'ma thug it to the fullest! Understandin' that You gave me this life for a reason... knowin' wholeheartedly that in this life thuggin represents freedom... and only the thugs will be free... so I'ma thug – young and proud – until you call a nigga home, Mal thought but more so prayed before chewing another pill.

Disco looked at his little homeboy and shook his head. *My lil' fool a certified pill head,* he reasoned, but thanked God for the real young nigga that squatted – *blacked out* – in his enemies' bushes with him – ready to kill for him. His mind drifted to the hours before, to the moment that led to this one.

$$$

He'd just woke up from almost a twenty-four hour slumber and was checking his messages and all of his missed calls – too many to detail. The most had been from Londa and surprisedly G. *Damn, I wonder what's up wit' my dog,* he wondered when Nephew Mal had came in talking loud and crazy.

"Bruh, my nigga, you shoulda came, got-damn! I done bussed 'bout a hunnid nuts. Got-damn, I fucked Halle and Lynn! Bruh, got-damn, Lynn got the best asshole in the world! I had them hoes kissin' each other, 69'ing each other, fightin' over my nut. Them hoes some animals, got-damn!" Mal went on and on about his sexual exploits with the two white girls – Halle and Lynn.

Disco gave him an occasional *yeah and un-huh* as he continued checking his messages, tuning Mal out but still hearing him ramble on.

There were long boring messages from both Blue and Jit, copping pleas and trying to reaffirm their allegiance with him. *Yeah right,* he mumbled.

Lil Will and Maine also had left messages claiming to have had no knowledge of Ziggy and Shelton's bullshit and wanted to make sure that he was good. *I bet,* he thought.

Messages had been left from Lil Disco and Shoniece, letting him know that they were safe on 30 Row. *Good*, he mused, knowing he'd be joining them in a few days.

There was a message with some bitches talking Spanish. He laughed, knowing it was the three *live-hoes* that he'd met with G at Club Levels. *I told them bitches I don't speak that gwalla-gwalla shit*, he said to himself.

Newphew Mal was still babbling, "I was fuckin' Lynn in the ass, but not from the back, I had that hoe in the buck. And bruh, Halle started ridin' that hoe face. I couldn't belive that shit... but then guess what that lil' momma tried to do? Kiss a nigga! Bruh, I spit right in that hoe face, got-damn! But that hoe just ate the spit and kept ridin' Lynn's face... you shoulda came, got-damn!... 'cause shit really got live when they two homeboys came over there, got-damn! Them niggas had it! They brought more pills, more 'dro, and a case of champagne. We was poppin' pills and bottles like we won the championship, got-damn. We jumped them hoes until 'bout one in the morning... then we went to *The After Hour* in Overtown. We left the rental and rode in they Chrysler 300. Them shits aiight, I might get one until I find me a '72 Vert... bruh-bruh, them two niggas know how to party, got-damn! They bought the bar, passed out pills, and got loose in that bitch. I ain't had to spend shit! Them boys grabbed two more hoes when that shit closed and we took 'em back to Lynn and Halle crib, gotdamn, and really *got-off-the-chain*! The nigga Varray remind me of you, dog! He a real-"

"What?! Who you said?!" Disco had cut Mal off.

"Varray. He a real nigga."

"Varray? You said the nigga took you to Town?"

"Hell yeah, got-damn, to *The After Hour*."

"And the nigga gotta Chrysler 300, black?" Disco asked.

"Yeah, I might snatch me a white one."

Disco had then explained everything that had transpired between himself and Varray.

"Damn, dog, that shit crazy!"

Disco nodded. "Call them hoes and see if they still 'round there."

"Shiid, we ain't gotta do that. The niggas live right next door!"

"Oh yeah?!" A smile – a wicked one – creased his face. He'd finally found Varray.

$$$

"Sco... dog... look, man. Get ready," Nephew Mal whispered from beside him, bringing Disco back from his reflections.

Disco looked and saw the all black 300 swing into its parking space in front of the house. Revenge was now certain. Retaliation a must.

He and Mal clutched their weapons and got ready to *thug-it-out*.

They never noticed the broken window on the side of the house...

Chapter 50

Yesterday Evening

G, Pito and Sombra had all been up to the ice cream parlor eating sundaes and making plans to get away for a few days. They all were in need of relieving a little stress. Sombra had suggested Vegas. G quickly shot that down, *been there and done that. From Tyson to Floyd, I've been on the floor,* he said.

Pito shrugged and suggested a boat trip.

G went the fuck off! Slammed his fist on the table and stated, "no fuckin' boats! No, not-a-me. No boats."

In his native tongue Sombra simply asked why. G had always been a laid back, easy going dude. Neither of his friends had ever seen him act that way before.

G pushed his sundae to the side and said, "Me fuckin' friend. Best-a-friend ever! He take a boat trip, with some guy. Something happened. Who knows?! Something. Me friend, eight-a-life sentences in prison. Fuck you! No boat trip for me. Fuck that shit."

Both men simply shrugged. They understood – *no fucking boat trips.*

Before they were able to resume their conversation – minus the boat trips – the cute little Spanish lady that worked at the parlor brought G the phone. He'd had to remove the phone from his ear upon saying hello, because the woman on the other end was screaming and carrying on badly.

"Calm down, please... I cannot under-a-stand you. You talkie-a-like you Cuban, come on, please," he'd said.

The woman did as G had told her, calmed down and told him what had happened.

Then he yelled, "What?! You fucking cra-zy! Somebody did what?!"

The woman began crying again and repeated her story.

"Fucking Christ sakes! Okay. Every-a-thing is okay. I be there soon. Like five-a-minute," he'd said and hung up.

But before he could get up and exit the parlor... she walked in.

Pito bit his closed fist and stared.

Sombra whistled and crossed himself like a Catholic.

"*Gggoooddamn*. Look-a-at what-a-the house-a-cat pulled in to-a-play with," G said.

Londa smiled a fake smile upon seeing all of the eyes on her. Her big nipples poking out through her loud baby-T and her little stank shorts still cutting into her big *worn-hole* and exposing her palms. The expensive Familiar Line bag hung over her shoulder as she stood before G.

"Can I holla atchu right quick, please?" she asked like a begging teenager.

G looked at his expensive time-piece and knew that he had very pressing business to attend to. But this was also his man's girlfriend, so it had to be important. He sighed and asked, "Is it important, very?"

"Umm, yeah... yeah, it's important," Londa had stuttered, already beginning to regret her decision.

G sighed again. "Okay, come on," he said and led her to an empty booth.

Londa sat, facing G, she took a deep breath and told G about the DVD's and where she'd gotten them from. She told him about her first time seeing the bag, but at the time, not knowing what was on the DVD's. Then she inquired about that reward money.

With a whistle, G brought Pito to the booth. He then pointed to the bag. Pito looked at the bag, shook his head, he knew the bag. Opening it, he whistled. The DVD's were Bertto's.

G spoke to the short man in Spanish. Pito nodded and took the bag. He returned five minutes later with ten neat thousand dollar stacks. The money was placed on the table and Pito went back to his table with Sombra, leaving G alone again with Londa.

"Remember, G, you said you ain't gone hurt him... be-because you can't hurt him or the deal is off. I'm only tellin' you this because, because you just need to cut him off. Don't deal wit' his ass. He's not a bad dude, he just don't appreciate shit. He don't appreciate good people... so, so just don't do no more business wit' his ass, G," Londa explained, wanting G to simply cut Disco off and leave him broke. What she didn't understand was that G couldn't *simply cut Disco off*. When someone transgressed in the game they were in, playing on the level they were operating on, violations meant *death*.

But G hadn't told her that. He'd asked, "Are you sure?"

Londa nodded yes.

G pushed the $10,000 across the table to her.

"Ut'un," Londa said. "You got yo' DVD's back. Now you can put that wit' whatever was taken and cut him off. That's all I want."

"It's fine. Every-a-thing is handsome ba-be. A deal is a deal. Take thee money. It's yours. I will take-a-care of every-a-thing else."

Londa had smiled, thanked G – kissing him on his cheek – and shook her big round ass right out of the ice cream parlor. Everything had worked out like a charm for her. Disco would be back broke in no time and back in her arms.

When she'd left, so did G, Pito and Sombra. G sped straight over to the two-story brick house. The big black lady fell into his arms as soon as he'd entered. She was once again crying. Once she settled down again she re-explained everything. Telling G things that she neglected to tell him over the phone. She was ashamed. One of the home invaders had made her perform oral sex on him. Telling her, *and swallow it all bitch, 'cause they can't get DNA outcha belly, hoe.*

"These fucking guys. I gonna kill them all. I swear!" he'd said.

Two muthafuckas had boldly ran up into his spot, took thirty kilos, and made his favorite auntie's best friend suck their dick. He was hot!

"Do you have any idea who... any thought, who-a-it may-a-be?" G'd asked.

He was surprised when she said, "Yeah. They had on masks, but I know it was them two niggas from across the street. I'd been seein' the lil' baldhead one peekin' over here, always watchin' me and the girls. Caught him on that porch over there, jackin' his dick a few times. The girls always laughed at his sick ass! I thought he was just a young pervert," she said and started back crying. "I-I didn't think he'd do no... no shit like this."

"It's okay. He will be gone! You-a-will never see him again. Now go to-a-me aunt house. I take-a-care of every-a-thing."

She nodded, kissed his cheek and left.

$$$

All fully strapped, the three men posted up at the windows and watched the house across the street all day. But no car ever came. Then, about 10:00 that night, a black Chrysler 300 pulled next door to the house. A blue-gray Impala and a white Jetta were already in the yard. Two men – one baldhead – had entered the house carrying a box. Nothing moved again until about 1:30 a.m., at which time G and his two men had decided to go across the street and break into the house in question. They entered through a side window – broke it and slid in. G wasn't surprised to find nineteen of the thirty kilos in the back bedroom. They all cocked their weapons and waited in the dark house. Because G knew that they'd have to come home sooner than later...

235

Chapter 51

Scarface's NEVER SAW A MAN CRY UNTIL I SAW A MAN DIE played loudly from the black Chrysler 300's sound system as Varray whipped it up into his driveway. Both he and Mac-90 tucked their *iron* before exiting the vehicle. They lived in a great neighborhood and didn't need their wonderful neighbors seeing them carrying guns.

"Varray, my nigga, lil' fool from Broward who partied wit' us last night was cool as fuck. I like lil' fool... I'on thank he really *'bout that life*... nigga too pretty, plus he red. Ain't too many red niggas *'bout that life*, but I like lil' fool," Mac-90 babbled on as they walked up the walkway, Varray in the front.

"Yeah, Nephew cool as fuck. We might can move them nineteen up his way, in Broward. You feel me?" Varray shot back, unlocking the door.

As soon as he opened the door a gun exploded, *Tat! Tat! Tat!*

Two shots chipped the wall, the third shot hit Varray in the shoulder and spun him. So he was now facing a scared Mac-90 when Mac-90 yelled, "oh shit!" and upped his .40.

Turning to run, Mac-90 opened the .40 up, firing as he ran off the porch, *Boom! Boom! Boom! Boom! Boom!* The .40 exploded, all six shots going through Varray's body and hitting one of the would-be assassins – Sombra – killing him where he stood.

Yak! Yak! Yak! Yak! Yak! Yak! Yak! Yak! Yak! Disco hopped out, hitting at Mac-90 as he fled.

Boom! Boom! Boom! Boom! Mac-90 fired back over his shoulder, never breaking his stride.

G and Pito came running out of the house. He and Disco locked eyes.

You sonofabitch! he thought, seeing Disco standing there, gun in hand, G assumed that he'd drove up with the home invaders. *I told his fucking ass not to cross me!*

$$$

His target had gotten away! Disco spun towards the house and locked eyes with G. *Fuck he doin' here?* he thought and lowered his assault rifle. A smile played at the corners of his mouth. Mal was coming up behind him.

Then, G's once stoic expression changed into a blanket of rage. His arm raised up, as if in slow motion, and an explosion occurred – sudden and bright. Time seemed to be suspended. A great force overwhelmed him, driving him backwards – his smile still in place.

More force... more explosions... pain... more force. Then Disco became aware of the blood and burning. The ground came up and slapped him in the back. *Damn!* he grunted inwardly and time exploded.

Yyyyyyyyyyyyyyyyyyyyyaaaaaaaaaaaaaaaaakkkkkkkkkkkkk!!! Mal unloaded, cutting Pito down like a tree.

G ducked and ran back into the house.

Yyyyyyyyyyyyyyyyyyyyyaaaaaaaaaaaaaaaaakkkkkkkkkkkkk!!! Mal let loose again, trying to kill G as well. But he'd gotten away.

Mal turned to Disco, who was hit up bad. Blood was leaking from everywhere.

"Damn, bruh!" Mal shook his head. "Not my dog... damn, dog."

Blood was running from his mouth and several holes in his shaking body.

"I'ma kill that fuck-nigga, dog! That's my word, dog. I put that on my grandma, dog!" Mal picked up the assault rifle that

Disco had been carrying and ran to the car. He hated to, but he had to leave his dog.

$$$

Disco felt himself being sucked into a hole – it was big, wet and hot. He thought about Londa's pussy. Wondered. She was mad at him. Why? He'd never get a chance to find out. Because he was dying. The thought of dying made him shiver. The big, wet hole was now cold. Cold. Like G's stare. *Why the fuck G shoot me?* he asked himself. Wondered. Shivered. A tear. *I can't cry!* he told himself. *But I'm dyin'!* Still he willed himself to live. *Gotta hold on… gotta daughter. My daughter needs me… gotta be there when my brutha come home…*

The smile never left his face. Warmth covered him. He saw the lights. Bright lights. There were voices. Many voices. He couldn't understand them. His focus was the lights. Bright lights. He remembered the lights… *Damn, I can fly*, he thought, staring into the light. He jumped. The chopping. He heard loud chopping. The lights. The chopping. The flying. The dying.

Images of his childhood. Images of his child. *I gotta daughter to look after*, he rememberd. But the hole was deep. Wet. Hot. Its pull was strong. Disco yield. Embraced the flight. Felt himself going under. Leaving. So young. So young to be leaving the world behind.

God forgive a nigga… bless my daughter and all my thug niggas… my momma and my sista. But God, be sho' to look out for my brutha, Disco prayed and was gone…

Chapter 52

Beep....Beep....Beep...Beep...Beeeeeeep! The monitor screamed.

"We're losing him!" the nurse said, excitedly.

"Everybody, calm down," the doctor said, rubbing the two fibrillator pads together. "Clear!"

Boop! The electrically charged pads sounded, causing the patient's body to jump.

The doctor rubbed the pads together again. "Clear!"

Boop! The body jumped again.

Beep...Beep...Beep...Beep.

"We've got a pulse!" the nurse yelled. "It's not very strong...if he goes under again, we'll lose him."

"Prep him for surgery...he's lost a lot of blood."

The team of nurses and doctors quickly scrambled to save the young man's life. He'd taken five shots to the back, neck and leg. Shots that were meant to end the life of Troy 'Disco' Jones. Yet, through God and the steady hand of the surgeon, his chances of surviving were increasing by the minute. Either the Grim Reaper had missed his mark or the young certified gangsta was too stubborn to call it quits...

90 DAYS LATER

A month had passed since Disco had been air lifted to Ryder Trauma Center, full of holes and bleeding like a muthafucka. During the course of his stay, he'd caught the attention of Nurse Parish. Every since she'd laid eyes on him, barely holding on to life, she could not get the handsome young man off of her mind. Everyday after she finished her rounds she would go into his room to check on him, and for the entire time of his stay she never ran into any ladyfriends of his. She found that quite odd, as handsome as he was.

Nurse Parish was open and aimed to see exactly what it was about Mr. Troy 'Disco' Jones that attracted her so strongly and seemed to repell all others...

To Be Continued....

PLEX PRESENTS:

GET IT HOW YOU LIVE

Volume 1NE

Big Gemo

PLEX PRESENTS

LOVE & THUGGIN

BY BO BROWN

CRUMBS TO BRICKS

BY CAPO CAT

GOLDIE

Part One

CASHMAN
DUVAL CO.

Erotic Desires

By Seven Supreme & The Book Gang

sOmEThInG 2 DiE 4

A Classic Novel
By PLEX

BADLAND PUBLISHING LLC
PO Box 11623
Riviera Beach, FL 33419-1623
www.badlandpub.com

Shipping address

Name:_____

Address:_____

City:_____State:_____Zip:_____

Title	Author	Price
STREET RAISED: The Beginning	Mike Harper	15.95
BOO BABY: The Secret Of...	PLEX	15.95
SERVED: With No Regard!	PLEX	15.95
STREET RAISED: The Raw Deal	PLEX	15.95
BUCKIN' DA' DICE Vol. 1	BOOK GANG	15.95
NO TURNING...	Big Nation	13.95
PROMISCUOUS	Calvin Williams	10.95
SUGAR	Mike Harper	15.00
CRUMBS TO BRICKS	Capo Cat	15.95
GET IT HOW YOU LIVE Vol. 1	Big Gemo	13.95
LOVE & THUGGIN	Bo Brown	15.00
EROTIC DESIRES	Seven Supreme	13.95
LIL ONE: Blood Investment	K-1 & Bino	15.00
ONE LOVE	PLEX	13.95
sOmEtHiNg 2 DiE 4	PLEX	14.95
GUTTA BOYZ	Stacey Culbert	15.00
GET IT HOW YOU LIVE 2	PLEX & Gemo	14.95

3.75 (S&H) for 1-3 Books _____
For Quantities over 3 add $ .75 per Book _____